FIC
ALC

Alcott, Louisa May,
1832-1888.

A double life

$17.45

DATE			

PLEASANTON

JUL - 1988   © THE BAKER & TAYLOR CO.

A DOUBLE LIFE

ALSO AVAILABLE

*The Selected Letters of
Louisa May Alcott*

*With an Introduction by
Madeleine B. Stern*

Joel Myerson and Daniel Shealy, Editors;
Madeleine B. Stern, Associate Editor

A DOUBLE LIFE

NEWLY DISCOVERED THRILLERS OF

Louisa May Alcott

WITH AN INTRODUCTION BY
MADELEINE B. STERN

Madeleine B. Stern, Editor
Joel Myerson and Daniel Shealy, Associate Editors

LITTLE, BROWN AND COMPANY • BOSTON • TORONTO

FIRST EDITION

All illustrations are reprinted by permission of the American
Antiquarian Society, Worcester, Massachusetts, except for the
illustration appearing on p. 191, which is reproduced courtesy of
the Brown University Library, Providence, Rhode Island.

Library of Congress Cataloging-in-Publication Data

Alcott, Louisa May, 1832–1888.
  A double life.

  1. Detective and mystery stories, American.   I. Stern,
Madeleine B. 1912–   II. Myerson, Joel.
III. Shealy, Daniel.   IV. Title.
PS1016.S73   1988   813′.4   87-37827
ISBN 0-316-03101-1

10 9 8 7 6 5 4 3 2 1

DESIGNED BY JEANNE ABBOUD

*Published simultaneously in Canada
by Little, Brown & Company (Canada) Limited*

PRINTED IN THE UNITED STATES OF AMERICA

Contents

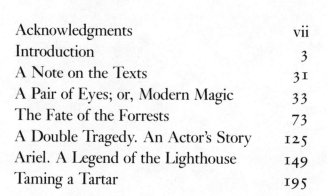

Acknowledgments

ALL THREE editors are grateful to the staffs of the American Antiquarian Society, Brown University Library, the New York Public Library, and the University of South Carolina Library for making available the original printings of the texts in *A Double Life*, and to the Houghton Library, Harvard University, and the University of Virginia Library for permission to publish material from their collections. We also wish to thank Armida Gilbert for her help in preparing the texts used in our edition. Joel Myerson acknowledges the support of Carol McGinnis Kay, Dean of the College of Humanities and Social Sciences of the University of South Carolina. Daniel Shealy is grateful to G. W. Koon, Chairman of the Department of English, and Robert A. Waller, Dean of the College of Liberal Arts, of Clemson University. Madeleine B. Stern acknowledges the unceasing support of her partner, Dr. Leona Rostenberg, who originally discovered many of Alcott's pseudonymous works.

A DOUBLE LIFE

Introduction

———◆———

BY MADELEINE B. STERN

N EVER AGAIN will you have quite the same image of this particular 'little woman.'"[1]

This remark, made in 1975 when the first volume of Louisa Alcott's sensational thrillers was published, was prophetic. The picture of the exemplary spinster of Concord, Massachusetts, who had created the perennial classic *Little Women* was shattered for all time. With publication of her anonymous and pseudonymous page turners, an amazed public learned that America's best-loved author of juvenile fiction had led a double literary life and that the creator of the greatest domestic novel of the New England family had also been the familiar of a world of darkness. Readers devoured her stories of madness and mind control, passionate and manipulating heroines, hashish and opium addiction. Some recalled that Jo March herself, the independent heroine of *Little Women*, had also

---

1. In a *Publishers Weekly* review of *Behind a Mask: The Unknown Thrillers of Louisa May Alcott*, ed. Madeleine B. Stern (New York: William Morrow, 1975). Other quoted reviews are from *Los Angeles Times* and *New York Times*.

written sensational stories in secret to earn money and enjoy an emotional catharsis. But most simply reveled in narratives whose themes were "deceit, sin, death," and whose heroines were "forceful, independent, sexually demanding, and don't do housework." And, during the decade or so that followed, between the mid-1970s and the mid-1980s, the scholarly world, depending upon the implications of her fiction, analyzed and psychoanalyzed the author, burrowed into her biography, and occasionally changed the biography to conform with the stories.[2]

All this was fascinating, but never so fascinating as the stories themselves, which were narrated with professional skill, insight into character, and a revelation of intimacy with satanic themes. And always, to those aware of the author's enormous productivity, there was the hope that more sensational thrillers would emerge from behind the mask of Louisa May Alcott, more stories written in secret, dispatched to a sensational newspaper, published anonymously or under a pseudonym, revolving about other macabre subjects.

That hope has been realized. Louisa Alcott's double literary life was even more productive and varied than had been estimated, and out of her inkstand have appeared five "new" astounding tales, discovered in 1986, that can be traced to her indefatigable pen. These tales will further alter her image, give fresh food for thought to literary scholars, but above all they will enthrall an avid readership.

Louisa Alcott's newly discovered thrillers were all published anonymously during the 1860s before she began *Little Women*. Why should a struggling young author hide her name from the public? Stephen King has written that "all novelists are inveterate role-players" and find it "fun to be someone else for a while."[3] The novelist's "someone else" may be nameless. Seeking money to support

2. See, for example, Judith Fetterley, "Impersonating 'Little Women': The Radicalism of Alcott's *Behind a Mask*," *Women's Studies* 10 (1983): 1–14; Martha Saxton, *Louisa May: A Modern Biography of Louisa May Alcott* (Boston: Houghton Mifflin, 1977).

3. Stephen King, *The Bachman Books* (New York: New American Library, 1986), p. viii.

the Alcott family, which included her philosopher father Bronson, her beloved and long-suffering mother Abby May, and her artist sister May, Louisa assumed the role of breadwinner. She also found it "fun" to be an anonymous someone else for a while, and the someone else who was able to turn sensational stories into fifty or seventy-five dollars was a writer who dwelled among shadows, pursuing strange and exotic themes of sadomasochism, mesmerism, East Indian Thuggism. These were no themes for Concord, Massachusetts, where Alcott's neighbors included the revered Ralph Waldo Emerson; indeed, they were no themes for her own family, especially not for her father, who could have conversed with Plato. They were themes to be embroidered in secret into melodramatic tales that were unsigned.

Because these "new" stories were all anonymous, their authorship was extremely elusive and, but for clues in unpublished journals and publisher's correspondence, would have remained unidentified.

The first hint surfaced in an examination of the 1863 journal entries made by Louisa Alcott, who, thanks to Bronson Alcott's pedagogical guidance, was addicted throughout her life to journal writing. In August 1863, having recently recuperated from a severe illness sustained when she served as an army nurse in the Civil War, she was more aware than ever of the need for contributions to the family treasury.[4] Her account of her experience at the Union Hotel Hospital had been well received as it appeared serially in the pages of the *Boston Commonwealth*. But neither the serialization nor the subsequent book appearance of *Hospital Sketches* would add appreciably to the Alcott coffers. Sensational stories paid better. And so, in August 1863, the author of *Hospital Sketches* wrote tersely in her journal: "Leslie [Frank Leslie, publisher of periodicals] sent $40 for 'A Whisper In The Dark,' & wanted another — Sent 'A Pair of Eyes.'"[5]

4. For biographical details throughout, see Madeleine B. Stern, *Louisa May Alcott* (Norman: University of Oklahoma Press, 1950, 1971, 1985).

5. Louisa May Alcott, unpublished journals (by permission of the Houghton Library, Harvard University), August 1863. I am indebted to my co-editors, Joel Myerson and Daniel Shealy, for transcripts of the journals.

"A Whisper in the Dark," a fairly innocuous story of mind control, was later to be acknowledged by its author and so is recognized as part of the Alcott canon. "A Pair of Eyes" turned out to be another matter altogether — a strange, extraordinary narrative focused upon a very particular kind of mind control. Searchers after unknown Alcott thrillers could be certain, then, that in August 1863 the author had indeed sent a tale entitled "A Pair of Eyes" to Leslie. But had it been accepted? Had it ever appeared? The reader of the journals found the answer under the date of November 1863: "Received $39 from Leslie for 'A Pair of Eyes' not enough, but I'm glad to get even that & be done with him. Paid debts with it as usual."[6] If the publisher Frank Leslie had paid for a story, the chances were he had published it. Another anonymous Alcott thriller now had a name and, somewhere in the pages of one of the Leslie periodicals, awaited the eye of the literary sleuth.

The Leslie correspondence — such as has survived — would supply the responses to the Alcott journal entries. In an undated letter, the editor of *Frank Leslie's Illustrated Newspaper* wrote to the "Dear Madam" who was Louisa May Alcott: "Mr Leslie informs me that you have a tale ready for us, and for which he has already settled with you by check. Will you be kind enough to let us have it at the earliest moment in your power." Beneath, the author, who was becoming quite pleased with herself, jotted: "Made them pay before hand."[7] Another sensation story might now be endowed with a title. In June 1864 Louisa supplied it, recording in her journal: "Wrote 'The Tale Of The Forrests' for Leslie who sent for a tale. Rubbish keeps the pot boiling."[8] "The Fate of the Forrests" might have helped keep the Alcott pot boiling, but, as its reading

6. Ibid., November 1863.

7. "Editor of F.L. Ill. Newsp. to [Louisa May Alcott]" (Louisa May Alcott Collection [#6255], Manuscripts Department, University of Virginia Library). The imprinted letterhead date is New York 1863, but the letter may well have been written later. My thanks to my co-editor Daniel Shealy for transcripts of Leslie letters. See also Daniel Shealy, "The Author-Publisher Relationships of Louisa May Alcott" (Ph.D. diss., University of South Carolina, 1985).

8. Louisa May Alcott, unpublished journals (by permission of the Houghton Library, Harvard University), June 1864.

would reveal, the story was not rubbish. In a way, it would turn out to be the most singular addition to the Alcott oeuvre.

And so a close perusal of Louisa May Alcott's unpublished journals produced the stunning revelations. In April 1865, having announced, "Richmond taken on the 2nd Hurrah! Went to Boston & enjoyed the grand jollification," the ex-nurse of the Union Hotel Hospital added a succinct paragraph: "Sewed, cleaned house & wrote a story for Leslie, 'A Double Tragedy.'"[9] The very next month, the author, glorying in her double life, made the following journal entry: "after I'd done the scrubbing up I went to my pen & wrote Leslie's second tale 'Ariel, A Legend Of The Light-house.'"[10] The puzzling expression "second tale" would become clear as soon as the story of the lighthouse and its legend was located.

The final, and perhaps the most powerful, new discovery contained in *A Double Life* did not first manifest itself until December 1866. By then, Louisa had returned from her first journey abroad, where she had served as companion to a young invalid. In August she confided to her journal: "Soon fell to work on some stories for things were, as I expected, behind hand when the money-maker was away." In December she was more specific: "Wrote . . . a wild Russian story 'Taming a Tartar.'"[11] An unpublished letter in the Leslie archive embroidered Miss Alcott's unadorned statement. On 13 June 1867, an assistant in the Frank Leslie Publishing House reported to "Miss L.M.Alcott": "Dear Madam: Your favor of the 10th inst acknowledging the receipt of $72 for 'Taming a Tartar' came to hand this morning."[12] As the Alcott bibliography expanded, Alcott prices rose. And so, the brief entries in the writer's unpublished journals, counterbalanced by statements in the Leslie

9. Ibid., April 1865.
10. Ibid., May 1865.
11. Ibid., August and December 1866.
12. "Benj. G. Smith for Frank Leslie to Miss L.M.Alcott, New York, 13 June 1867" (Louisa May Alcott Collection [#6255], Manuscripts Department, University of Virginia Library). Smith went on to discuss an apparent misunderstanding about "the amount paid per page. . . . I was not aware that any agreement existed between you and Mr. Leslie binding him to pay $100 per story. . . . To avoid difficulty in future you might mark the price on the first page of the MS."

business correspondence, have yielded up fresh secrets. The prolific author of *Flower Fables*, *Hospital Sketches*, and *Moods*, the future
creator of *Little Women*, was even more prolific than had been believed. She was also, as the reader of these stories will discover,
more skillful in her narrative development, more varied in her literary motifs. As her already extraordinary productivity increased,
her frame of reference widened. The stories in *A Double Life* add
still a new dimension to the image of Louisa May Alcott.

All those stories were published anonymously, and all appeared
in the pages of Frank Leslie periodicals.[13] Louisa had had dealings
with the House of Leslie before the August 1863 journal entry that
announced the dispatch of "A Pair of Eyes." Actually her first
known sensation tale had been submitted to a competition announced by *Frank Leslie's Illustrated Newspaper*, offering one hundred
dollars for the best story. "Pauline's Passion and Punishment," a
fast-paced narrative revolving about the manipulating heroine Pauline Valary, had won the prize and in January 1863 appeared in the
weekly, where it was ascribed to "a lady of Massachusetts." To most
ladies and gentlemen of Massachusetts and other states of the
Union in those Civil War years, *Frank Leslie's Illustrated Newspaper*
was a familiar journal. Indeed, Frank Leslie was a household
word.[14]

Frank Leslie was also a pseudonym — a fact probably unknown
to the author of "Pauline's Passion and Punishment." In all likelihood she never met the short, broad, black-bearded newspaperman
who exuded dynamic magnetism, although she may well have seen
his published likeness. Born Henry Carter in Ipswich, England, a
glove manufacturer's son, he had turned his back on the family
business and early evinced the artistic propensities that would dom-

13. For the original discovery of Alcott's anonymous and pseudonymous
stories, see Leona Rostenberg, "Some Anonymous and Pseudonymous Thrillers
of Louisa M. Alcott," *Papers of the Bibliographical Society of America* 37 (2d Quarter
1943).

14. For details about Leslie and his publishing empire, see Madeleine B. Stern,
Purple Passage: The Life of Mrs. Frank Leslie (Norman: University of Oklahoma
Press, 1953, 1970).

inate his career. As Frank Leslie he pursued the skills of engraving and pictorial printing for the *Illustrated London News* until 1848, when he immigrated to America. By the mid-fifties he had begun to establish a place for himself in the field of illustrated journalism. Within ten years he had become a colossus on New York's Publishers' Row.

The flagship of his fleet of weeklies and monthlies was *Frank Leslie's Illustrated Newspaper*. That weekly catered aggressively to most facets of popular taste. Murder and horror, executions and assassinations, prizefights and revolutions — every cause célèbre, every sensation, every exposure — were grist for its mill. Leslie's emphasis was pictorial. His approach, since he was basically an artist, was visual. And so his weekly ran just enough text to float the pictures that reanimated contemporary history (especially its gorier aspects) for the American household. In single woodcuts or in huge double-page engravings, the *Illustrated Newspaper* reproduced for its vast readership authentic Civil War battle scenes, volcanoes and earthquakes, private scandals and public revelations. In addition, it ran the illustrated serials that lured the old from the fireside and the young from their play — serials that appeared anonymously under such titles as "A Pair of Eyes," "The Fate of the Forrests," and "Taming a Tartar."

The remaining two thrillers in *A Double Life* were dispatched to yet another Leslie journal. *Frank Leslie's Chimney Corner* was planned, started, and edited by the femme fatale Miriam Squier, apex of a melodramatic triangle, soon to become the wife of Frank Leslie. This fascinating beauty was also an astute editor, and she planned her *Chimney Corner* as an illustrated fireside friend that would provide American mothers with domestic stories, their daughters with romances, their sons with dramatic escapades, and youngsters with adventures and fairy tales. On 3 June 1865, in the words of the editor:

We present herewith, just as the aurora of peace irradiates the horizon, the first number of The Chimney Corner . . . which shall be a welcome messenger of instruction and amusement to the young and old, in the family and by the fireside — that altar around which cluster our holiest and most cherished recollections. . . . We give a story a day all the year around, some to touch by their tragic power, some to thrill with love's vicissitudes, some to hold in suspense with dramatic interest. . . . Come then, and welcome, to our Chimney Corner, sure of a feast of good things.[15]

Part of that feast had been requisitioned from the Leslie prize-winner Louisa May Alcott, who wrote in her journal: "Leslie asked me to be a regular contributor to his new paper 'The Chimney Corner,' & I agreed if he'd pay before hand, he said he would & bespoke two tales at once $50 each. Longer ones as often as I could, & whatever else I liked to send. So here's another source of income & Alcott brains seem in demand, whereat I sing 'Hallyluyer,' & fill up my inkstand."[16] And so "A Double Tragedy" was given a place of honor on page 1 of the first issue of America's "Great Family Paper," while "Ariel. A Legend of the Lighthouse," the author's "second" *Chimney Corner* tale, followed in July.

All five stories in this collection reveal Louisa May Alcott as a writer sensitive to the cultural and social currents of her time. She employs as themes art and the theater — two lifelong passions — as well as the contemporary interest in what might now be termed the occult. Always present, too, are examples of the struggle between the sexes, reflecting the rise of feminism.

Alcott's preoccupation with the art theme is thoroughly understandable. Her sister May was an eager art student, who illustrated her sister's effusions, studied at the School of Design in Boston, served as drawing teacher in Syracuse, and took anatomical drawing lessons under the distinguished Dr. William Rimmer.[17] Even-

15. *Frank Leslie's Chimney Corner* 1:1 (3 June 1865); Stern, *Purple Passage*, pp. 45–46.

16. Louisa May Alcott, unpublished journals (by permission of the Houghton Library, Harvard University), March 1865, printed with deletions in Ednah Dow Cheney, *Louisa May Alcott: Her Life, Letters, and Journals* (Boston: Roberts Brothers, 1889), p. 165.

17. It is interesting to note that Rimmer was drawn to Shakespearean subjects. His paintings include scenes from *The Tempest*, *Macbeth*, and *Romeo and Juliet*. See Jeffrey Weidman et al., *William Rimmer: A Yankee Michelangelo* (Hanover, N.H.: University Press of New England, 1985).

tually she would go abroad to study art, and after her tragic death her box of paintings would be sent home to Concord. Now, in the early 1860s, the two young women shared their excitement over literature and art just as they shared lodgings in Boston. Between May's enthusiastic reports and her own exposure to art exhibitions, Louisa May Alcott was enabled to inject the art motif into at least two of these tales, "A Pair of Eyes" and "Ariel."

In the former, published in *Frank Leslie's Illustrated Newspaper* in October 1863,[18] the black-bearded artist Max Erdmann (who, curiously, bears a close resemblance to Frank Leslie) finds a model for his portrait of Lady Macbeth in Agatha Eure, whom he later marries. Agatha, however, jealous of Max's better-loved mistress Art, practices mesmeric powers upon him and so subdues him in one of Alcott's more remarkable versions of the power struggle between man and woman.

In "Ariel," Philip Southesk, a poet-artist, sketches the nymph Ariel, making "the likeness perfect with a happy stroke or two,"[19] a tribute to economy in brushwork. In "A Pair of Eyes," Max Erdmann creates a far more arresting painting. Erdmann is the artist incarnate, going far beyond Frank Leslie or May Alcott in his devotion to a muse that was to him "wife, child, friend, food and fire." And the portrait of Lady Macbeth for which a mesmerist acts as model sets the weird and sinister tone of this tale. Alcott describes the portrait in detail: "the dimly lighted chamber, the listening attendants, the ghostly figure with wan face framed in hair, that streamed shadowy and long against white draperies, and whiter arms, whose gesture told that the parted lips were uttering that mournful cry — 'Here's the smell of blood still! / All the perfumes of Arabia will not / Sweeten this little hand — '"

Was the portrait a copy, or a Louisa Alcott original? The great eighteenth-century Swiss artist John Henry Fuseli produced a pen and gray wash of Lady Macbeth sleepwalking that has much in common with Max Erdmann's portrait, including the listening at-

---

18. "A Pair of Eyes; or, Modern Magic," *Frank Leslie's Illustrated Newspaper* (24 and 31 October 1863), 69–71, 85–87.

19. All quotations are from the stories that follow, unless otherwise indicated.

tendants, the gesture of Lady Macbeth's arms, her long streaming hair. But Fuseli's work was in the British Museum, which Louisa had not yet visited, and unless she had seen a reproduction of it somewhere, she probably had transposed her own vision of the sleepwalking queen into a net of words.[20]

The vision was of course an outcome of Louisa Alcott's lifelong fascination with the theater; the theme of theatricality in general, and of Shakespeare in particular, run markedly through nearly all these tales.

The plays the young Louisa had co-authored and coproduced with her sister Anna for performance in the barn before the Concord neighbors were published after her death as *Comic Tragedies*.[21] She dramatized one of her early stories, "The Rival Prima Donnas," and wrote a farce, "Nat Bachelor's Pleasure Trip" that actually saw a single performance at the Howard Athenaeum in 1860. In addition, Louisa Alcott's addiction to the footlights was reflected in her amateur acting in Walpole, New Hampshire, in Concord, and in Boston, and though her major role was that of the Dickensian Mrs. Jarley of the waxworks, she elocuted her way through a variety of popular parlor comedies.

She was, in short, stagestruck. In 1855, on her twenty-third birthday, she wrote to her father from Boston: "I go to the theatre once or twice a week."[22] Three years later she mentioned in her journal: "Saw Charlotte Cushman, and had a stagestruck fit. . . . Worked off my stage fever in writing a story, and felt better." And

---

20. For the Fuseli suggestion I am grateful to Charles Colbert of Newton, Massachusetts. See also Caroline Keay, *Henry Fuseli* (New York: St. Martin's Press, 1974), p. 29, No. 24: Lady Macbeth sleepwalking. Alcott's interest in art persisted. See, for example, Louisa May Alcott, *Diana & Persis*, ed. Sarah Elbert (New York: Arno Press, 1978). In that "art novel," Persis, modeled upon May Alcott, is the young woman painter, while the character of Diana is based upon the sculptor Harriet Hosmer.

21. *Comic Tragedies Written by "Jo" and "Meg" and Acted by the "Little Women"* (Boston: Roberts Brothers, 1893).

22. Louisa May Alcott to Amos Bronson Alcott, 28 November [1855], *The Selected Letters of Louisa May Alcott*, eds. Joel Myerson and Daniel Shealy (Boston: Little, Brown, 1987).

when that renowned American actress descended upon Concord, Louisa was lost in admiration.[23]

Charlotte Cushman was of course a famous Lady Macbeth, and Louisa Alcott was becoming a connoisseur of Macbeth performers. Of Edwin Forrest she commented: "Tho Forrest does not act Shakespere well the beauty of the play shines thro the badly represented parts, & imagining what I should like to see, I can make up a better Macbeth . . . than Forrest with his gaspings & shoutings can give me."[24] Alcott confined her own greenroom roles to those in comedies and farces. In her sensational stories she also indulged in melodrama and tragedy, and even attempted to "make up a better Macbeth."

Macbeth pervades much of Alcott's "A Pair of Eyes." That story opens in the theater where the artist Max Erdmann and the woman who is to mesmerize him are both watching a performance of that tragedy. The painting of Lady Macbeth that Erdmann finally completes, having used Agatha Eure as his model, crashes from the wall during the second and last installment — a symbolic omen of the tragedy that is to follow.

In place of *Macbeth*, *The Tempest* provided Alcott with suggestions for her "Ariel. A Legend of the Lighthouse,"[25] the only one of these five tales in which setting is more important than plot, character, or theme. Indeed, as in *The Tempest* itself, an enchanted island surrounded by "deep water, heavy surf and a spice of danger" dominates all three. Out of the background emerges the character of Alcott's Ariel, to whom the author prophetically gave the surname March. And out of the background arise many of the plot developments: Ariel's life on the island; her love of the hero Philip South-

23. Cheney, pp. 99 and 113. As late as 1886, in her last domestic novel, *Jo's Boys*, Alcott created in the actress Miss Cameron "a near-translation" of Charlotte Cushman. See Joseph Leach, *Bright Particular Star: The Life & Times of Charlotte Cushman* (New Haven, Conn.: Yale University Press, 1970), p. 283.

24. Louisa May Alcott to Amos Bronson Alcott, 28 November [1855], *The Selected Letters of Louisa May Alcott*.

25. "Ariel. A Legend of the Lighthouse," *Frank Leslie's Chimney-Corner* (8 and 15 July 1865), 81–83, 99–101.

esk, himself "as changeable as the ocean" he loves so well; the revelation of their true identities; their thwarted romance; and finally their happy reunion.

If the author based her background upon scenes near Gloucester, Massachusetts, where she camped out on Norman's Woe,[26] she found much else in Shakespeare's *Tempest*. Throughout this "Legend of the Lighthouse" there are overt and covert allusions to Shakespeare's play. In much of the conversation and characterization, the source is obvious. Philip, for example, comments to Ariel: "It only needs a Miranda to make a modern version of the Tempest," and she replies: "Perhaps I am to lead you to her as the real Ariel led Ferdinand to Miranda. . . . " When Philip asks Ariel what she knows of Shakespeare, she answers: "I know and love Shakespeare better than any of my other books, and can sing every song he wrote." Indeed, she frequently sings "Oh, come unto the yellow sands," an appropriate lyric for one who is "a spirit singing to itself between sea and sky." Philip's gift to his beloved Ariel is "a beautiful volume of Shakespeare, daintily bound, richly illustrated," and as he sketches, she reads. Gazing at "a fine illustration of the Tempest," she remarks: "Here we all are! Prospero is not unlike my father, but Ferdinand is much plainer than you. Here's Ariel swinging in a vine, as I've often done, and Caliban watching her. . . . " Alcott's narrative adaptation is complete to its Caliban, the lighthouse keeper's humpbacked companion, whose massive head is set upon a stunted body and who loves Ariel and wreaks much evil.

On the nineteenth-century American stage, theatergoers could watch a winged Ariel fly in and out of the scenes of *The Tempest* on "visible ropes."[27] In *Frank Leslie's Chimney Corner*, readers of sensa-

26. See Louisa May Alcott, unpublished journals (by permission of the Houghton Library, Harvard University), August 1864, and Cheney, p. 159, for the fortnight in Gloucester. For scenes similar to those described in "Ariel. A Legend of the Lighthouse," see Charles Boardman Hawes, *Gloucester by Land and Sea: The Story of a New England Seacoast Town* (Boston: Little, Brown, 1923); Edward Rowe Snow, *Famous New England Lighthouses* (Boston: Yankee Publishing Company, 1945); John S. Webber, Jr., *In and Around Cape Ann* (Gloucester: Cape Ann Advertiser Office, 1885), p. 36 and *passim*.

27. Charles H. Shattuck, *Shakespeare on the American Stage from the Hallams to Edwin Booth* (Washington: Folger Shakespeare Library, 1976), p. 114.

tion stories could enjoy a modern version of that play ingeniously contrived by the future author of *Little Women*.

The great British actor David Garrick succeeded in reducing Shakespeare's *Taming of the Shrew* to a three-act farce called *Katharine and Petruchio*, which was performed from time to time at the Boston Theatre.[28] Since the author of "The Rival Prima Donnas" had a pass to the Boston, she might well have enjoyed Garrick's adaptation of Shakespeare upon several occasions and been moved to write her own modern version. This she did in "Taming a Tartar," the "wild Russian story" she contributed to *Frank Leslie's Illustrated Newspaper*. Her Russian melodrama is a well-paced, neatly plotted story of the power struggle between the defiant, fearless, freedom-loving Sybil Varna and the Slavic autocrat Prince Alexis Demidoff, whose Tartar blood has made him a tyrant. Step by step, in bout after bout, her Petruchio succumbs to her Katharine, feminism rises victorious, and where William Shakespeare tamed a shrew, Miss Alcott tames a Tartar.

It is, however, in the story Louisa Alcott contributed to the first issue of *Frank Leslie's Chimney Corner* that her devotion to the theater and her preoccupation with Shakespeare are crystallized. "A Double Tragedy" is precisely what its subtitle indicates: "An Actor's Story."[29] This, the shortest of the narratives in *A Double Life*, is quintessentially a story of the stage. It opens with a performance by the two protagonists — lovers in life as well as on the stage — in "a Spanish play" whose cast includes a lover disguised as a monk, a Grand Inquisitor, and a stern old duke and whose plot involves a state secret, a duel, and long immurement in a dungeon. What Spanish play had Alcott in mind? Her Spanish play seems to have derived more from her own early dramatic effort performed in the Concord barn and entitled "The Captive of Castile" than from any

28. Ibid., p. xi. See also, for the performances of the time and Alcott's addiction to the theater, Cheney, p. 65; Madeleine B. Stern, "Louisa Alcott, Trouper," *New England Quarterly* 16:2 (June 1943): 188; Stern, *Louisa May Alcott*, p. 78; Eugene Tompkins, *The History of the Boston Theatre 1854–1901* (Boston: Houghton Mifflin, 1908).

29. "A Double Tragedy. An Actor's Story," *Frank Leslie's Chimney Corner* (3 June 1865), 1–3.

extant professional drama. During the nightmares that accompanied her illness after serving at the Union Hotel Hospital, Alcott had had visions of a "stout, handsome Spaniard" who pursued her, "appearing out of closets, in at windows, or threatening me dreadfully all night long."[30] Perhaps the shade of that Spaniard was upon her.

Whatever sources may have contributed to the Spanish play that opens "A Double Tragedy," there is no doubt about the play that shaped its architecture. The sudden reappearance of her husband, St. John, so maddens the actress Clotilde Varian, who is in love with the actor Paul Lamar, that she murders her spouse. When Paul becomes aware of her guilt, he finds her abhorrent: "What devil devised and helped you execute a crime like this?" Following the murder, the two enact the only tragedy possible under the circumstances: *Romeo and Juliet*. On the night of the performance, Clotilde performs Juliet to the life and kills herself on stage. Paul Lamar never acts again.

When Louisa Alcott was given a free pass to the Boston Theatre, she was also conducted by the manager all over the building on Boston's Washington Street. She was shown how a dancing floor could be fitted over the orchestra chairs and the house converted into a ballroom, and she was introduced to the mysteries of theatrical apparatus and effects. In "A Double Tragedy" a platform has been hastily built for the launching of an aerial car in some grand spectacle; there is also a roped gallery from which there is a fine view of the stage. This area becomes the scene of Clotilde's murder of her husband. She simply cuts the rope that would have protected him from falling. And so, having studied the secrets behind the scenes of the Boston Theatre, Alcott shaped them to her own dramatic purposes.

Clotilde Varian's acting credo has much in common with Louisa May Alcott's credo as a writer of sensational fiction. Actors, Clotilde believed, must have neither hearts nor nerves while on stage. As an actress "she seldom played a part twice alike, and left much

30. Louisa May Alcott, unpublished journals (by permission of the Houghton Library, Harvard University), [January] 1863, and Cheney, pp. 146–147.

to the inspiration of the moment." She held that an actor must learn to live a double life. Louisa Alcott also, often relying upon the inspiration of the moment, seldom wrote a sensational story twice alike. In this particular story she created her own "hapless Italian lovers" who "never found better representatives" than in Clotilde and Paul that night. Juliet's grave clothes became Clotilde's. The "mimic tragedy . . . slowly darkened to its close."

The world of art and the world of the theater were entwined in Alcott's double life. So too was a more dangerous art. The third of Louisa Alcott's sensational themes was named after an Austrian physician and was known to the nineteenth century as mesmerism.

Although Alcott's involvement with art and with the stage are easily traceable to their sources in her life, her interest in mesmerism seems to have developed as a shared interest of her time rather than from personal experience. It is true that, toward the end of her life, when mesmerism had taken a "religious turn, in spiritualism and in Christian Science,"[31] Alcott did submit to a treatment called mind cure to rid herself of various ills. She found the treatment interesting and described it for the *Woman's Journal*: "No effect was felt except sleepiness for the first few times; then mesmeric sensations occasionally came, sunshine in the head, a sense of walking on the air, and slight trances, when it was impossible to stir for a few moments."[32] During the 1880s, when she was trying this mind cure, was Louisa Alcott remembering the 1860s, when she had used mesmerism as a pivot in a sensational story?

During the eighteenth century, "the great enchanter" Franz Anton Mesmer had developed a theory of hypnotism based upon the existence of some magnetic force or fluid that permeated the universe and insinuated itself into the nervous system of man. This force he called animal magnetism. The theory, introduced to Boston, had created a furor, and the pseudoscience originated by Mesmer attracted a stream of followers in this country — mesmerists and clairvoyants, etherologists and psychometrists, along with a

31. Taylor Stoehr, "Hawthorne and Mesmerism," *Huntington Library Quarterly* 33:1 (November 1969): 37.
32. "Miss Alcott on Mind-Cure," *Woman's Journal* 16:16 (18 April 1885): 121.

fascinated if sometimes skeptical public. Among the last were Nathaniel Hawthorne, who, while rejecting the hocus-pocus, was much taken up with such matters as the evil eye; and Edgar Allan Poe, whose "Mesmeric Revelation" consisted of a dialogue between magnetizer and magnetized and ended with the death of the sleepwalker. As for Louisa Alcott's revered neighbor Ralph Waldo Emerson, the god of her early idolatry, he reacted to the pseudoscience with characteristic equanimity, writing: "Mesmerism, which broke into the inmost shrines, attempted the explanation of miracle and prophecy, as well as of creation. . . . a certain success attended it. . . . It was human, it was genial, it affirmed unity and connection between remote points."[33] Alcott was well aware of all these points of view. Moreover, she had access to the library of books eventually published on such subjects as electrical psychology, magnetic revelation, and mesmeric influence. She was drawn to the theme, as Hawthorne and Poe had been drawn. She perceived, as Hawthorne especially perceived, the violation of the human soul that might result from the penetrating intrusions of the mesmerist. And whether she believed in it or was skeptical, she knew that the subject of mesmerism would make a colorful thread to weave into a sensation tale.

The author of "A Pair of Eyes" writes as an expert on the hypnotic function of the mesmerist's eye, the effects of hypnotic influence upon the subject, and the use of mesmerism as an exercise in power. The eyes of Agatha Eure are "two dark wells . . . tranquil yet . . . fathomless." Her first exercise in mesmerism is perpetrated upon her unknowing victim, the painter Max Erdmann, who reacts almost clinically:

It seemed as if my picture had left its frame. . . . My hand moved slower and slower. . . . my eyelids began to be weighed down by a delicious

33. Stoehr, "Hawthorne and Mesmerism," 35, quoting from Emerson's "Historic Notes on Life and Letters in New England," and 54–55, discussing Hawthorne and the unpardonable sin. See also Nathaniel Hawthorne, *The American Notebooks . . . edited by Randall Stewart* (New Haven, Conn.: Yale University Press, 1933), pp. lxxiv-lxxvi; Madeleine B. Stern, *Heads & Headlines: The Phrenological Fowlers* (Norman: University of Oklahoma Press, 1971), pp. 70–85, discussing Poe's "Mesmeric Revelation."

drowsiness. . . . Everything grew misty. . . . a sensation of wonderful airiness came over me, and I felt as if I could float away like a thistledown. Presently every sense seemed to fall asleep . . . I drifted away into a sea of blissful repose. . . . I seemed to be looking down at myself, as if soul and body had parted company and I was gifted with a double life. . . . then my sleep deepened into utter oblivion. . . .

Erdmann is expertly roused from the mesmeric state. "A pungent odor seemed to recall me to the same half wakeful state. . . . an unseen hand stirred my hair with the grateful drip of water, and once there came a touch like the pressure of lips upon my forehead. . . . I clearly saw a bracelet on the arm [of Agatha] and read the Arabic characters engraved upon the golden coins that formed it; I . . . felt the cool sweep of a hand passing to and fro across my forehead." Alcott seems to have studied seriously the mesmeric process, the efficacy of mesmeric passes, and even the use of a bracelet as a magnetic aid.

Later in "A Pair of Eyes," in the course of their tempestuous marriage, Agatha exercises her mesmeric powers upon Max with the sole purpose of subduing his will to hers. Aware of the telepathic influence being exerted upon him, Erdmann consults a physician. "Dr. L —— " is temporarily absent, and while Max awaits his arrival, his attention is drawn to a book on magnetism, which opens "a new world" to him. In all likelihood, the book that elucidates his victimization is Theodore Leger's *Animal Magnetism; or Psycodunamy*,[34] a volume that includes a general history of the subject, a chapter on Mesmer, and an account of the progress of the pseudoscience in the United States. "These operations," Leger expounded, "are as simple as possible; . . . No apparatus is necessary. . . . It is only necessary that you find a person of impressible temperament, which is indicated generally by the largeness of the pupils of the eyes." Theodore Leger happened also to have been physician to the great American feminist Margaret Fuller, and his office was the place of assignation for her and her lover James Na-

---

34. Theodore Leger, *Animal Magnetism; or Psycodunamy* (New York: Appleton, 1846), p. 386 and *passim*.

than. Had Louisa Alcott, who admired Margaret Fuller all her life, been aware of this?[35]

In any event, Alcott was fully aware of the method of mesmerism and the nature of the mesmerist. In Agatha Eure she painted the practitioner par excellence: "sitting . . . erect and motionless as an inanimate figure of intense thought; her eyes were fixed, face colorless, with an expression of iron determination, as if every energy of mind and body were wrought up to the achievement of a single purpose." And so, the heroine whose pair of eyes gives the story its title, uses those eyes to conquer and control a will. If this is a variation upon Hawthorne's "unpardonable sin" — the exploitation of a human soul — it is a variation that Alcott made peculiarly her own. All her magnetic revelations are loaded with sexual overtones, and her victim is no helpless female, but the male.

Like Agatha Eure, the evil genius of "The Fate of the Forrests" has "mysterious eyes [that] both attracted and repelled, with a subtle magnetism." As in "A Pair of Eyes," the focal theme is a *diablerie* shaped to literary ends. "The Fate of the Forrests," however, hinges not upon mesmerism or any other pseudoscience but upon the far more remote motif of Hindu Thuggee.

Of all the Alcott thrillers in *A Double Life*, "The Fate of the Forrests"[36] has the most complicated plot line and the most exotic theme. The characters are introduced at the moment when they wish to pry into the future, and their wish is granted — with devastating results — by the seeming "magician" Felix Stähl. His whispered prophecies presage tragic consequences for all. As for the heroine, Ursula Forrest, who loves and is loved by her cousin Evan, Stähl's prophetic whisper is a single word that turns her into a "marble Medusa" and changes her life forever. Instead of marrying her beloved Evan, she unaccountably marries Stähl!

And so the stage is set, the mystery presented: Who is this Stähl

---

35. Madeleine B. Stern, *The Life of Margaret Fuller* (New York: Dutton, 1942), pp. 347–349, 351.
36. "The Fate of the Forrests," *Frank Leslie's Illustrated Newspaper* (11, 18, and 25 February 1865), 325–326, 341–343, 362–363.

and what has he whispered? Ursula and Evan are "dimly conscious of some unseen yet controlling hand that ruled their intercourse and shaped events." The reader is aware that Ursula has been metamorphosed into Stähl's "very passive bride." When Stähl exclaims, "But now, when I have made you wholly mine . . . I find a cold, still creature in my arms," Ursula retorts that she had vowed obedience, not love.

Why has she done so? Although the reader senses that Ursula is attempting to save Evan from some dire, unnamed fate, the answer to the enigma is not vouchsafed until the last installment. By then a poison plot has further complicated the tale, for Stähl has prophesied that "before the month is out the city will be startled by a murder, and the culprit will elude justice by death." Stähl's prophecies are invariably fulfilled. He has engineered his own death, making sure that Ursula will be charged with it. Before he dies he manages to snatch "her to him with an embrace almost savage in its passionate fervor," while later he mutters to himself, "I won my rose . . . but my blight is on her." It is indeed. Stähl dies; Ursula is imprisoned for the crime of murder; eventually — after her hair whitens — she too dies.

It is, as Alcott puts it, "the romance within a romance, which had made a tragedy of three lives." The romance within a romance is a theme directly out of the heart of India. Leslie readers, Alcott knew, were interested in the mysteries of Indian mores and the fascinations of their ceremonies. That she too was drawn by the lure of the East is indicated by scattered references in her tales. In "Ariel," the hero Southesk had been born on a long voyage to India; in "A Pair of Eyes," Max Erdmann, the susceptible victim of mesmerism, describes himself as having "Indian blood in my veins, and superstition lurked there still."

In June 1861, Louisa Alcott mentioned in her journal that "Emerson recommended Hodson's India, and I got it, and liked it."[37] While W.S.R. Hodson's *Twelve Years of a Soldier's Life in India*

---

37. Cheney, p. 128.

informed Alcott of the Delhi campaign of 1857 and 1858, there was little or nothing in it about the horror known as Hindu Thuggee.[38] The details of that barbarous and "abnormal excrescence upon Hinduism" may have been appropriated by Alcott from another popular book, *The Confessions of a Thug*, by Meadows Taylor, which created a furor when first published as a British three-decker and doubtless later titillated the lurid fancies of the Concord spinner of tales.[39] Amir Ali, Taylor's protagonist, was a professional murderer who strangled seven hundred human beings with pride and pleasure. Surely he was not only one of the most successful devotees of Thuggism but one capable of elucidating its secrets and its horrors to an author in search of shocking themes.

And Hindu Thuggism was a shocking theme. The Thugs of India, first mentioned in the fourteenth century and all but stamped out by the British in the nineteenth, formed a secret "confederacy of professional assassins" who, after performing certain religious rites in worship of the Hindu goddess of destruction, strangled their victims and regarded their plunder as a reward for the observance of a religious duty. Their use of the noose gave them the name Phansigars, or "noose operators." The fraternity employed secret signs by which they recognized each other. The goddess of destruction whom they worshiped — variously known as Kali, Bhowanee, or Bhawani — at one time demanded human sacrifice as an essential of her ritual. Her will was revealed to her worshipers by "a complicated series of omens." As Meadows Taylor explained, omens and incantations formed an important part of Thug ritual. Louisa Alcott, seeking themes for her thrillers, pounced upon the paraphernalia of Thuggism to explain the mystery of Felix Stähl. Stähl, it develops, was Indian on his mother's side, belonged to the Thuggee league, bore on his left arm the insignia of Bhawani, and had inherited, along with his devotion to the goddess of destruc-

38. Major W.S.R. Hodson, *Twelve Years of a Soldier's Life in India* (Boston: Ticknor and Fields, 1860).

39. Meadows Taylor, *The Confessions of a Thug*, ed. F. Yeats-Brown (London: Eyre and Spottiswoode, 1938). See also, for Thugs, Thuggism, and Kali, *Encyclopaedia Britannica*, 11th ed., vol. XIV, pp. 412–413; vol. XV, p. 641; vol. XXVI, p. 896.

tion, his family's vow of vengeance against the Forrests. The word he had whispered to Ursula, who was aware of the curse on her family, was Bhawani's name. By marrying her, Stähl wreaks vengeance not only upon her, but upon her beloved cousin Evan.

Perhaps the most interesting Thuggist regulation in Louisa Alcott's view was that regarding women. According to the rites of the confederacy, a woman could not be killed. Hence Stähl cannot and will not murder Ursula directly. The fate he inflicts upon her becomes a fate worse than death. Thus Stähl's black art and power are explained as the Indian goddess of destruction is propitiated in a brew concocted by the future author of the Little Women series.

In "The Fate of the Forrests" Evan and Stähl ostensibly contend, "like spirits of good and evil," for the beautiful Ursula. In reality, the struggle takes place where it almost inevitably does in Alcott sensation stories, between the man and the woman, between Stähl, representing Eastern vengeance and brutality, and Ursula, who wins only through dying. In succumbing to Stähl but never returning his passion, Ursula is "both mistress and slave."

Louisa Alcott made much of the theme of slave and master in her thrillers, and the power struggle between the sexes runs like a scarlet thread consistently through most of these stories. In varying degrees the woman is victorious, until, in the final narrative of *A Double Life*, "Taming a Tartar," she reigns supreme.

Interested as she was in the arts of painting and the theater and in the blacker arts of mesmerism and Thuggee, Alcott was dominated by the theme of the conflict between men and women. Her fascination with the relations between master and slave is explained to some extent by episodes of her early life, but by and large her interest in the subject was pragmatic, professional, designed to satisfy subscribers to Leslie periodicals. In her hands involvement with sexual conflict became an enormously productive literary theme.

Attempts have been made from time to time to analyze the often contradictory relationship between Louisa Alcott and her father Bronson. As one scholar commented recently, "Louisa May Alcott seized upon melodrama as a source of emotional excitement and catharsis, which she indulged in as part of her rebellion against her father's utopian domestic ideal. The family stage thus became an important arena for the well-known conflict between father and daughter."[40] An outcome of the love-hate relationship that doubtless existed between Louisa and Bronson, this discord was due in large measure to differences in temperament between the rebellious, independent, hardworking daughter and the idealistic, philosophic dreamer who was her father. Louisa's rebellion was surely intensified when she witnessed the effects of Bronson's inability to earn a living upon her mother and her sisters. This background, tempestuous though always tinged with love, was in itself a power struggle of sorts and in all likelihood helped germinate the battles she would imagine for her characters.

The seven weeks spent by the nineteen-year-old Louisa Alcott as a domestic servant in Dedham, Massachusetts, must have brought to a crescendo the conflict she had experienced at home. In Dedham the conflict of wills was between a young and inexperienced girl and her taskmaster-pursuer James Richardson, whose demands went beyond the drudgeries of domestic service. Stored in her writer's mind, this experience would later provide kindling for the inflammatory theme of the power struggle.[41]

In addition to these personal experiences, the climate of the 1850s gave Alcott cause for the anger she would infuse into her theme. Any observant woman of the time was aware of the inequality of the sexes in the economic world, in government, in law, in marriage, and in the home. Taxed but not represented, the woman of mid-nineteenth-century America lived in an antifeminist world in which the war between the sexes could be carried on far more successfully in fiction than in life.

Most of the narratives in *A Double Life* are basically exercises in that struggle. Because she was so gifted a writer, Louisa Alcott portrayed that fight with intriguing diversity, creating many variations on the dominant theme. In "A Pair of Eyes" the conflict

40. Karen Halttunen, "The Domestic Drama of Louisa May Alcott," *Feminist Studies* 10:2 (Summer 1984): 233.

41. See Louisa May Alcott, "How I Went Out to Service," *The Independent* 26 (4 June 1874); *Behind a Mask*, pp. ix-x.

between man and woman is reduced to a simplistic level: It becomes a matter of responding to or resisting telepathic commands. Supremely significant is the fact that it is the woman who mesmerizes, the man who is mesmerized. Agatha confesses to Max that she used her powers until she had "subjugated" his "arrogant spirit," to make herself master. "Henceforth you are the slave of the ring, and when I command you must obey. . . . You have brought this fate upon yourself, accept it, submit to it, for I have bought you with my wealth, I hold you with my mystic art, and body and soul, Max Erdmann, you are mine!" For all the man's resistance, in the end the woman conquers. Here, as in most of these tales, the reiteration of certain words alerts the reader to the author's intention: *power, slavery, master, slave, subjugate, submit, subject, conquer, control.* The words signal the recurrent theme.

Even in "The Fate of the Forrests," in which Stähl exercises his power with the aid of Hindu Thuggee, the villain-hero realizes that, though he brings Ursula to submission, he can never bring her to love. In effect he has lost his slave and found a master — a subtle variation on the power struggle motif.

The conflict in "A Double Tragedy" exonerates, for the reader at least, Clotilde of the murder of her husband. The husband, St. John, is an arrogant lord of creation who regards his wife with the "pride which a master bestows upon a handsome slave." He is certain she will "submit with a good grace" and return to him. "I am convinced," he smugly remarks, "it would be best for this adorable woman to submit without defiance or delay — and I do think she will." Of course she does not. Instead, armed with her writer's anger, Louisa Alcott turns Clotilde into a murderess who annihilates the male contender.

It is in the last of the shockers in *A Double Life* that the struggle is most explicit and most dramatic.[42] From the start of "Taming a Tartar" — indeed from its very title — the author's purpose is made

---

42. "Taming a Tartar," *Frank Leslie's Illustrated Newspaper* (30 November, and 7, 14, and 21 December 1867), 166–167, 186–187, 202–203, 219. See Louisa May Alcott, *A Modern Mephistopheles and Taming a Tartar*, ed. Madeleine B. Stern (New York: Praeger, 1987).

clear. The Tartar is the "swarthy, black-eyed, scarlet-lipped" Prince Alexis, a man of "fearful temper, childish caprices. . . . impetuous . . . moods." His Tartar blood has made him a tyrant; he is mad for "wolves, . . . ice and . . . barbarous delights." He has the "savage strength and spirit of one in whose veins flowed the blood of men reared in tents, and born to lead wild lives in a wild land." What more delicious foil could be invented for Mademoiselle Sybil Varna, the slender, pale-faced English teacher in a *Pensionnat pour Demoiselles* who was "bent on" having her own way?

The contest between the two constitutes the entire plot of the tale. The question is not who will yield to whom, the answer to which is implicit in the title, but how long the struggle will take and what steps the taming process will encompass. Each round in the battle of wills becomes more intense: The first bout concerns the trifling question of the return to St. Petersburg; the second, the prince's cruelty to his hound. As she succeeds in these minor conflicts, Sybil gains a renewed sense of her power. "Once conquer his will, . . . and I had gained a power possessed by no other person. I liked the trial."

The third and penultimate round ends in a draw, a kind of mutual taming, highly sexual in nature. Sybil refuses to accompany the prince to his estate in Volnoi, and as a result Alexis abducts her, accompanying the physical act with a very purple passage: "Submit, and no harm will befall you. Accept the society of one who adores you, and permit yourself to be conquered by one who never yields — except to you." At Volnoi the struggle ends, but not before the serfs have set fire to the estate and wounded the prince. Sybil's wish to see her "haughty lover thoroughly subdued before I put my happiness into his keeping" is realized at last. The masterful Russian humbles himself, obeys her commands, and wins her as wife. Moreover, at her demand he frees his serfs. Victory is hers, and with the final dialogue the curtain falls:

"I might boast that I also had tamed a fiery spirit, but I am humble, and content myself with the knowledge that the proudest woman ever born has promised to love, honor, and —"

"*Not* obey you."

And so, guided by the New England spinster Louisa May Alcott, the woman Sybil Varna tamed a tyrannical Tartar. In the power struggle between the sexes, surely the ultimate has been achieved.

In this quintet of tales, Louisa Alcott achieved much else as well. From her arsenal of skills she drew forth literary techniques that made an artistic craft of the sensational narrative. One thinks of the wonderful opening sentences of "A Pair of Eyes," combining the writer's focus upon art and the theater with the suspenseful allusion to the sought-for pair of eyes. The mesmerism theme is introduced subtly but immediately, and the threads of art, the stage, and mesmerism are woven seamlessly together.

In the structure of her most complicated story, "The Fate of the Forrests," Alcott demonstrated her skillful response to the demands of the serial. Here, the omens of Felix Stähl pose the mystery; the omens are fulfilled and the poison plot introduced; the denouement provides the explanation in the exotic Hindu theme.

In "A Double Tragedy," the plot moves inexorably to its tragic end, each episode mounting in tension: the performance of the Spanish play; the appearance of Clotilde's husband, St. John; the incident of the bouquet; the costume party; the crime of murder; Paul's reaction to it; Clotilde's suicide on stage in the role of Juliet.

Similarly, "Taming a Tartar" is paced to meet the requirements of the serial, its episodes steadily increasing in interest till the culmination and the victory of the heroine.

Max Erdmann, artist of the sleepwalking Lady Macbeth; Felix Stähl, "beardless, thin lipped, sharply featured," with a face "colorless as ivory" and "eyes of the intensest black"; the Tartar prince Alexis — all are colorful figures. Especially vivid are Alcott's heroines: Ursula Forrest, who "looks like one born to live a romance" and whose "unconscious queenliness" betrays "traces of some hidden care, some haunting memory, or . . . that vague yet melancholy prescience which often marks those fore-doomed to tragic lives"; Agatha Eure, "strong-willed, imperious . . . used to command all about her"; Sybil Varna of the lustrous gray eyes and firm mouth, proud nose and chestnut hair, tamer of a Tartar. These women, joining the gallery of Alcott heroines, are all memorable creations.

Skilled too is the use made by Louisa Alcott of scenes and episodes of her life that she saw fit to entwine in these tales. A Russian baron, encountered at the Pension Victoria in Vevey, Switzerland, where she was companion to an invalid in 1865, is recognizable in the Tartar tamed by Sybil Varna.[43] A visit to Gloucester and Norman's Woe in 1864 had literary consequences the following year when "Ariel. A Legend of the Lighthouse" was produced. This tale of a creature of the sea is set in a lighthouse on an island. On the island's further side is a chasm, a great split in the rock on Gull's Perch through which the sea flows. The chasm bears likeness to that deeply cut fissure in the ledge near Magnolia, Massachusetts, known as Rafe's Chasm, a rockbound channel through which the sea rushes with tremendous force.[44] What she saw, Louisa Alcott used, molding scenes and characters — along with her convictions and her furies — into the tales she told.

The connections between Alcott's life and literature may now be further explored. Assuredly, there are intriguing queries still awaiting firm answers. Which particular performance of *Macbeth* induced her to pick up her pen and indite "A Pair of Eyes"? Was it indeed Fuseli's portrait of Lady Macbeth or some other that she depicted on Max Erdmann's canvas? Was it her own "Captive of Castile" or another Spanish play she had in mind when she wrote "A Double Tragedy" for Frank Leslie? Was she herself ever mesmerized, or did she rely simply upon the text of Dr. Theodore Leger? What initially attracted her to the dark theme of Hindu Thuggism? Was it Meadows Taylor's triple-decker alone? Most important, what power struggles beyond father-daughter relations and the experience in domestic service — struggles thus far hidden from her biographers — did she win or lose and weave into her

43. Louisa May Alcott, "Life in a Pension," *The Independent* (7 November 1867), 2.

44. Although "Rafe's Chasm is at the water's edge in Magnolia, a section of Gloucester, and not on an island" (Marion A. Harding, Cape Ann Historical Association), it bears a striking resemblance to the chasm in "Ariel."

stories? As more of her sensational tales emerge, so too do enigmas that call for solutions.

Always one persistent question remains: What further anonymous Alcott stories with still more varied themes lie buried in the crumbling pages of nineteenth-century periodicals, how many more graphically illustrated installments of other tales of darkness — written in secret and published without a name — await the pursuit of researcher, the delight of avid reader?

Although it may not be necessary to rewrite Alcott's biography, it is necessary to rewrite more radically our concept of this Concord author, this delver into dark and diverse themes, this keeper of many secrets. Her achievement, ranging from the exotic to the domestic, appears to be even grander and more varied than had been suspected. It is time it was fully recognized and reassessed.

A Note on the Texts

A DOUBLE LIFE reprints five stories written by Louisa May Alcott and published anonymously in nineteenth-century newspapers and magazines. The sources for these texts are:

"A Pair of Eyes; or, Modern Magic," *Frank Leslie's Illustrated Newspaper*, 24 and 31 October 1863, 69–71, 85–87.

"The Fate of the Forrests," *Frank Leslie's Illustrated Newspaper*, 11, 18, and 25 February 1865, 325–326, 341–343, 362–363.

"A Double Tragedy. An Actor's Story," *Frank Leslie's Chimney Corner*, 3 June 1865, 1–3.

"Ariel. A Legend of the Lighthouse," *Frank Leslie's Chimney Corner*, 8 and 15 July 1865, 81–83, 99–101.

"Taming a Tartar," *Frank Leslie's Illustrated Newspaper*, 30 November, and 7, 14, and 21 December 1867, 166–167, 186–187, 202–203, 219.

In preparing these stories for publication, we have made emendations only where the text would be obviously in error or unclear without them. For example, we have corrected obvious spelling and typographical errors, inserted words and punctuation marks for clarity, and provided missing single or double quotation marks. We have let stand nineteenth-century spellings (such as "to-day") and inconsistencies in capitalization, hyphenation, and commas in series. We have also declined to alter such technical matters as the error in "The Fate of the Forrests" when in Part I Felix whispers "three words" in Kate's ear and in Part II tells Ursula that they were "'To win my heart.'" Alcott was careless in preparing her manuscripts for publication, and compositors for nineteenth-century newspapers and magazines were not particularly careful in setting type from even the best-prepared copy, so we have in general tried to modernize or "correct" these texts as little as possible.

A Pair of Eyes; or, Modern Magic

PART I

I WAS DISAPPOINTED — the great actress had not given me what I wanted, and my picture must still remain unfinished for want of a pair of eyes. I knew what they should be, saw them clearly in my fancy, but though they haunted me by night and day I could not paint them, could not find a model who would represent the aspect I desired, could not describe it to any one, and though I looked into every face I met, and visited afflicted humanity in many shapes, I could find no eyes that visibly presented the vacant yet not unmeaning stare of Lady Macbeth in her haunted sleep. It fretted me almost beyond endurance to be delayed in my work so near its completion, for months of thought and labor had been bestowed upon it; the few who had seen it in its imperfect state had elated me with commendation, whose critical sincerity I knew the worth of; and the many not admitted were impatient for a sight of that which others praised, and to which the memory of former successes lent an interest beyond mere curiosity. All was done, and well done, except the eyes; the dimly lighted chamber, the listening attendants, the ghostly figure with wan face framed in hair, that streamed shadowy and long against white draperies, and whiter arms, whose gesture told that the parted lips were uttering that mournful cry —

> "Here's the smell of blood still!
> All the perfumes of Arabia will not
> Sweeten this little hand — "

The eyes alone baffled me, and for want of these my work waited, and my last success was yet unwon.

I was in a curious mood that night, weary yet restless, eager yet impotent to seize the object of my search, and full of haunting images that would not stay to be reproduced. My friend was absorbed in the play, which no longer possessed any charm for me, and leaning back in my seat I fell into a listless reverie, still harping on the one idea of my life; for impetuous and resolute in all things, I had given myself body and soul to the profession I had chosen and followed through many vicissitudes for fifteen years. Art was wife, child, friend, food and fire to me; the pursuit of fame as a reward for my long labor was the object for which I lived, the hope which gave me courage to press on over every obstacle, sacrifice and suffering, for the word "defeat" was not in my vocabulary. Sitting thus, alone, though in a crowd, I slowly became aware of a disturbing influence whose power invaded my momentary isolation, and soon took shape in the uncomfortable conviction that some one was looking at me. Every one has felt this, and at another time I should have cared little for it, but just then I was laboring under a sense of injury, for of all the myriad eyes about me none would give me the expression I longed for; and unreasonable as it was, the thought that I was watched annoyed me like a silent insult. I sent a searching look through the boxes on either hand, swept the remoter groups with a powerful glass, and scanned the sea of heads below, but met no answering glance; all faces were turned stageward, all minds seemed intent upon the tragic scenes enacting there.

Failing to discover any visible cause for my fancy, I tried to amuse myself with the play, but having seen it many times and being in an ill-humor with the heroine of the hour, my thoughts soon wandered, and though still apparently an interested auditor, I heard nothing, saw nothing, for the instant my mind became abstracted the same uncanny sensation returned. A vague consciousness that some stronger nature was covertly exerting its power upon my own; I smiled as this whim first suggested itself, but it rapidly grew upon me, and a curious feeling of impotent resistance took possession of me, for I was indignant without knowing why, and longed to rebel against — I knew not what. Again I looked far and wide, met several inquiring glances from near neighbors, but none that answered my demand by any betrayal of especial interest or malicious pleasure. Baffled, yet not satisfied, I turned to myself, thinking to find the cause of my disgust there, but did not succeed. I seldom drank wine, had not worked intently that day, and except the picture had no anxiety to harass me; yet without any physical or mental cause that I could discover, every nerve seemed jangled out of tune, my temples beat, my breath came short, and the air seemed feverishly close, though I had not perceived it until then. I did not understand this mood and with an impatient gesture took the playbill from my friend's knee, gathered it into my hand and fanned myself like a petulant woman, I suspect, for Louis turned and surveyed me with surprise as he asked:

"What is it, Max; you seem annoyed?"

"I am, but absurd as it is, I don't know why, except a foolish fancy that someone whom I do not see is looking at me and wishes me to look at him."

Louis laughed — "Of course there is, aren't you used to it yet? And are you so modest as not to know that many eyes take stolen glances at the rising artist, whose ghosts and goblins make their hair stand on end so charmingly? I had the mortification to discover some time ago that, young and comely as I take the liberty of thinking myself, the upturned lorgnettes are not levelled at me, but at the stern-faced, black-bearded gentleman beside me, for he looks particularly moody and interesting to-night."

"Bah! I just wish I could inspire some of those starers with gratitude enough to set them walking in their sleep for my benefit and their own future glory. Your suggestion has proved a dead failure, the woman there cannot give me what I want, the picture will never get done, and the whole affair will go to the deuce for want of a pair of eyes."

I rose to go as I spoke, and there they were behind me!

What sort of expression my face assumed I cannot tell, for I forgot time and place, and might have committed some absurdity if Louis had not pulled me down with a look that made me aware that I was staring with an utter disregard of common courtesy.

"Who are those people? Do you know them?" I demanded in a vehement whisper.

"Yes, but put down that glass and sit still or I'll call an usher to put you out," he answered, scandalized at my energetic demonstrations.

"Good! then introduce me — now at once — Come on," and I rose again, to be again arrested.

"Are you possessed to-night? You have visited so many fever wards and madhouses in your search that you've unsettled your own wits, Max. What whim has got into your brain now? And why do you want to know those people in such haste?"

"Your suggestion has not proved failure, a woman can give me what I want, the picture will be finished, and nothing will go to the deuce, for I've found the eyes — now be obliging and help me to secure them."

Louis stared at me as if he seriously began to think me a little mad, but restrained the explosive remark that rose to his lips and answered hastily, as several persons looked round as if our whispering annoyed them.

"I'll take you in there after the play if you must go, so for heaven's sake behave like a gentleman till then, and let me enjoy myself in peace."

I nodded composedly, he returned to his tragedy and shading my eyes with my hand, I took a critical survey, feeling more and more assured that my long search was at last ended. Three persons occupied the box, a well-dressed elderly lady dozing behind her fan, a lad leaning over the front absorbed in the play, and a young lady looking straight before her with the aspect I had waited for with such impatience. This figure I scrutinized with the eye of an artist which took in every accessory of outline, ornament and hue.

Framed in darkest hair, rose a face delicately cut, but cold and colorless as that of any statue in the vestibule without. The lips were slightly parted with the long slow breaths that came and went, the forehead was femininely broad and low, the brows straight and black, and underneath them the mysterious eyes fixed on vacancy, full of that weird regard so hard to counterfeit, so impossible to describe; for though absent, it was not expressionless, and through its steadfast shine a troubled meaning wandered, as if soul and body could not be utterly divorced by any effort of the will. She seemed unconscious of the scene about her, for the fixture of her glance never changed, and nothing about her stirred but the jewel on her bosom, whose changeful glitter seemed to vary as it rose and fell. Emboldened by this apparent absorption, I prolonged my scrutiny and scanned this countenance as I had never done a woman's face before. During this examination I had forgotten myself in her, feeling only a strong desire to draw nearer and dive deeper into those two dark wells that seemed so tranquil yet so fathomless, and in the act of trying to fix shape, color and expression in my memory, I lost them all; for a storm of applause broke the attentive hush as the curtain fell, and like one startled from sleep a flash of intelligence lit up the eyes, then a white hand was passed across them, and long downcast lashes hid them from my sight.

Louis stood up, gave himself a comprehensive survey, and walked out, saying, with a nod,

"Now, Max, put on your gloves, shake the hair out of your eyes, assume your best 'deportment,' and come and take an observation which may immortalize your name."

Knocking over a chair in my haste, I followed close upon his heels, as he tapped at the next door; the lad opened it, bowed to my conductor, glanced at me and strolled away, while we passed in. The elderly lady was awake, now, and received us graciously; the younger was leaning on her hand, the plumy fan held between her and the glare of the great chandelier as she watched the moving throng below.

"Agatha, here is Mr. Yorke and a friend whom he wishes to present to you," said the old lady, with a shade of deference in her manner which betrayed the companion, not the friend.

Agatha turned, gave Louis her hand, with a slow smile dawning on her lip, and looked up at me as if the fact of my advent had no particular interest for her, and my appearance promised no great pleasure.

"Miss Eure, my friend Max Erdmann yearned to be made happy by a five minutes audience, and I ventured to bring him without sending an *avant courier* to prepare the way. Am I forgiven?" with which half daring, half apologetic introduction, Louis turned to the chaperone and began to rattle.

Miss Eure bowed, swept the waves of silk from the chair beside her, and I sat down with a bold request waiting at my lips till an auspicious moment came, having resolved not to exert myself for nothing. As we discussed the usual topics suggested by the time and place, I looked often into the face before me and soon found it difficult to look away again, for it was a constant surprise to me. The absent mood had passed and with it the frost seemed to have melted from mien and manner, leaving a living woman in the statue's place. I had thought her melancholy, but her lips were dressed in smiles, and frequent peals of low-toned laughter parted them like pleasant music; I had thought her pale, but in either cheek now bloomed a color deep and clear as any tint my palette could have given; I had thought her shy and proud at first, but with each moment her manner warmed, her speech grew franker and her whole figure seemed to glow and brighten as if a brilliant lamp were lit behind the pale shade she had worn before. But the eyes were the greatest surprise of all — I had fancied them dark, and found them the light, sensitive gray belonging to highly nervous temperaments. They were remarkable eyes; for though softly fringed with shadowy lashes they were not mild, but fiery and keen, with many lights and shadows in them as the pupils dilated, and the irids shone with a transparent lustre which varied with her varying words, and proved the existence of an ardent, imperious nature underneath the seeming snow.

They exercised a curious fascination over me and kept my own obedient to their will, although scarce conscious of it at the time and believing mine to be the controlling power. Wherein the charm

lay I cannot tell; it was not the influence of a womanly
alone, for fairer faces had smiled at me in vain; yet as I sat there i
felt a pleasant quietude creep over me, I knew my voice had fallen
to a lower key, my eye softened from its wonted cold indifference,
my manner grown smooth and my demeanor changed to one almost as courtly as my friend's, who well deserved his soubriquet of
"Louis the Debonnair."

"It is because my long fret is over," I thought, and having something to gain, exerted myself to please so successfully that, soon
emboldened by her gracious mood and the flattering compliments
bestowed upon my earlier works, I ventured to tell my present
strait and the daring hope I had conceived that she would help me
through it. How I made this blunt request I cannot tell, but remember that it slipped over my tongue as smoothly as if I had
meditated upon it for a week. I glanced over my shoulder as I
spoke, fearing Louis might mar all with apology or reproof; but he
was absorbed in the comely duenna, who was blushing like a girl
at the half playful, half serious devotion he paid all womankind;
and reassured, I waited, wondering how Miss Eure would receive
my request. Very quietly; for with no change but a peculiar dropping of the lids, as if her eyes sometimes played the traitor to her
will, she answered, smilingly,

"It is I who receive the honor, sir, not you, for genius possesses
the privileges of royalty, and may claim subjects everywhere, sure
that its choice ennobles and its power extends beyond the narrow
bounds of custom, time and place. When shall I serve you, Mr.
Erdmann?"

At any other time I should have felt surprised both at her and at
myself; but just then, in the ardor of the propitious moment, I
thought only of my work, and with many thanks for her great kindness left the day to her, secretly hoping she would name an early
one. She sat silent an instant, then seemed to come to some determination, for when she spoke a shadow of mingled pain and patience swept across her face as if her resolve had cost her some
sacrifice of pride or feeling.

"It is but right to tell you that I may not always have it in my power to give you the expression you desire to catch, for the eyes you honor by wishing to perpetuate are not strong and often fail me for a time. I have been utterly blind once and may be again, yet have no present cause to fear it, and if you can come to me on such days as they will serve your purpose, I shall be most glad to do my best for you. Another reason makes me bold to ask this favor of you, I cannot always summon this absent mood, and should certainly fail in a strange place; but in my own home, with all familiar things about me, I can more easily fall into one of my deep reveries and forget time by the hour together. Will this arrangement cause much inconvenience or delay? A room shall be prepared for you — kept inviolate as long as you desire it — and every facility my house affords is at your service, for I feel much interest in the work which is to add another success to your life."

She spoke regretfully at first, but ended with a cordial glance as if she had forgotten herself in giving pleasure to another. I felt that it must have cost her an effort to confess that such a dire affliction had ever darkened her youth and might still return to sadden her prime; this pity mingled with my expressions of gratitude for the unexpected interest she bestowed upon my work, and in a few words the arrangement was made, the day and hour fixed, and a great load off my mind. What the afterpiece was I never knew; Miss Eure stayed to please her young companion, Louis stayed to please himself, and I remained because I had not energy enough to go away. For, leaning where I first sat down, I still looked and listened with a dreamy sort of satisfaction to Miss Eure's low voice, as with downcast eyes, still shaded by her fan, she spoke enthusiastically and well of art (the one interesting theme to me) in a manner which proved that she had read and studied more than her modesty allowed her to acknowledge.

We parted like old friends at her carriage door, and as I walked away with Louis in the cool night air I felt like one who had been asleep in a close room, for I was both languid and drowsy, though a curious undercurrent of excitement still stirred my blood and tingled along my nerves. "A theatre is no place for me," I decided, and anxious to forget myself said aloud:

"Tell me all you know about that woman."

"What woman, Max?"

"Miss Agatha Eure, the owner of the eyes."

"Aha! smitten at last! That ever I should live to see our Benedict the victim of love at first sight!"

"Have done with your nonsense, and answer my question. I don't ask from mere curiosity, but that I may have some idea how to bear myself at these promised sittings; for it will never do to ask after her papa if she has none, to pay my respects to the old lady as her mother if she is only the duenna, or joke with the lad if he is the heir apparent."

"Do you mean to say that you asked her to sit to you?" cried Louis, falling back a step and staring at me with undisguised astonishment.

"Yes, why not?"

"Why, man, Agatha Eure is the haughtiest piece of humanity ever concocted; and I, with all my daring, never ventured to ask more than an occasional dance with her, and feel myself especially favored that she deigns to bow to me, and lets me pick up her gloves or carry her bouquet as a mark of supreme condescension. What witchcraft did you bring to bear upon her? and how did she grant your audacious request?"

"Agreed to it at once."

"Like an empress conferring knighthood, I fancy."

"Not at all. More like a pretty woman receiving a compliment to her beauty — though she is not pretty, by the way."

Louis indulged himself in the long, low whistle, which seems the only adequate expression for masculine surprise. I enjoyed his amazement, it was my turn to laugh now, and I did so, as I said:

"You are always railing at me for my avoidance of all womankind, but you see I have not lost the art of pleasing, for I won your haughty Agatha to my will in fifteen minutes, and am not only to paint her handsome eyes, but to do it at her own house, by her own request. I am beginning to find that, after years of effort, I have mounted a few more rounds of the social ladder than I was aware of, and may now confer as well as receive favors; for she seemed to think me the benefactor, and I rather enjoyed the novelty of the thing. Now tell your story of 'the haughtiest piece of humanity' ever known. I like her the better for that trait."

Louis nodded his head, and regarded the moon with an aspect of immense wisdom, as he replied:

"I understand it now; it all comes back to me, and my accusation holds good, only the love at first sight is on the other side. You shall have your story, but it may leave the picture in the lurch if it causes you to fly off, as you usually see fit to do when a woman's name is linked with your own. You never saw Miss Eure before; but what you say reminds me that she has seen you, for one day last autumn, as I was driving with her and old madame — a mark of uncommon favor, mind you — we saw you striding along, with your hat over your eyes, looking very much like a comet streaming down the street. It was crowded, and as you waited at the crossing you spoke to Jack Mellot, and while talking pulled off your hat and tumbled your hair about, in your usual fashion, when very earnest. We were blockaded by cars and coaches for a moment, so Miss Eure had a fine opportunity to feast her eyes upon you, 'though you are not pretty, by the way.' She asked your name, and when I told her she gushed out into a charming little stream of interest in your daubs, and her delight at seeing their creator; all of which was not agreeable to me, for I considered myself much the finer work of art of the two. Just then you caught up a shabby child with a big basket, took them across, under our horses' noses, with never a word for me, though I called to you, and, diving into the crowd, disappeared. 'I like that,' said Miss Eure; and as we drove on she asked questions, which I answered in a truly Christian manner, doing you no harm, old lad; for I told all you had fought through, with the courage of a stout-hearted man, all you had borne with the patience of a woman, and what a grand future lay open to you, if you chose to accept and use it, making quite a fascinating little romance of it, I assure you. There the matter dropped. I forgot it till this minute, but it accounts for the ease with which you gained your first suit, and is prophetic of like success in a second and more serious one. She is young, well-born, lovely to those who love her, and has a fortune and position which will lift you at once to the topmost round of the long ladder you've been climbing all these years. I wish you joy, Max."

"Thank you. I've no time for lovemaking, and want no fortune but that which I earn for myself. I am already married to a fairer wife than Miss Eure, so you may win and wear the lofty lady yourself."

Louis gave a comical groan.

"I've tried that, and failed; for she is too cold to be warmed by any flame of mine, though she is wonderfully attractive when she likes, and I hover about her even now like an infatuated moth, who beats his head against the glass and never reaches the light within. No; you must thankfully accept the good the gods bestow. Let Art be your Leah, but Agatha your Rachel. And so, good-night!"

"Stay and tell me one thing — is she an orphan?"

"Yes; the last of a fine old race, with few relatives and few friends, for death has deprived her of the first, and her own choice of the last. The lady you saw with her plays propriety in her establishment; the lad is Mrs. Snow's son, and fills the role of *cavaliere-servente*; for Miss Eure is a Diana toward men in general, and leads a quietly luxurious life among her books, pencils and music, reading and studying all manner of things few women of two-and-twenty care to know. But she has the wit to see that a woman's mission is to be charming, and when she has sufficient motive for the exertion she fulfils that mission most successfully, as I know to my sorrow. Now let me off, and be for ever grateful for the good turn I have done you to-night, both in urging you to go to the theatre and helping you to your wish when you got there."

We parted merrily, but his words lingered in my memory, and half unconsciously exerted a new influence over me, for they flattered the three ruling passions that make or mar the fortunes of us all — pride, ambition and self-love. I wanted power, fame and ease, and all seemed waiting for me, not in the dim future but the actual present, if my friend's belief was to be relied upon; and remembering all I had seen and heard that night, I felt that it was not utterly without foundation. I pleased myself for an idle hour in dreaming dreams of what might be; finding that amusement began to grow dangerously attractive, I demolished my castles in the air with the last whiff of my meerschaum, and fell asleep, echoing my own words:

"Art is my wife, I will have no other!"

Punctual to the moment I went to my appointment, and while waiting an answer to my ring took an exterior survey of Miss Eure's house. One of an imposing granite block, it stood in a West End square, with every sign of unostentatious opulence about it. I was very susceptible to all influences, either painful or pleasant, and as I stood there the bland atmosphere that surrounded me seemed most attractive; for my solitary life had been plain and poor, with little time for ease, and few ornaments to give it grace. Now I seemed to have won the right to enjoy both if I would; I no longer felt out of place there, and with this feeling came the wish to try the sunny side of life, and see if its genial gifts would prove more inspiring than the sterner masters I had been serving so long.

The door opened in the middle of my reverie, and I was led through an anteroom, lined with warmhued pictures, to a large apartment, which had been converted into an impromptu studio by some one who understood all the requisites for such a place. The picture, my easel and other necessaries had preceded me, and I thought to have spent a good hour in arranging matters. All was done, however, with a skill that surprised me; the shaded windows, the carefully-arranged brushes, the proper colors already on the palette, the easel and picture placed as they should be, and a deep curtain hung behind a small dais, where I fancied my model was to sit. The room was empty as I entered, and with the brief message, "Miss Eure will be down directly," the man noiselessly departed.

I stood and looked about me with great satisfaction, thinking, "I cannot fail to work well surrounded by such agreeable sights and sounds." The house was very still, for the turmoil of the city was subdued to a murmur, like the far-off music of the sea; a soft gloom filled the room, divided by one strong ray that fell athwart my picture, gifting it with warmth and light. Through a half-open door I saw the green vista of a conservatory, full of fine blendings of color, and wafts of many odors blown to me by the west wind rustling through orange trees and slender palms; while the only sound that broke the silence was the voice of a flame-colored foreign bird, singing a plaintive little strain like a sorrowful lament. I liked this scene, and, standing in the doorway, was content to look, listen and enjoy, forgetful of time, till a slight stir made me turn and for a moment look straight before me with a startled aspect. It seemed as if my picture had left its frame; for, standing on the narrow dais, clearly defined against the dark background, stood the living likeness of the figure I had painted, the same white folds falling from neck to ankle, the same shadowy hair, and slender hands locked together, as if wrung in slow despair; and fixed full upon my own the weird, unseeing eyes, which made the face a pale mask, through which the haunted spirit spoke eloquently, with its sleepless anguish and remorse.

"Good morning, Miss Eure; how shall I thank you?" I began, but stopped abruptly, for without speaking she waved me towards the easel with a gesture which seemed to say, "Prove your gratitude by industry."

"Very good," thought I, "if she likes the theatrical style she shall have it. It is evident she has studied her part and will play it well, I will do the same, and as Louis recommends, take the good the gods send me while I may."

Without more ado I took my place and fell to work; but, though never more eager to get on, with each moment that I passed I found my interest in the picture grow less and less intent, and with every glance at my model found that it was more and more difficult to look away. Beautiful she was not, but the wild and woful figure seemed to attract me as no Hebe, Venus or sweet-faced Psyche had ever done. My hand moved slower and slower, the painted face grew dimmer and dimmer, my glances lingered longer and longer, and presently palette and brushes rested on my knee, as I leaned back in the deep chair and gave myself up to an uninterrupted stare. I knew that it was rude, knew that it was a trespass on Miss Eure's kindness as well as a breach of good manners, but I could not help it, for my eyes seemed beyond my control, and though I momentarily expected to see her color rise and hear some warning of the lapse of time, I never looked away, and soon forgot to imagine her feelings in the mysterious confusion of my own.

I was first conscious of a terrible fear that I ought to speak or move, which seemed impossible, for my eyelids began to be weighed down by a delicious drowsiness in spite of all my efforts to keep them open. Everything grew misty, and the beating of my heart sounded like the rapid, irregular roll of a muffled drum; then a strange weight seemed to oppress and cause me to sigh long and deeply. But soon the act of breathing appeared to grow unnecessary, for a sensation of wonderful airiness came over me, and I felt as if I could float away like a thistledown. Presently every sense seemed to fall asleep, and in the act of dropping both palette and brush I drifted away into a sea of blissful repose, where nothing disturbed me but a fragmentary dream that came and went like a lingering gleam of consciousness through the new experience which had befallen me.

I seemed to be still in the quiet room, still leaning in the deep chair with half-closed eyes, still watching the white figure before me, but that had changed. I saw a smile break over the lips, something like triumph flash into the eyes, sudden color flush the cheeks, and the rigid hands lifted to gather up and put the long hair back; then with noiseless steps it came nearer and nearer till it stood beside me. For awhile it paused there mute and intent, I felt the eager gaze searching my face, but it caused no displeasure; for I seemed to be looking down at myself, as if soul and body had parted company and I was gifted with a double life. Suddenly the vision laid a light hand on my wrist and touched my temples, while a shade of anxiety seemed to flit across its face as it turned and vanished. A dreamy wonder regarding its return woke within me, then my sleep deepened into utter oblivion, for how long I cannot tell. A pungent odor seemed to recall me to the same half wakeful state. I dimly saw a woman's arm holding a glittering object before me, when the fragrance came; an unseen hand stirred my hair with the grateful drip of water, and once there came a touch like the pressure of lips upon my forehead, soft and warm, but gone in an instant. These new sensations grew rapidly more and more defined; I clearly saw a bracelet on the arm and read the Arabic characters engraved upon the golden coins that formed it; I heard the rustle of garments, the hurried breathing of some near presence, and felt

The Artist and His Model

the cool sweep of a hand passing to and fro across my forehead. At this point my thoughts began to shape themselves into words, which came slowly and seemed strange to me as I searched for and connected them, then a heavy sigh rose and broke at my lips, and the sound of my own voice woke me, drowsily echoing the last words I had spoken:

"Good morning, Miss Eure; how shall I thank you?"

To my great surprise the well-remembered voice answered quietly:

"Good morning, Mr. Erdmann; will you have some lunch before you begin?"

How I opened my eyes and got upon my feet was never clear to me, but the first object I saw was Miss Eure coming towards me with a glass in her hand. My expression must have been dazed and imbecile in the extreme, for to add to my bewilderment the tragic robes had disappeared, the dishevelled hair was gathered in shining coils under a Venetian net of silk and gold, a white embroidered wrapper replaced the muslins Lady Macbeth had worn, and a countenance half playful, half anxious, now smiled where I had last seen so sorrowful an aspect. The fear of having committed some great absurdity and endangered my success brought me right with a little shock of returning thought. I collected myself, gave a look about the room, a dizzy bow to her, and put my hand to my head with a vague idea that something was wrong there. In doing this I discovered that my hair was wet, which slight fact caused me to exclaim abruptly:

"Miss Eure, what have I been doing? Have I had a fit? been asleep? or do you deal in magic and rock your guests off into oblivion without a moment's warning?"

Standing before me with uplifted eyes, she answered, smiling:

"No, none of these have happened to you; the air from the Indian plants in the conservatory was too powerful, I think; you were a little faint, but closing the door and opening a window has restored you, and a glass of wine will perfect the cure, I hope."

She was offering the glass as she spoke. I took it but forgot to thank her, for on the arm extended to me was the bracelet never seen so near by my waking eyes, yet as familiar as if my vision had come again. Something struck me disagreeably, and I spoke out with my usual bluntness.

"I never fainted in my life, and have an impression that people do not dream when they swoon. Now I did, and so vivid was it that I still remember the characters engraved on the trinket you wear, for that played a prominent part in my vision. Shall I describe them as proof of it, Miss Eure?"

Her arm dropped at her side and her eyes fell for a moment as I spoke; then she glanced up unchanged, saying as she seated herself and motioned me to do the same:

"No, rather tell the dream, and taste these grapes while you amuse me."

I sat down and obeyed her. She listened attentively, and when I ended explained the mystery in the simplest manner.

"You are right in the first part of your story. I did yield to a whim which seized me when I saw your picture, and came down *en costume*, hoping to help you by keeping up the illusion. You began, as canvas and brushes prove; I stood motionless till you turned pale and regarded me with a strange expression; at first I thought it might be inspiration, as your friend Yorke would say, but presently you dropped everything out of your hands and fell back in your chair. I took the liberty of treating you like a woman, for I bathed your temples and wielded my vinaigrette most energetically till you revived and began to talk of 'Rachel, art, castles in the air, and your wife Lady Macbeth;' then I slipped away and modernized myself, ordered some refreshments for you, and waited till you wished me 'Good-morning.'"

She was laughing so infectiously that I could not resist joining her and accepting her belief, for curious as the whole affair seemed to me I could account for it in no other way. She was winningly kind, and urged me not to resume my task, but I was secretly disgusted with myself for such a display of weakness, and finding her hesitation caused solely by fears for me, I persisted, and seating her, painted as I had never done before. Every sense seemed unwontedly acute, and hand and eye obeyed me with a docility they seldom showed. Miss Eure sat where I placed her, silent and intent, but her face did not wear the tragic aspect it had worn before, though she tried to recall it. This no longer troubled me, for the memory of the vanished face was more clearly before me than her own, and with but few and hasty glances at my model, I reproduced it with a speed and skill that filled me with delight. The striking of a clock reminded me that I had far exceeded the specified time, and that even a woman's patience has limits; so concealing my regret at losing so auspicious a mood, I laid down my brush, leaving my work unfinished, yet glad to know I had the right to come again, and complete it in a place and presence which proved so inspiring.

Miss Eure would not look at it till it was all done, saying in reply to my thanks for the pleasant studio she had given me — "I was not quite unselfish in that, and owe you an apology for venturing to meddle with your property; but it gave me real satisfaction to arrange these things, and restore this room to the aspect it wore three years ago. I, too, was an artist then, and dreamed aspiring dreams here, but was arrested on the threshold of my career by loss of sight; and hard as it seemed then to give up all my longings, I see now that it was better so, for a few years later it would have killed me. I have learned to desire for others what I can never hope for myself, and try to find pleasure in their success, unembittered by regrets for my own defeat. Let this explain my readiness to help you, my interest in your work and my best wishes for your present happiness and future fame."

The look of resignation, which accompanied her words, touched me more than a flood of complaints, and the thought of all she had lost woke such sympathy and pity in my frosty heart, that I involuntarily pressed the hand that could never wield a brush again. Then for the first time I saw those keen eyes soften and grow dim with unshed tears; this gave them the one charm they needed to be beautiful as well as penetrating, and as they met my own, so womanly sweet and grateful, I felt that one might love her while that mood remained. But it passed as rapidly as it came, and when we parted in the anteroom the cold, quiet lady bowed me out, and the tender-faced girl was gone.

I never told Louis all the incidents of that first sitting, but began my story where the real interest ended; and Miss Eure was equally silent, through forgetfulness or for some good reason of her own. I went several times again, yet though the conservatory door stood open I felt no ill effects from the Indian plants that still bloomed there, dreamed no more dreams, and Miss Eure no more enacted the somnambulist. I found an indefinable charm in that pleasant room, a curious interest in studying its mistress, who always met me with a smile, and parted with a look of unfeigned regret. Louis rallied me upon my absorption, but it caused me no uneasiness, for it was not love that led me there, and Miss Eure knew it. I never had forgotten our conversation on that first night, and with every interview the truth of my friend's suspicions grew more and more apparent to me. Agatha Eure was a strong-willed, imperious woman, used to command all about her and see her last wish gratified; but now she was conscious of a presence she could not command, a wish she dare not utter, and, though her womanly pride sealed her lips, her eyes often traitorously betrayed the longing of her heart. She was sincere in her love for art, and behind that interest in that concealed, even from herself, her love for the artist; but the most indomitable passion given humanity cannot long be hidden. Agatha soon felt her weakness, and vainly struggled to subdue it. I soon knew my power, and owned its subtle charm, though I disdained to use it.

The picture was finished, exhibited and won me all, and more than I had dared to hope; for rumor served me a good turn, and whispers of Miss Eure's part in my success added zest to public curiosity and warmth to public praise. I enjoyed the little stir it caused, found admiration a sweet draught after a laborious year, and felt real gratitude to the woman who had helped me win it. If my work had proved a failure I should have forgotten her, and been an humbler, happier man; it did not, and she became a part of my success. Her name was often spoken in the same breath with mine, her image was kept before me by no exertion of my own, till the memories it brought with it grew familiar as old friends, and slowly ripened into a purpose which, being born of ambition and not love, bore bitter fruit, and wrought out its own retribution for a sin against myself and her.

The more I won the more I demanded, the higher I climbed the

The Painting Finished

more eager I became; and, at last, seeing how much I could gain by a single step, resolved to take it, even though I knew it to be a false one. Other men married for the furtherance of their ambitions, why should not I? Years ago I had given up love of home for love of fame, and the woman who might have made me what I should be had meekly yielded all, wished me a happy future, and faded from my world, leaving me only a bitter memory, a veiled picture and a quiet grave my feet never visited but once. Miss Eure loved me, sympathised in my aims, understood my tastes; she could give all I asked to complete the purpose of my life, and lift me at once and for ever from the hard lot I had struggled with for thirty years. One word would win the miracle, why should I hesitate to utter it?

I did not long — for three months from the day I first entered that shadowy room I stood there intent on asking her to be my wife. As I waited I lived again the strange hour once passed there, and felt as if it had been the beginning of another dream whose awakening was yet to come. I asked myself if the hard healthful reality was not better than such feverish visions, however brilliant, and the voice that is never silent when we interrogate it with sincerity answered, "Yes." "No matter, I choose to dream, so let the phantom of a wife come to me here as the phantom of a lover came to me so long ago." As I uttered these defiant words aloud, like a visible reply, Agatha appeared upon the threshold of the door. I knew she had heard me — for again I saw the soft-eyed, tender girl, and opened my arms to her without a word. She came at once, and clinging to me with unwonted tears upon her cheek, unwonted fervor in her voice, touched my forehead, as she had done in that earlier dream, whispering like one still doubtful of her happiness —

"Oh, Max! be kind to me, for in all the world I have only you to love."

I promised, and broke that promise in less than a year.

PART II

WE WERE MARRIED QUIETLY, went away till the nine days
gossip was over, spent our honeymoon as that absurd month is usually spent, and came back to town with the first autumnal frosts;
Agatha regretting that I was no longer entirely her own, I secretly
thanking heaven that I might drop the lover, and begin my work
again, for I was as an imprisoned creature in that atmosphere of
"love in idleness," though my bonds were only a pair of loving
arms. Madame Snow and son departed, we settled ourselves in the
fine house and then endowed with every worldly blessing, I looked
about me, believing myself master of my fate, but found I was its
slave.

If Agatha could have joined me in my work we might have been
happy; if she could have solaced herself with other pleasures and
left me to my own, we might have been content; if she had loved
me less, we might have gone our separate ways, and yet been
friends like many another pair; but I soon found that her affection
was of that exacting nature which promises but little peace unless
met by one as warm. I had nothing but regard to give her, for it
was not in her power to stir a deeper passion in me; I told her this
before our marriage, told her I was a cold, hard man, wrapt in a
single purpose; but what woman believes such confessions while
her heart still beats fast with the memory of her betrothal? She said
everything was possible to love, and prophesied a speedy change;
I knew it would not come, but having given my warning left the
rest to time. I hoped to lead a quiet life and prove that adverse
circumstances, not the want of power, had kept me from excelling
in the profession I had chosen; but to my infinite discomfort Agatha turned jealous of my art, for finding the mistress dearer than
the wife, she tried to wean me from it, and seemed to feel that
having given me love, wealth and ease, I should ask no more, but
play the obedient subject to a generous queen. I rebelled against
this, told her that one-half my time should be hers, the other belonged to me, and I would so employ it that it should bring honor
to the name I had given her. But, Agatha was not used to seeing
her will thwarted or her pleasure sacrificed to another, and soon

felt that though I scrupulously fulfilled my promise, the one task was irksome, the other all absorbing; that though she had her husband at her side his heart was in his studio, and the hours spent with her were often the most listless in his day. Then began that sorrowful experience old as Adam's reproaches to Eve; we both did wrong, and neither repented; both were self-willed, sharp tongued and proud, and before six months of wedded life had passed we had known many of those scenes which so belittle character and lessen self-respect.

Agatha's love lived through all, and had I answered its appeals by patience, self-denial and genial friendship, if no warmer tie could exist, I might have spared her an early death, and myself from years of bitterest remorse; but I did not. Then her forbearance ended and my subtle punishment began.

"Away again to-night, Max? You have been shut up all day, and I hoped to have you to myself this evening. Hear how the storm rages without, see how cheery I have made all within for you, so put your hat away and stay, for this hour belongs to me, and I claim it."

Agatha took me prisoner as she spoke, and pointed to the cosy nest she had prepared for me. The room was bright and still; the lamp shone clear; the fire glowed; warm-hued curtains muffled the war of gust and sleet without; books, music, a wide-armed seat and a woman's wistful face invited me; but none of these things could satisfy me just then, and though I drew my wife nearer, smoothed her shining hair, and kissed the reproachful lips, I did not yield.

"You must let me go, Agatha, for the great German artist is here, I had rather give a year of life than miss this meeting with him. I have devoted many evenings to you, and though this hour is yours I shall venture to take it, and offer you a morning call instead. Here are novels, new songs, an instrument, embroidery and a dog, who can never offend by moody silence or unpalatable conversation — what more can a contented woman ask, surely not an absent-minded husband?"

"Yes, just that and nothing more, for she loves him, and he can supply a want that none of these things can. See how pretty I have tried to make myself for you alone; stay, Max, and make me happy."

"Dear, I shall find my pretty wife to-morrow, but the great painter will be gone; let me go, Agatha, and make me happy."

She drew herself from my arm, saying with a flash of the eye — "Max, you are a tyrant!"

"Am I? then you made me so with too much devotion."

"Ah, if you loved me as I loved there would be no selfishness on your part, no reproaches on mine. What shall I do to make myself dearer, Max?"

"Give me more liberty."

"Then I should lose you entirely, and lead the life of a widow. Oh, Max, this is hard, this is bitter, to give all and receive nothing in return."

She spoke passionately, and the truth of her reproach stung me, for I answered with that coldness that always wounded her:

"Do you count an honest name, sincere regard and much gratitude as nothing? I have given you these, and ask only peace and freedom in return. I desire to do justice to you and to myself, but I am not like you, never can be, and you must not hope it. You say love is all-powerful, prove it upon me, I am willing to be the fondest of husbands if I can; teach me, win me in spite of myself, and make me what you will; but leave me a little time to live and labor for that which is dearer to me than your faulty lord and master can ever be to you."

"Shall I do this?" and her face kindled as she put the question.

"Yes, here is an amusement for you, use what arts you will, make your love irresistible, soften my hard nature, convert me into your shadow, subdue me till I come at your call like a pet dog, and when you make your presence more powerful than painting I will own that you have won your will and made your theory good."

I was smiling as I spoke, for the twelve labors of Hercules seemed less impossible than this, but Agatha watched me with her glittering eyes; and answered slowly —

"I will do it. Now go, and enjoy your liberty while you may, but remember when I have conquered that you dared me to it, and keep your part of the compact. Promise this." She offered me her hand with a strange expression — I took it, said good-night, and hurried away, still smiling at the curious challenge given and accepted.

The Domestic Feud Culminates

Agatha told me to enjoy my liberty, and I tried to do so that very night, but failed most signally, for I had not been an hour in the brilliant company gathered to meet the celebrated guest before I found it impossible to banish the thought of my solitary wife. I had left her often, yet never felt disturbed by more than a passing twinge of that uncomfortable bosom friend called conscience; but now the interest of the hour seemed lessened by regret, for through varying conversation held with those about me, mingling with the fine music that I heard, looking at me from every woman's face, and thrusting itself into my mind at every turn, came a vague, disturbing self-reproach, which slowly deepened to a strong anxiety. My attention wandered, words seemed to desert me, fancy to be frostbound, and even in the presence of the great man I had so ardently desired to see I could neither enjoy his society nor play my own part well. More than once I found myself listening for Agatha's voice; more than once I looked behind me expecting to see her figure, and more than once I resolved to go, with no desire to meet her.

"It is an acute fit of what women call nervousness; I will not yield to it," I thought, and plunged into the gayest group I saw, supped, talked, sang a song, and broke down; told a witty story, and spoiled it; laughed and tried to bear myself like the lightest-hearted guest in the rooms; but it would not do, for stronger and stronger grew the strange longing to go home, and soon it became uncontrollable. A foreboding fear that something had happened oppressed me, and suddenly leaving the festival at its height I drove home as if life and death depended on the saving of a second. Like one pursuing or pursued I rode, eager only to be there; yet when I stood on my own threshold I asked myself wonderingly, "Why such haste?" and stole in ashamed at my early return. The storm beat without, but within all was serene and still, and with noiseless steps I went up to the room where I had left my wife, pausing a moment at the half open door to collect myself, lest she should see the disorder of both mind and mien. Looking in I saw her sitting with neither book nor work beside her, and after a momentary glance began to think my anxiety had not been causeless, for she sat erect and motionless as an in-

animate figure of intense thought; her eyes were fixed, face colorless, with an expression of iron determination, as if every energy of
mind and body were wrought up to the achievement of a single
purpose. There was something in the rigid attitude and stern aspect
of this familiar shape that filled me with dismay, and found vent in
the abrupt exclamation,

"Agatha, what is it?"

She sprang up like a steel spring when the pressure is removed,
saw me, and struck her hands together with a wild gesture of surprise, alarm or pleasure, which I could not tell, for in the act she
dropped into her seat white and breathless as if smitten with sudden death. Unspeakably shocked, I bestirred myself till she recovered, and though pale and spent, as if with some past exertion,
soon seemed quite herself again.

"Agatha, what were you thinking of when I came in?" I asked,
as she sat leaning against me with half closed eyes and a faint smile
on her lips, as if the unwonted caresses I bestowed upon her were
more soothing than any cordial I could give. Without stirring she
replied,

"Of you, Max. I was longing for you, with heart and soul and
will. You told me to win you in spite of yourself; and I was sending
my love to find and bring you home. Did it reach you? did it lead
you back and make you glad to come?"

A peculiar chill ran through me as I listened, though her voice
was quieter, her manner gentler than usual as she spoke. She
seemed to have such faith in her tender fancy, such assurance of its
efficacy, and such a near approach to certain knowledge of its success, that I disliked the thought of continuing the topic, and answered cheerfully,

"My own conscience brought me home, dear; for, discovering
that I had left my peace of mind behind me, I came back to find it.
If your task is to cost a scene like this it will do more harm than
good to both of us, so keep your love from such uncanny wander-
ings through time and space, and win me with less dangerous arts."

She smiled her strange smile, folded my hand in her own, and
answered, with soft exultation in her voice,

"It will not happen so again, Max; but I am glad, most glad you came, for it proves I have some power over this wayward heart of yours, where I shall knock until it opens wide and takes me in."

The events of that night made a deep impression on me, for from that night my life was changed. Agatha left me entirely free, never asked my presence, never upbraided me for long absences or silences when together. She seemed to find happiness in her belief that she should yet subdue me, and though I smiled at this in my indifference, there was something half pleasant, half pathetic in the thought of this proud woman leaving all warmer affections for my negligent friendship, the sight of this young wife laboring to win her husband's heart. At first I tried to be all she asked, but soon relapsed into my former life, and finding no reproaches followed, believed I should enjoy it as never before — but I did not. As weeks passed I slowly became conscious that some new power had taken possession of me, swaying my whole nature to its will; a power alien yet sovereign. Fitfully it worked, coming upon me when least desired, enforcing its commands regardless of time, place or mood; mysterious yet irresistible in its strength, this mental tyrant led me at all hours, in all stages of anxiety, repugnance and rebellion, from all pleasures or employments, straight to Agatha. If I sat at my easel the sudden summons came, and wondering at myself I obeyed it, to find her busied in some cheerful occupation, with apparently no thought or wish for me. If I left home I often paused abruptly in my walk or drive, turned and hurried back, simply because I could not resist the impulse that controlled me. If she went away I seldom failed to follow, and found no peace till I was at her side again. I grew moody and restless, slept ill, dreamed wild dreams, and often woke and wandered aimlessly, as if sent upon an unknown errand. I could not fix my mind upon my work; a spell seemed to have benumbed imagination and robbed both brain and hand of power to conceive and skill to execute.

At first I fancied this was only the reaction of entire freedom after long captivity, but I soon found I was bound to a more exacting mistress than my wife had ever been. Then I suspected that it was only the perversity of human nature, and that having gained my wish it grew valueless, and I longed for that which I had lost;

but it was not this, for distasteful as my present life had become, the other seemed still more so when I recalled it. For a time I believed that Agatha might be right, that I was really learning to love her, and this unquiet mood was the awakening of that passion which comes swift and strong when it comes to such as I. If I had never loved I might have clung to this belief, but the memory of that earlier affection, so genial, entire and sweet, proved that the present fancy was only a delusion; for searching deeply into myself to discover the truth of this, I found that Agatha was no dearer, and to my own dismay detected a covert dread lurking there, harmless and vague, but threatening to deepen into aversion or resentment for some unknown offence; and while I accused myself of an unjust and ungenerous weakness, I shrank from the thought of her, even while I sought her with the assiduity but not the ardor of a lover.

Long I pondered over this inexplicable state of mind, but found no solution of it; for I would not own, either to myself or Agatha, that the shadow of her prophecy had come to pass, though its substance was still wanting. She sometimes looked inquiringly into my face with those strange eyes of hers, sometimes chid me with a mocking smile when she found me sitting idly before my easel without a line or tint given though hours had passed; and often, when driven by that blind impulse I sought her anxiously among her friends, she would glance at those about her, saying, with a touch of triumph in her mien, "Am I not an enviable wife to have inspired such devotion in this grave husband?" Once, remembering her former words, I asked her playfully if she still "sent her love to find and bring me home?" but she only shook her head and answered, sadly,

"Oh, no; my love was burdensome to you, so I have rocked it to sleep and laid it where it will not trouble you again."

At last I decided that some undetected physical infirmity caused my disquiet, for years of labor and privation might well have worn the delicate machinery of heart or brain, and this warning suggested the wisdom of consulting medical skill in time. This thought grew as month after month increased my mental malady and began to tell upon my hitherto unbroken health. I wondered if Agatha knew how listless, hollow-eyed and wan I had grown; but she never spoke of it, and an unconquerable reserve kept me from uttering a complaint to her.

One day I resolved to bear it no longer, and hurried away to an old friend in whose skill and discretion I had entire faith. He was out, and while I waited I took up a book that lay among the medical works upon his table. I read a page, then a chapter, turning leaf after leaf with a rapid hand, devouring paragraph after paragraph with an eager eye. An hour passed, still I read on. Dr. L —— did not come, but I did not think of that, and when I laid down the book I no longer needed him, for in that hour I had discovered a new world, had seen the diagnosis of my symptoms set forth in unmistakable terms, and found the key to the mystery in the one word — Magnetism. This was years ago, before spirits had begun their labors for good or ill, before ether and hashish had gifted humanity with eternities of bliss in a second, and while Mesmer's mystical discoveries were studied only by the scientific or philosophical few. I knew nothing of these things, for my whole life had led another way, and no child could be more ignorant of the workings or extent of this wonderful power. There was Indian blood in my veins, and superstition lurked there still; consequently the knowledge that I was a victim of this occult magic came upon me like an awful revelation, and filled me with a storm of wrath, disgust and dread.

Like an enchanted spirit who has found the incantation that will free it from subjection, I rejoiced with a grim satisfaction even while I cursed myself for my long blindness, and with no thought for anything but instant accusation on my part, instant confession and atonement on hers, I went straight home, straight into Agatha's presence, and there, in words as brief as bitter, told her that her reign was over. All that was sternest, hottest and most unforgiving ruled me then, and like fire to fire roused a spirit equally strong and high. I might have subdued her by juster and more generous words, but remembering the humiliation of my secret slavery I forgot my own offence in hers, and set no curb on tongue or temper, letting the storm she had raised fall upon her with the suddenness of an unwonted, unexpected outburst.

As I spoke her face changed from its first dismay to a defiant calmness that made it hard as rock and cold as ice, while all expression seemed concentrated in her eye, which burned on me with an unwavering light. There was no excitement in her manner, no sign of fear, or shame, or grief in her mien, and when she answered me her voice was untremulous and clear as when I heard it first.

"Have you done? Then hear me: I knew you long before you dreamed that such a woman as Agatha Eure existed. I was solitary, and longed to be sincerely loved. I was rich, yet I could not buy what is unpurchasable; I was young, yet I could not make my youth sweet with affection; for nowhere did I see the friend whose nature was akin to mine until you passed before me, and I felt at once, 'There is the one I seek!' I never yet desired that I did not possess the coveted object, and believed I should not fail now. Years ago I learned the mysterious gift I was endowed with, and fostered it; for, unblessed with beauty, I hoped its silent magic might draw others near enough to see, under this cold exterior, the woman's nature waiting there. The first night you saw me I yielded to an irresistible longing to attract your eye, and for a moment see the face I had learned to love looking into mine. You know how well I succeeded — you know your own lips asked the favor I was so glad to give, and your own will led you to me. That day I made another trial of my skill and succeeded beyond my hopes, but dared not repeat it, for your strong nature was not easily subdued, it was too perilous a game for me to play, and I resolved that no delusion should make you mine. I would have a free gift or none. You offered me your hand, and believing that it held a loving heart, I took it, to find that heart barred against me, and another woman's name engraved upon its door. Was this a glad discovery for a wife to make? Do you wonder she reproached you when she saw her hopes turn to ashes, and could no longer conceal from herself that she was only a stepping-stone to lift an ambitious man to a position which she could not share? You think me weak and wicked; look back upon the year nearly done and ask yourself if many young wives have such a record of neglect, despised love, unavailing sacrifices, long suffering patience and deepening despair? I had been reading the tear-stained pages of this record when you bid me win you if I could; and with a bitter sense of the fitness of such a punishment, I resolved to do it, still cherishing a hope that some spark of affection might be found. I soon saw the vanity of such a hope, and this hard truth goaded me to redouble my efforts till I had entirely subjugated that arrogant spirit of yours, and made myself master where I would so gladly have been a loving subject. Do you think I have not suffered? have not wept bitter tears in secret, and been wrung by sharper anguish than you have ever known? If you had given any sign of affection, shown any wish to return to me, any shadow of regret for the wrong you had done me, I would have broken my wand like Prospero, and used no magic but the pardon of a faithful heart. You did not, and it has come to this. Before you condemn me, remember that you dared me to do it — that you bid me make my presence more powerful than Art — bid me convert you to my shadow, and subdue you till you came like a pet dog at my call. Have I not obeyed you? Have I not kept my part of the compact? Now keep yours."

There was something terrible in hearing words whose truth wounded while they fell, uttered in a voice whose concentrated passion made its tones distinct and deep, as if an accusing spirit read them from that book whose dread records never are effaced. My hot blood cooled, my harsh mood softened, and though it still burned, my resentment sank lower, for, remembering the little life to be, I wrestled with myself, and won humility enough to say, with regretful energy:

"Forgive me, Agatha, and let this sad past sleep. I have wronged you, but I believed I sinned no more than many another man who, finding love dead, hoped to feed his hunger with friendship and ambition. I never thought of such an act till I saw affection in your face; that tempted me, and I tried to repay all you gave me by the offer of the hand you mutely asked. It was a bargain often made in this strange world of ours, often repented as we repent now. Shall we abide by it, and by mutual forbearance recover mutual peace? or shall I leave you free, to make life sweeter with a better man, and find myself poor and honest as when we met?"

Something in my words stung her; and regarding me with the same baleful aspect, she lifted her slender hand, so wasted since I made it mine, that the single ornament it wore dropped into her palm, and holding it up, she said, as if prompted by the evil genius that lies hidden in every heart:

"I will do neither. I have outlived my love, but pride still remains; and I will not do as you have done, take cold friendship or selfish ambition to fill an empty heart; I will not be pitied as an injured woman, or pointed at as one who staked all on a man's faith and lost; I will have atonement for my long-suffering — you owe me this, and I claim it. Henceforth you are the slave of the ring, and when I command you must obey, for I possess a charm you cannot defy. It is too late to ask for pity, pardon, liberty or happier life; law and gospel joined us, and as yet law and gospel cannot put us asunder. You have brought this fate upon yourself, accept it, submit to it, for I have bought you with my wealth, I hold you with my mystic art, and body and soul, Max Erdmann, you are mine!"

I knew it was all over then, for a woman never flings such taunts in her husband's teeth till patience, hope and love are gone. A desperate purpose sprung up within me as I listened, yet I delayed a moment before I uttered it, with a last desire to spare us both.

"Agatha, do you mean that I am to lead the life I have been leading for three months — a life of spiritual slavery worse than any torment of the flesh?"

"I do."

"Are you implacable? and will you rob me of all self-control, all peace, all energy, all hope of gaining that for which I have paid so costly a price?"

"I will."

"Take back all you have given me, take my good name, my few friends, my hard-earned success; leave me stripped of every earthly blessing, but free me from this unnatural subjection, which is more terrible to me than death!"

"I will not!"

"Then your own harsh decree drives me from you, for I will break the bond that holds me, I will go out of this house and never cross its threshold while I live — never look into the face which has wrought me all this ill. There is no law, human or divine, that can give you a right to usurp the mastery of another will, and if it costs life and reason I will not submit to it."

"Go when and where you choose, put land and sea between us, break what ties you may, there is one you cannot dissolve, and when I summon you, in spite of all resistance, you must come."

"I swear I will not!"

I spoke out of a blind and bitter passion, but I kept my oath. How her eyes glittered as she lifted up that small pale hand of hers, pointed with an ominous gesture to the ring, and answered:

"Try it."

As she spoke like a sullen echo came the crash of the heavy picture that hung before us. It bore Lady Macbeth's name, but it was a painted image of my wife. I shuddered as I saw it fall, for to my superstitious fancy it seemed a fateful incident; but Agatha laughed a low metallic laugh that made me cold to hear, and whispered like a sibyl:

"Accept the omen; that is a symbol of the Art you worship so idolatrously that a woman's heart was sacrificed for its sake. See where it lies in ruins at your feet, never to bring you honor, happiness or peace; for I speak the living truth when I tell you that your ambitious hopes will vanish the cloud now rising like a veil between us, and the memory of this year will haunt you day and night, till the remorse you painted shall be written upon heart, and face, and life. Now go!"

Her swift words and forceful gesture seemed to banish me for ever, and, like one walking in his sleep, I left her there, a stern, still figure, with its shattered image at its feet.

That instant I departed, but not far — for as yet I could not clearly see which way duty led me. I made no confidante, asked no sympathy or help, told no one of my purpose, but resolving to take no decisive step rashly, I went away to a country house of Agatha's, just beyond the city, as I had once done before when busied on a work that needed solitude and quiet, so that if gossip rose it might be harmless to us both. Then I sat down and thought. Submit I would not, desert her utterly I could not, but I dared defy her, and I did; for as if some viewless spirit whispered the suggestion in my ear, I determined to oppose my will to hers, to use her weapons if

[66]

I could, and teach her to be merciful through suffering like my own. She had confessed my power to draw her to me, in spite of coldness, poverty and all lack of the attractive graces women love; that clue inspired me with hope. I got books and pored over them till their meaning grew clear to me; I sought out learned men and gathered help from their wisdom; I gave myself to the task with indomitable zeal, for I was struggling for the liberty that alone made life worth possessing. The world believed me painting mimic woes, but I was living through a fearfully real one; friends fancied me busied with the mechanism of material bodies, but I was prying into the mysteries of human souls; and many envied my luxurious leisure in that leafy nest, while I was leading the life of a doomed convict, for as I kept my sinful vow so Agatha kept hers.

She never wrote, or sent, or came, but day and night she called me — day and night I resisted, saved only by the desperate means I used — means that made my own servant think me mad. I bid him lock me in my chamber; I dashed out at all hours to walk fast and far away into the lonely forest; I drowned consciousness in wine; I drugged myself with opiates, and when the crisis had passed, woke spent but victorious. All arts I tried, and slowly found that in this conflict of opposing wills my own grew stronger with each success, the other lost power with each defeat. I never wished to harm my wife, never called her, never sent a baneful thought or desire along that mental telegraph which stretched and thrilled between us; I only longed to free myself, and in this struggle weeks passed, yet neither won a signal victory, for neither proud heart knew the beauty of self-conquest and the power of submission.

One night I went up to the lonely tower that crowned the house, to watch the equinoctial storm that made a Pandemonium of the elements without. Rain streamed as if a second deluge was at hand; whirlwinds tore down the valley; the river chafed and foamed with an angry dash, and the city lights shone dimly through the flying mist as I watched them from my lofty room. The tumult suited me, for my own mood was stormy, dark and bitter, and when the cheerful fire invited me to bask before it I sat there wrapped in reveries as gloomy as the night. Presently the well-known premonition came with its sudden thrill through blood and nerves, and with a revengeful strength never felt before I gathered up my energies for the trial, as I waited some more urgent summons. None came, but in its place a sense of power flashed over me, a swift exultation dilated within me, time seemed to pause, the present rolled away, and nothing but an isolated memory remained, for fixing my thoughts on Agatha, I gave myself up to the dominant spirit that possessed me. I sat motionless, yet I willed to see her. Vivid as the flames that framed it, a picture started from the red embers, and clearly as if my bodily eye rested on it, I saw the well-known room, I saw my wife lying in a deep chair, wan and wasted as if with suffering of soul and body, I saw her grope with outstretched hands, and turn her head with eyes whose long lashes never lifted from the cheek where they lay so dark and still, and through the veil that seemed to wrap my senses I heard my own voice, strange and broken, whispering:

"God forgive me, she is blind!"

For a moment, the vision wandered mistily before me, then grew steady, and I saw her steal like a wraith across the lighted room, so dark to her; saw her bend over a little white nest my own hands placed there, and lift some precious burden in her feeble arms; saw her grope painfully back again, and sitting by that other fire — not solitary like my own — lay her pale cheek to that baby cheek and seem to murmur some lullaby that mother-love had taught her. Over my heart strong and sudden gushed a warmth never known before, and again, strange and broken through the veil that wrapped my senses, came my own voice whispering:

"God be thanked, she is not utterly alone!"

As if my breath dissolved it, the picture faded; but I willed again and another rose — my studio, dim with dust, damp with long disuse, dark with evening gloom — for one flickering lamp made the white shapes ghostly, and the pictured faces smile or frown with fitful vividness. There was no semblance of my old self there, but in the heart of the desolation and the darkness Agatha stood alone, with outstretched arms and an imploring face, full of a love and longing so intense that with a welcoming gesture and a cry that echoed through the room, I answered that mute appeal:

"Come to me! come to me!"

A gust thundered at the window, and rain fell like stormy tears, but nothing else replied; as the bright brands dropped the flames died out, and with it that sad picture of my deserted home. I longed to stir but could not, for I had called up a power I could not lay, the servant ruled the master now, and like one fastened by a spell I still sat leaning forward intent upon a single thought. Slowly from the gray embers smouldering on the hearth a third scene rose behind the smoke wreaths, changeful, dim and strange. Again my former home, again my wife, but this time standing on the threshold of the door I had sworn never to cross again. I saw the wafture of the cloak gathered about her, saw the rain beat on her shelterless head, and followed that slight figure through the deserted streets, over the long bridge where the lamps flickered in the wind, along the leafy road, up the wide steps and in at the door whose closing echo startled me to consciousness that my pulses were beating with a mad rapidity, that a cold dew stood upon my forehead, that every sense was supernaturally alert, and that all were fixed upon one point with a breathless intensity that made that little span of time as fearful as the moment when one hangs poised in air above a chasm in the grasp of nightmare. Suddenly I sprang erect, for through the uproar of the elements without, the awesome hush within, I heard steps ascending, and stood waiting in a speechless agony to see what shape would enter there.

One by one the steady footfalls echoed on my ear, one by one they seemed to bring the climax of some blind conflict nearer, one by one they knelled a human life away, for as the door swung open Agatha fell down before me, storm-beaten, haggard, spent, but loving still, for with a faint attempt to fold her hands submissively, she whispered:

"You have conquered, I am here!" and with that act grew still for ever, as with a great shock I woke to see what I had done.

*   *   *

Ten years have passed since then. I sit on that same hearth a feeble, white-haired man, and beside me, the one companion I shall ever know, my little son — dumb, blind and imbecile. I lavish ten-

"You have conquered, I am here!"

der names upon him, but receive no sweet sound in reply; I gather him close to my desolate heart, but meet no answering caress; I look with yearning glance, but see only those haunting eyes, with no gleam of recognition to warm them, no ray of intellect to inspire them, no change to deepen their sightless beauty; and this fair body moulded with the Divine sculptor's gentlest grace is always here before me, an embodied grief that wrings my heart with its pathetic innocence, its dumb reproach. This is the visible punishment for my sin, but there is an unseen retribution heavier than human judgment could inflict, subtler than human malice could conceive, for with a power made more omnipotent by death Agatha still calls me. God knows I am willing now, that I long with all the passion of desire, the anguish of despair to go to her, and He knows that the one tie that holds me is this aimless little life, this duty that I dare not neglect, this long atonement that I make. Day and night I listen to the voice that whispers to me through the silence of these years; day and night I answer with a yearning cry from the depths of a contrite spirit; day and night I cherish the one sustaining hope that Death, the great consoler, will soon free both father and son from the inevitable doom a broken law has laid upon them; for then I know that somewhere in the long hereafter my remorseful soul will find her, and with its poor offering of penitence and love fall down before her, humbly saying:

"You have conquered, I am here!"

The Fate of the Forrests

PART I

A GROUP OF FOUR, two ladies and two gentlemen, leaned or lounged together in the soft brilliance of mingled moonlight and lamplight, that filled the luxurious room. Through the open windows came balmy gusts of ocean air, up from below rose the murmurous plash of waves, breaking on a quiet shore, and frequent bursts of music lent another charm to place and hour. A pause in the gay conversation was broken by the younger lady's vivacious voice:

"Now if the day of witches and wizards, astrologers and fortune-tellers was not over, how I should enjoy looking into a magic mirror, having my horoscope cast, or hearing my fate read by a charming black-eyed gipsy."

"The age of enchantment is not yet past, as all who are permitted to enter this magic circle confess; and one need not go far for 'a charming black-eyed gipsy' to decide one's destiny."

And with a half-serious, half-playful gesture the gentleman offered his hand to the fair-faced girl, who shook her head and answered, smilingly:

"No, I'll not tell your fortune, Captain Hay; and all your compliments cannot comfort me for the loss of the delightful *diablerie* I love to read about and long to experience. Modern gipsies are commonplace. I want a genuine Cagliostro, supernaturally elegant, gifted and mysterious. I wish the fable of his eternal youth were true, so that he might visit us, for where would he find a fitter company? You gentlemen are perfect sceptics, and I am a firm believer, while Ursula would inspire the dullest wizard, because she looks like one born to live a romance."

She did indeed. The beautiful woman, sitting where the light showered down upon her, till every charm seemed doubled. The freshest bloom of early womanhood glowed in a face both sweet and spirited, eloquent eyes shone lustrous and large, the lips smiled as if blissful visions fed the fancy, and above the white forehead dark, abundant hair made a graceful crown for a head which bore itself with a certain gentle pride, as if the power of beauty, grace and intellect lent an unconscious queenliness to their possessor. In the personal atmosphere of strength, brilliancy and tenderness that surrounded her, an acute observer would detect the presence of a daring spirit, a rich nature, a deep heart; and, looking closer, might also discover, in the curves of that sensitive mouth, the depths of those thoughtful eyes, traces of some hidden care, some haunting memory, or, perhaps, only that vague yet melancholy prescience which often marks those fore-doomed to tragic lives. As her companions chatted this fleeting expression touched her face like a passing shadow, and the gentleman who had not yet spoken leaned nearer, as if eager to catch that evanescent gloom. She met his wistful glance with one of perfect serenity, saying, as an enchanting smile broke over her whole face:

"Yes, my life has been a romance thus far; may it have a happy ending. Evan, you were born in a land of charms and spells, can you not play the part of a Hindoo conjuror, and satisfy Kate's longing?"

"I can only play the part of a Hindoo devotee, and exhaust myself with strivings after the unattainable, like this poor little fire-worshipper," replied the young man, watching, with suspicious interest, a moth circling round the globe of light above his head, as if he dared not look at the fair speaker, lest his traitorous eyes should say too much.

"You are both sadly unromantic and ungallant men not to make an effort in our favor," exclaimed the lively lady. "I am in just the mood for a ghostly tale, a scene of mystery, a startling revelation, and where shall I look for an obliging magician to gratify me?"

"Here!"

The voice, though scarcely lifted above a whisper, startled the group as much as if a spirit spoke, and all eyes were turned towards the window, where white draperies were swaying in the wind. No uncanny apparition appeared behind the tentlike aperture, but the composed figure of a small, fragile-looking man, reclining in a lounging-chair. Nothing could have been more unimpressive at first glance, but at a second the eye was arrested, the attention roused, for an indefinable influence held one captive against one's will. Beardless, thin lipped, sharply featured and colorless as ivory was the face. A few locks of blonde hair streaked the forehead, and underneath it shone the controlling feature of this singular countenance. The eyes, that should have been a steely blue to match the fair surroundings, were of the intensest black, varying in expression with a startling rapidity, unless mastered by an art stronger than nature; by turns stealthily soft, keenly piercing, fiercely fiery or utterly expressionless, these mysterious eyes both attracted and repelled, with a subtle magnetism which few wills could resist, and which gave to this otherwise insignificant man a weird charm, which native grace and the possession of rare accomplishments made alluring, even to those who understood the fateful laws of temperament and race.

Languidly leaning in his luxurious chair, while one pale hand gathered back the curtain from before him, the new comer eyed the group with a swift glance, which in an instant had caught the meaning of each face and transferred it to the keeping of a memory which nothing could escape. Annoyance was the record set down against Ursula Forrest's name; mingled joy and shame against the other lady's; for, with the perfect breeding which was one of the man's chief attractions, he gave the precedence to women even in this rapid mental process. Aversion was emphatically marked against

Evan Forrest's name, simple amusement fell to his companion's share. Captain Hay was the first to break the sudden silence which followed that one softly spoken word:

"Beg pardon, but upon my life I forgot you, Stähl. I thought you went half an hour ago, in your usual noiseless style, for who would dream of your choosing to lounge in the strong draught of a sea-breeze?"

"It is I who should beg pardon for forgetting myself in such society, and indulging in the reveries that will come unbidden to such poor shadows as I."

The voice that answered, though low-toned, was singularly persuasive, and the words were uttered with an expression more engaging than a smile.

"Magician, you bade me look to you. I take you at your word. I dare you to show your skill, and prove that yours is no empty boast," said Kate Heath, with evident satisfaction at the offer and interest in its maker.

Rising slowly, Felix Stähl advanced towards her, and, despite his want of stature and vigor, which are the manliest attributes of manhood, no one felt the lack of them, because an instantaneous impression of vitality and power was made in defiance of external seeming. With both hands loosely folded behind him, he paused before Miss Heath, asking, tranquilly:

"Which wish shall I grant? Will you permit me to read your palm? Shall I show you the image of your lover in yonder glass? or shall I whisper in your ear the most secret hope, fear or regret, which you cherish? Honor me by choosing, and any one of these feats I will perform."

Kate stole a covert glance at the tall mirror, saw that it reflected no figure but that of the speaker, and with an irrepressible smile she snatched her eyes away, content, saying hastily:

"As the hardest feat of the three, you shall tell me what I most ardently desire, if the rest will submit to a like test. Can you read their hearts as well as mine?"

His eye went slowly round the little circle, and from each face the smile faded, as that searching gaze explored it. Constrained by its fascination, more than by curiosity or inclination, each person bowed their acquiescence to Kate's desire, and as Stähl's eye came back to her, he answered briefly, like one well assured of his own power:

"I can read their hearts. Shall I begin with you?"

For a moment she fluttered like a bird caught in a fowler's net, then with an effort composed both attitude and aspect, and looked up half-proudly, half-pleadingly, into the colorless countenance that bent till the lips were at her ear. Only three words, and the observers saw the conscious blood flush scarlet to her forehead, burning hotter and deeper as eyes fell, lips quivered and head sank in her hands, leaving a shame-stricken culprit where but an instant ago a bright, happy-hearted woman sat.

Before Ursula could reach her friend, or either gentleman exclaim, Stähl's uplifted hand imposed passive silence and obtained it, for already the magnetism of his presence made itself felt, filling the room with a supernatural atmosphere, which touched the commonplace with mystery, and woke fantastic fears or fancies like a spell. Without a look, a word for the weeping girl before him, he turned sharply round on Evan Forrest, signified by an imperious gesture that he should bend his tall head nearer, and when he did so, seemed to stab him with a breath. Pale with indignation and surprise, the young man sprang erect, demanding in a smothered voice:

"Who will prevent me?"

"I will."

As the words left Stähl's lips, Evan stirred as if to take him by the throat, but that thin, womanish hand closed like a steel spring round his wrist and held the strong arm powerless, as, with a disdainful smile, and warning "Remember where you are!" the other moved on undisturbed. Evan flung himself into a seat, vainly attempting self-control, while Stähl passed to Captain Hay, who sat regarding him with undisguised interest and amazement, which latter sentiment reached its climax as the magic whisper came.

"How in Heaven's name did you know that?" he cried, starting like one stupefied; then overturning his chair in his haste, he dashed out of the room with every mark of uncontrollable excitement and alarm.

"Dare you let me try my power on you, Miss Forrest?" asked Stähl, pausing at her side, with the first trace of emotion visible in his inscrutable face.

"I dare everything!" and as she spoke, Ursula's proud head rose erect, Ursula's dauntless eyes looked full into his own.

"In truth you do dare everything," he murmured below his breath, with a glance of passionate admiration. But the soft ardor that made his eyes wonderfully lovely for an instant flamed as suddenly into a flash of anger, for there was a perceptible recoil of the white shoulder as his breath touched it in bending, and when he breathed a single word into her ear, his face wore the stealthy ferocity of a tiger in the act of springing upon his unsuspecting prey. Had she been actually confronted with the veritable beast, it could scarcely have wrought a swifter panic than that one word. Fixed in the same half-shrinking, half-haughty attitude, she sat as if changed suddenly to stone. Her eyes, dark and dilated with some unconquerable horror, never left his face while light, color, life itself seemed to ebb slowly from her own, leaving it as beautiful yet woful to look upon as some marble Medusa's countenance. So sudden, so entire was the change in that blooming face, that Kate forgot her own dismay, and cried:

"Ursula, what is it?" while Evan, turning on the worker of the miracle, demanded hotly:

"What right have you to terrify women and insult men by hissing in their ears secret information dishonorably obtained?"

Neither question received an answer, for Ursula and Stähl seemed unconscious of any presence but their own, as each silently regarded the other with a gaze full of mutual intelligence, yet opposing emotions of triumph and despair. At the sound of Evan's voice, a shudder shook Ursula from head to foot, but her eye never wavered, and the icy fixture of her features remained unchanged as she asked in a sharp, shrill whisper —

"Is it true?"

"Behold the sign!" and with a gesture, too swift and unsuspected for any but herself to see or understand the revelation made, Stähl bared his left arm, held it before her eyes, and dropped it in the drawing of a breath. Whatever Ursula saw confirmed her dread; she uttered neither cry nor exclamation, but wrung her hands together in dumb anguish, while her lips moved without uttering a sound.

Kate Heath's over-wrought nerves gave way, and weeping hysterically, she clung to Evan, imploring him to take her home. Instantly assuming his usual languid courtesy of mien and manners, Stähl murmured regretful apologies, rang the bell for Miss Heath's carriage, and bringing her veil and mantle from the ante-room, implored the privilege of shawling her with a penitent devotion wonderfully winning, yet which did not prevent her shrinking from him and accepting no services but such as Evan half-unconsciously bestowed.

"You are coming with me? You promised mama to bring me safely back. Mr. Forrest, take pity on me, for I dare not go alone."

She spoke tearfully, still agitated by the secret wound inflicted by a whisper.

"Hay will gladly protect you, Kate; I cannot leave Ursula," began Evan, but a smooth, imperious voice took the word from his lips.

"Hay is gone, I shall remain with Ursula, and you, Forrest, will not desert Miss Heath in the distress which I have unhappily caused by granting her wish. Forgive me, and good-night."

As Stähl spoke, he kissed the hand that trembled in his own, with a glance that lingered long in poor Kate's memory, and led her towards her friend. But Evan's dark face kindled with the passion that he had vainly striven to suppress, and though he tried to curb his tongue, his eye looked a defiance as he placed himself beside his cousin, saying doggedly:

"I shall not leave Ursula to the tender mercies of a charlatan unless she bids me go. Kate, stay with us and lend your carriage to this gentleman, as his own is not yet here."

Bowing with a face of imperturbable composure, Stähl answered in his softest tones, bending an inquiring glance on Ursula:

"Many thanks, but I prefer to receive my dismissal from the lady of the house, not from its would-be master. Miss Forrest, shall I leave you to begin the work marked out for me? or shall I remain to unfold certain matters which nearly concern yourself, and which, if neglected, may result in misfortune to more than one of us?"

As if not only the words but the emphasis with which they were pronounced recalled some forgotten fact, woke some new fear, Ursula started from her stupor of surprise and mental suffering into sudden action. All that had passed while she sat dumb seemed to return to her, and a quick glance from face to face appeared to decide her in the course she must pursue.

Rising she went to Kate, touched her wet cheek with lips that chilled it, and turning to her companions regarded them with an eye that seemed to pierce to the heart's core of each. What she read there none knew, but some purpose strong enough to steady and support her with a marvellous composure seemed born of that long scrutiny, for motioning her cousin from her she said:

"Go, Evan, I desire it."

"Go! and leave you with that man? I cannot, Ursula!"

"You must, you will, if I command it. I wish to be alone with him; I fear nothing, not even this magician, who in an instant has changed my life by a single word. See! I trust myself to his protection; I throw myself upon his mercy, and implore you to have faith in me."

With an air of almost pathetic dignity, a gesture of infinite grace, she stretched a hand to either man, and as each grasped the soft prize a defiant glance was exchanged between them, a daring one was fixed upon the beautiful woman for whom, like spirits of good and ill, they were henceforth to contend.

"I shall obey you, but may I come to-morrow?" Evan whispered, as he pressed the hand that in his own was tremulous and warm.

"Yes, come to me early, I shall need you then — if ever."

And as the words left her lips that other hand in Felix Stähl's firm hold grew white and cold as if carved in marble.

With Kate still trembling on his arm, Evan left them; his last glance showing him his rival regarding his departure with an air of tranquil triumph, and Ursula, his proud, high-hearted cousin, sinking slowly on her knees before this man, who in an hour seemed to have won the right to make or mar her happiness for ever.

How the night passed Evan Forrest never knew. He took Kate home, and then till day dawned haunted beach and cliff like a restless ghost, thinking only of Ursula, remembering only that she bade him come early, and chiding the tardy sun until it rose upon a day that darkened all his life. As the city bells chimed seven from the spires that shone across the little bay, Evan re-entered his cousin's door; but before he could pronounce her name the lady who for years had filled a mother's place to the motherless girl came hurrying to meet him, with every mark of sleepless agitation in her weary yet restless face and figure.

"Thank heaven, you are come!" she ejaculated, drawing him aside into the ante-room. "Oh, Mr. Forrest, such a night as I have passed, so strange, so unaccountable, I am half distracted."

"Where is Ursula?" demanded Evan.

"Just where you left her, sir; she has not stirred since that dreadful Mr. Stähl went away."

"When was that?"

"Past midnight. At eleven I went down to give him a hint, but the door was fast, and for another hour the same steady sound of voices came up to me as had been going on since you left. When he did go at last it was so quietly I only knew it by the glimpse I caught of him gliding down the walk, and vanishing like a spirit in the shadow of the great gate."

"Then you went to Ursula?"

"I did, sir; I did, and found her sitting as I saw her when I left the room in the evening."

"What did she say? what did she do?"

"She said nothing, and she looked like death itself, so white, so cold, so still; not a sigh, a tear, a motion; and when I implored her to speak she only broke my heart with the look she gave me, as she whispered, 'Leave me in peace till Evan comes.'"

With one stride he stood before the closed door, but when he tapped no voice bade him enter, and opening he noiselessly glided in. She was there, sitting as Mrs. Yorke described her, and looking more like a pale ghost than a living woman. Evan's eye wandered round the room, hungry to discover some clue to the mystery, but nothing was changed. The lamps burned dimly in the glare of early sunshine streaming through the room; the curtains were still wafted to and fro by balmy breezes; the seats still stood scattered here and there as they were quitted; Captain Hay's chair still lay overthrown; Kate's gloves had been trodden under foot, and round the deep chair in the window still glowed the scattered petals of the rose with which Felix Stähl had regaled himself while lying there.

"Ursula!"

No answer came to his low call, and drawing nearer, Evan whispered tenderly:

"My darling, speak to me! It breaks my heart to see you so, and have no power to help you."

The dark eyes fixed on vacancy relaxed in their strained gaze, the cold hands locked together in her lap loosened their painful pressure, and with a long sigh Ursula turned towards him, saying, like one wakened from a heavy dream:

"I am glad you are come;" then as if some fear stung her, added with startling abruptness, "Evan! what did he whisper in your ear last night?"

Amazed at such a question, yet not ill pleased to answer it even then, for his full heart was yearning to unburden itself, the young man instantly replied, while his face glowed with hope, and his voice grew tender with the untold love that had long hovered on his lips:

"He said, 'You will never win your cousin;' but, Ursula, he lied, for I will win you even if he bring the powers of darkness to confound me. He read in my face what you must have read there long ago, and did not rebuke by one cold look, one forbidding word. Let me tell my love now; let me give you the shelter of my heart if you need it, and whatever grief or shame or fear has come to you let me help you bear it if I cannot banish it."

She did not speak, till kneeling before her he said imploringly:

"Ursula, you bade me trust you; I do entirely. Can you not place a like confidence in me?"

"No, Evan."

"Then you do not love as I love," he cried, with a foreboding fear heavy at his heart.

"No, I do not love as you love." The answer came like a soft echo, and her whole frame trembled for an instant as if some captive emotion struggled for escape and an iron hand restrained it. Her cousin saw it, and seizing both her hands, looked deep into her eyes, demanding, sternly:

"Do you love this man?"

"I shall marry him."

Evan stared aghast at the hard, white resolution stamped upon her face, as she looked straight before her with a blank yet steady gaze, seeming to see and own allegiance to a master invisible to him. A moment he struggled with a chaos of conflicting passions, then fought his way to a brief calmness, intent on fathoming the mystery that had wrought such a sudden change in both their lives.

"Ursula, as the one living relative whom you possess, I have a right to question you. Answer me truly, I conjure you, and deal honestly with the heart that is entirely your own. I can forget myself, can put away my own love and longing, can devote my whole time, strength, life to your service, if you need me. Something has happened that affects you deeply, let me know it. No common event would move you so, for lovers do not woo in this strange fashion, nor betrothed brides wear their happiness with such a face as you now wear."

"Few women have such lovers as mine, or such betrothals to tell. Ask me nothing, Evan, I have told you all I may; go now, and let me rest, if any rest remains for me."

"Not yet," he answered, with as indomitable a purpose in his face as that which seemed to have fixed and frozen hers. "I must know more of this man before I give you up. Who and what is he?"

"Study, question, watch and analyse him. You will find him what he seems — no more, no less. I leave you free to do what you will, and claim an equal liberty for myself," she said.

"I thought he was a stranger to you as to me and others. You must have known him elsewhere, Ursula?"

"I never saw or knew him till a month ago."

Evan struck his hands together with a gesture of despair, as he sprang up, saying:

"Ah! I see it now. A month ago I left you, and in that little time you learned to love."

"Yes, in that little time I did learn to love."

Again the soft echo came, again the sadder tremor shook her, but she neither smiled, nor wept, nor turned her steady eyes away from the unseen but controlling presence that for her still seemed to haunt the room.

Evan Forrest was no blind lover, and despite his own bitter loss he was keen-eyed enough to see that some emotion deeper than caprice, stronger than pity, sharper than regret, now held possession of his cousin's heart. He felt that some tie less tender than that which bound him to her bound her to this man, who exercised such power over her proud spirit and strong will. Bent on reading the riddle, he rapidly glanced through the happy past, so shared with Ursula that he believed no event in the life of either was unknown to the other; yet here was a secret lying dark between them, and only one little month of absence had sowed the seed that brought such a harvest of distrust and pain. Suddenly he spoke:

"Ursula, has this man acquired power over you through any weakness of your own?"

A haughty flash kindled in her eyes, and for an instant her white face glowed with womanly humiliation at the doubt implied.

"I am as innocent of any sin or shame, any weakness or wrong, as when I lay a baby in my mother's arms. Would to God I lay there now as tranquilly asleep as she!"

The words broke from her with a tearless sob, and spreading her hands before her face he heard her murmur like a broken-hearted child:

"How could he, oh, how could he wound me with a thought like that?"

"I will not! I do not! Hear me, Ursula, and forgive me, if I cannot submit to see you leave me for a man like this without one effort to fathom the inexplicable change I find in you. Only tell me that he is worthy of you, that you love him and are happy, and I will be dumb. Can you do this to ease my heart and conscience, Ursula?"

"Yes, I can do more than that. Rest tranquil, dearest Evan. I know what I do; I do it freely, and in time you will acknowledge that I did well in marrying Felix Stähl."

"You are betrothed to him?"

"I am; his kiss is on my cheek, his ring is on my hand; I accept both."

With a look and gesture which he never could forget she touched the cheek where one deep spot of color burned as if branded there, and held up the hand whose only ornament beside its beauty was a slender ring formed of two twisted serpents, whose diamond eyes glittered with an uncanny resemblance of life.

"And you will marry him?" repeated Evan, finding the hard fact impossible to accept.

"I will."

"Soon, Ursula?"

"Very soon."

"You wish it so?"

"I wish what he wishes."

"You will go away with him?"

"To the end of the earth if he desires it."

"My God! is this witchcraft or infatuation?"

"Neither, it is woman's love, which is quick and strong to dare and suffer all things for those who are dearer to her than her life."

He could not see her face, for she had turned it from him, but in her voice trembled a tender fervor which could not be mistaken, and with a pang that wrung his man's heart sorely he relinquished all hope, and bade farewell to love, believing that no mystery existed but that which is inexplicable, the workings of a woman's heart.

"I am going, Ursula," he said; "you no longer have any need of me, and I must fight out my fight alone. God bless you, and remember whatever befalls, while life lasts you have one unalterable friend and lover in me."

As he spoke with full eyes, broken voice and face eloquent with love, regret and pity, Ursula rose suddenly and fell upon his bosom, clinging there with passionate despair that deepened his ever growing wonder.

"God help you, Evan! love me, trust me, pity me, and so goodbye! good-bye!" she cried, in that strange paroxysm of emotion, as tearless, breathless, trembling and wearied, yet still self-controlled, she kissed and blessed and led him to the door. No pause upon the threshold; as he lingered she put him from her, closed and bolted it: then as if with him the sustaining power of her darkened life departed, she fell down upon the spot where he had stood, and lay there, beautiful and pale and still as some fair image of eternal sleep.

PART II

THE NINE DAYS' WONDER at the sudden wedding which followed that strange betrothal had died away, the honeymoon was over, and the bridal pair were alone together in their new home. Ursula stood at the window looking out, with eyes as wistful as a caged bird's, upon the fading leaves that fluttered in the autumn wind. Her husband lay on his couch, apparently absorbed in a vellum-covered volume, the cabalistic characters of which were far easier to decipher than the sweet, wan face he was studying covertly. The silence which filled the room was broken by a long sigh of pain as the book fell from Stähl's hand, and his head leaned wearily upon the pillow. Ursula heard the sigh, and, like a softly moving shadow, glided to his side, poured wine from an antique flask, and kneeling, held it to his lips. He drank thirstily, but the cordial seemed to impart neither strength nor comfort, for he drew his wife's head down beside him, saying:

"Kiss me, Ursula; I am so faint and cold, nothing seems to warm my blood, and my body freezes, while my heart burns with a never-dying fire."

With a meek obedience that robbed the act of all tenderness, she touched her ruddy lips to the paler ones that ardently returned the pressure, yet found no satisfaction there. Leaning upon his arm, he held her to him with a fierce fondness, in strange contrast to his feeble frame, saying earnestly:

"Ursula, before I married you I found such strength and solace, such warmth and happiness in your presence, that I coveted you as a precious healing for my broken health. Then I loved you, forgetful of self — loved you as you never will be loved again, and thanked heaven that my fate was so interwoven with your own that the utterance of a word secured my life's desire. But now, when I have made you wholly mine, and hope to bask in the sunshine of your beauty, youth and womanhood, I find a cold, still creature in my arms, and no spark of the fire that consumes me ever warms the image of my love. Must it be so? Can I never see you what you were again?"

"Never!" she answered, leaning there as pale and passive as if she were in truth a marble woman. "I vowed obedience at the altar, nothing more. I did not love you; I could not honor you, but I felt that I might learn to obey. I have done so, be content."

"Not I! Colder women have been taught love as well as obedience; you, too, shall be a docile pupil, and one day give freely what I sue for now. Other men woo before they wed, my wooing and my winning will come later — if I live long enough."

He turned her face towards him as he spoke and scanned it closely; but no grateful sign of softness, pity or regret appeared, and, with a broken exclamation, he put her from him, locked both hands across his eyes and lay silent, till some uncontrollable paroxysm of emotion had passed by. Presently he spoke, and the words betrayed what the pain had been.

"My mother — heaven bless her for her tenderness! — used to pray that her boy's life might be a long and happy one; it is a bitter thing to feel that the only woman now left me to love prays for the shortening of that same life, and can bestow no look or word to make its failing hours happy."

The unwonted tone of filial affection, the keen sorrow and the mournful acknowledgment of an inevitable doom touched Ursula as no ardent demonstration or passionate reproach had ever done. She softly lifted up the folded hands, saw that those deep eyes were wet with tears, and in that pallid countenance read the melancholy record of a life burdened with a sad heritage of pain, thwarted by unhappy love and darkened by allegiance to a superstitious vow. Great as her sacrifice had been, deep as the wound still was, and heavily as her captivity weighed on her proud heart, it was still womanly, generous and gentle; and, despite all wrongs, all blemishes, all bitter memories, she felt the fascination of this wild and wayward nature, as she had never done before, and yielded to its persuasive potency. Laying her cool hand on his hot forehead, she leaned over him, saying, with an accent of compassion sweeter to his ear than her most perfect song:

"No, Felix, I pray no prayers that heaven would refuse to grant. I only ask patience for myself, a serener spirit for you, and God's blessing upon Evan, wherever he may be."

Before the words of tender satisfaction which rose to Stähl's lips could be uttered, a noiseless servant brought a black-edged card. Ursula read and handed it to her husband.

"Mrs. Heath. Shall we see her, love?" he asked.

"As you please," was the docile answer, though an expression of mingled pain and sorrow passed across her face in speaking.

He half frowned at her meekness, then smiled and bade the man deny them, adding, as he left the room,

"I am too well content with this first glimpse of the coming happiness to be saddened by the lamentations of that poor lady over her wilful daughter, who had the bad taste to drown herself upon our wedding-day."

"Felix, may I ask you a question?"

"Anything of me, Ursula."

"Tell me what you whispered in Kate's ear on the evening which both of us remember well."

Questions were so rare, and proving a sign of interest, that Stähl made haste to answer, with a curious blending of disdain and pity,

"She bade me tell her the most ardent desire of her life, and I dared to answer truly, 'To win my heart.'"

"A true answer, but a cruel one," Ursula said.

"That cruel truthfulness is one of the savage attributes which two generations of civilization cannot entirely subdue in my race.

Those who tamely submit to me I despise, but those who oppose me I first conquer and then faithfully love."

"Had you made poor Kate happy, you would not now regret the possession of a cold, untender wife."

"Who would gather a gay tulip when they can reach a royal rose, though thorns tear the hand that seizes it? For even when it fades its perfume lingers, gifting it with an enduring charm. Love, I have found my rose, so let the tulip fade — "

There he paused abruptly in his flowery speech, for with the swift instinct of a temperament like his, he was instantly conscious of the fact when her thoughts wandered, and a glance showed him that, though her attitude was unaltered, she was listening intently. A far-off bell had rung, the tones of a man's voice sounded from below, and the footsteps of an approaching servant grew audible. Stähl recognised the voice, fancied that Ursula did also, and assured himself of it by an unsuspected test that took the form of a caress. Passing his arm about her waist, his hand lay lightly above her heart, and as her cousin's name was announced he felt the sudden bound that glad heart gave, and counted the rapid throbs that sent the color to her cheeks and made her lips tremble. A black frown lowered on his forehead, and his eyes glittered ominously for an instant, but both betrayals were unseen, and nothing marred the gracious sweetness of his voice.

"Of course you will see your cousin, Ursula. I shall greet him in passing, and return when you have enjoyed each other alone."

"Alone!" she echoed, with a distrustful look at him, an anxious one about the room, as if no place seemed safe or sacred in that house where she was both mistress and slave.

He understood the glance, and answered with one so reproachful that she blushed for the ungenerous suspicion, as he said, with haughty emphasis:

"Yes, Ursula, alone. Whatever evil names I may deserve, those of spy and eavesdropper cannot be applied to me; and though my wife can neither love nor honor me, I will prove that she may trust me."

With that he left her, and meeting Evan just without, offered his hand frankly, and gave his welcome with a cordial grace that was irresistible. Evan could not refuse the hand, for on it shone a little ring which Ursula once wore, and yielding to the impulse awakened by that mute reminder of her, he betrayed exactly what his host desired to know, for instantaneous as was both recognition and submission, Stähl's quick eye divined the cause.

"Come often to us, Evan; forget the past, and remember only that through Ursula we are kindred now. She is waiting for you; go to her and remain as long as you incline, sure of a hearty welcome from both host and hostess."

Then he passed on, and Evan hurried to his cousin; eager, yet reluctant to meet her, lest in her face he should read some deeper mystery or greater change than he last saw there. She came to meet him smiling and serene, for whatever gust of joy or sorrow had swept over her, no trace of it remained; yet, when he took her in his arms, there broke from him the involuntary exclamation:

"Is this my cousin Ursula?"

"Yes, truly. Am I then so altered?"

"This is a reflection of what you were; that of what you are. Look, and tell me if I have not cause for wonder."

She did look as he drew a miniature from his bosom and led her to the mirror. The contrast was startling even to herself, for the painted face glowed with rosy bloom, hope shone in the eyes, happiness smiled from the lips, while youthful purity and peace crowned the fair forehead with enchanting grace. The living face was already wan and thin, many tears had robbed the cheeks of color, sleepless nights had dimmed the lustre of the eyes, much secret suffering and strife had hardened the soft curves of the mouth and deepened the lines upon the brow. Even among the dark waves of her hair silver threads shone here and there, unbidden, perhaps unknown; and over the whole woman a subtle blight had fallen, more tragical than death. Silently she compared the two reflections, for the first time realising all that she had lost, yet as she returned the miniature she only said, with pathetic patience:

"I am not what I was, but my heart remains unchanged, believe that, Evan."

"I do. Tell me, Ursula, are you happy now?"

Her eyes rose to his, and over her whole face there shone the sudden magic of a glow warmer and brighter than a smile.

"I am supremely happy now."

It was impossible to doubt her truth, however past facts or present appearances might seem to belie it, and Evan was forced to believe, despite his disappointment.

"He is kind to you, Ursula? You suffer no neglect, no tyranny nor wrong from this strange man?" he asked, still haunted by vague doubts.

She waved her hand about the lovely room, delicately dainty as a bride's bower should be, and answered, with real feeling:

"Does this look as if I suffered any neglect or wrong? Every want and whim is seen and gratified before expressed; I go and come unwatched, unquestioned; the winds of heaven are not allowed to visit me too roughly, and as for kindness, look there and see a proof of it."

She pointed to the garden where her husband walked alone, never quitting the wide terrace just below her window, though the sunshine that he loved had faded from the spot, and the autumn winds he dreaded blew gustily about him. He never lifted up his eyes, nor paused, nor changed his thoughtful attitude, but patiently paced to and fro, a mute reproach for Ursula's unjust suspicion.

"How frail he looks; if life with you cannot revive him he must be past hope."

Evan spoke involuntarily, and Ursula's hand half checked the words upon his lips; but neither looked the other in the face, and neither owned, even to themselves, how strong a hidden wish had grown.

"He will live because he resolves to live, for that frail body holds the most indomitable spirit I have ever known. But let me tell you why he lingers where every breath brings pain," said Ursula, and having told him, she added:

"Is not that both a generous and a gentle rebuke for an unkind doubt?"

"It is either a most exquisite piece of loverlike devotion or of consummate art. I think it is the latter, for he knows you well, and repays great sacrifices by graceful small ones, which touch and charm your woman's heart."

"You wrong him, Evan, and aversion blinds you to the better traits I have learned to see. An all absorbing love ennobles the most sinful man, and makes it possible for some woman to forgive and cling to him."

"I have no right to ask, but the strange spirit that has taken possession of you baffles and disquiets me past endurance. Tell me, Ursula, what you would not tell before, do you truly, tenderly love this man whom you have married?"

The question was uttered with an earnestness so solemn that it forced a truthful answer, and she looked up at him with the old frankness unobscured by any cloud, as she replied:

"But for one thing I should long ago have learned to love him. I know this, because even now I cannot wholly close my heart against the ardent affection that patiently appeals to it."

"And that one thing, that cursed mystery which has wrecked two lives, when am I to know it, Ursula?"

"Never till I lie on my deathbed, and not even then, unless — "

She caught back the words hovering on her lips, but her eye glanced furtively upon the solitary figure pacing there below, and Evan impetuously finished the broken sentence:

"Unless he is already dead — let it be so; I shall wait and yet prove his prophecy a false one by winning and wearing you when his baleful love is powerless."

"He is my husband, Evan, remember that. Now come with me, I am going to him, for he must not shiver there when I can give him the warmth his tropical nature loves."

But Evan would not go, and soon left her plunged in a new sea of anxious conjectures, doubts and dreads. Stähl awaited his wife's approach, saying within himself as he watched her coming under the gold and scarlet arches of the leafy walk, with unwonted elasticity in her step, color on her cheeks and smiles upon her lips:

"Good! I have found the spell that turns my snow image into flesh and blood; I will use it and enjoy the summer of her presence while I may."

He did use it, but so warily and well that though Ursula and Evan were dimly conscious of some unseen yet controlling hand that ruled their intercourse and shaped events, they found it hard to believe that studious invalid possessed and used such power. Evan came daily, and daily Ursula regained some of her lost energy and bloom, till an almost preternatural beauty replaced the pale loveliness her face had worn, and she seemed to glow and brighten with an inward fire, like some brilliant flower that held the fervor of a summer in its heart and gave it out again in one fair, fragrant hour.

Like a watchful shadow Evan haunted his cousin, conscious that they were drifting down a troubled stream without a pilot, yet feeling powerless to guide or govern his own life, so inextricably was it bound up in Ursula's. He saw that the vigor and vitality his presence gave her was absorbed by her husband, to whom she was a more potent stimulant than rare winds, balmy airs or costly drugs. He knew that the stronger nature subdued the weaker, and the failing life sustained itself by draining the essence of that other life, which, but for some sinister cross of fate, would have been an ever springing fountain of joy to a more generous and healthful heart.

The blind world applauded Felix Stähl's success, and envied him the splendid wife in whose affluent gifts of fortune, mind and person he seemed to revel with luxurious delight. It could not see the secret bitterness that poisoned peace; could not guess the unavailing effort, unappeased desire and fading hope that each day brought him; nor fathom the despair that filled his soul as he saw and felt the unmistakable tokens of his coming fate in hollow temples, wasting flesh and a mortal weariness that knew no rest; a despair rendered doubly bitter by the knowledge of his impotence to prevent another from reaping what he had sown with painful care.

Ursula's hard won submission deserted her when Evan came, for in reanimating the statue Stähl soon felt that he had lost his slave and found a master. The heart which had seemed slowly yielding to his efforts closed against him in the very hour of fancied conquest. No more meek services, no more pity shown in spite of pride, no more docile obedience to commands that wore the guise of entreaties. The captive spirit woke and beat against its bars, passionately striving to be free, though not a cry escaped its lips. Very soon her recovered gaiety departed, and her life became a vain effort to forget, for like all impetuous natures she sought oblivion in excitement and hurried from one scene of pleasure to another, finding rest and happiness in none. Her husband went with her everywhere, recklessly squandering the strength she gave him in a like fruitless quest, till sharply checked by warnings which could no longer be neglected.

One night in early spring when winter gaieties were drawing to a close, Ursula came down to him shining in festival array, with the evening fever already burning in her cheeks, the expectant glitter already kindling in her eyes, and every charm heightened with that skill which in womanly women is second nature. Not for his pride or pleasure had she made herself so fair, he knew that well, and the thought lent its melancholy to the tone in which he said:

"Ursula, I am ready, but so unutterably weak and weary that I cannot go."

"I can go without you. Be so good," and quite unmoved by the suffering that rarely found expression, she held her hand to him that he might clasp her glove. He rose to perform the little service with that courtesy which never failed him, asking, as he bent above the hand with trembling fingers and painful breath,

"Does Evan go with you?"

"Yes, he never fails me, he has neither weakness nor weariness to mar my pleasure or to thwart my will."

"Truly a tender and a wifely answer."

"I am not tender nor wifely; why assume the virtues which I never shall possess? They were not set down in the bond; that I fulfilled to the letter when I married you, and beyond the wearing of your name and ring I owe you nothing. Do I?"

"Yes, a little gratitude for the sincerity that placed a doomed life in your keeping; a little respect for the faith I have kept unbroken through all temptations; a little compassion for a malady that but for you would make my life a burden I would gladly lay down."

Time was when words like these would have touched and softened her, but not now, for she had reached the climax of her suffering, the extent of her endurance, and turning on him she gave vent to the passionate emotion which could no longer be restrained:

"I should have given you much gratitude if in helping me to save one life you had not doomed another. I should honestly respect the faith you boast of if such costly sacrifices were not demanded for its keeping. I should deeply pity that mortal malady if you had bravely borne it alone instead of seeking a selfish solace in bequeathing it to another. I tell you, Felix, you are killing me swiftly and surely by this dreadful life. Better end me at once than drive me mad, or leave me a strong soul prisoned in a feeble body like yourself."

For the first time in his life Stähl felt the touch of fear, not for himself but for her, lest that terrible affliction which so baffles human skill and science should fall upon the woman whom he loved with a selfish intensity which had tangled two lives and brought them to this pass.

"Hush, Ursula," he said, soothingly, "have patience, I shall soon be gone, and then — what will you do then?"

The question leaped to his lips, for at the word "gone" he saw the gloom lift from her face, leaving an expression of relief that unmistakably betrayed how heavily her burden had oppressed her. Undaunted by the almost fierce inquiry she fixed her eyes upon him, and answered steadily:

"I shall put off my bridal white, wear widow's weeds for a single year, and then" — there she, too, paused abruptly; but words were needless, for as Evan's step sounded on the stair she turned and hurried towards him, as if love, liberty and life all lay waiting for her there. Stähl watched them with a jealous pang that pierced the deeper as, remembering Ursula's taunt, he compared the young man with himself; the one rich in the stature, vigor, comeliness that make a manly man; the other, in sad truth, a strong spirit imprisoned in a ruined body. As he looked he clenched his pale hand hard, and muttered low between his set teeth:

"He shall not have her, if I sell my soul to thwart him!"

To Ursula's intense surprise and Evan's annoyance Stähl followed them into the carriage, with a brief apology for his seeming caprice. No one spoke during the short drive, but as they came into the brilliant rooms Ursula's surprise deepened to alarm, for in the utter change of mien and manner which had befallen her husband she divined the presence of some newborn purpose, and trembled for the issue. Usually he played the distasteful part of invalid with a grace and skill which made the undisguisable fact a passport to the sympathy and admiration of both men and women. But that night no vigorous young man bore himself more debonnairly, danced more indefatigably, or devoted himself more charmingly to the service of matron, maid and grateful hostess. Lost in amazement, Ursula and Evan watched him, gliding to and fro, vivacious, blithe and bland, leaving a trail of witty, wise or honied words behind him, and causing many glances of approval to follow that singular countenance, for now its accustomed pallor was replaced by a color no art could counterfeit, and the mysterious eyes burned with a fire that fixed and fascinated other eyes.

"What does it mean, Evan?" whispered Ursula, standing apart with her faithful shadow.

"Mischief, if I read it rightly," was the anxious answer, and at that moment, just before them, the object of their thoughts was accosted by a jovial gentleman, who exclaimed:

"God bless me, Stähl! Rumor said you were dying, like a liar as she is, and here I find you looking more like a bridegroom than when I left you at the altar six months ago."

"For once rumor tells the truth, Coventry. I am dying, but one may make their exit gracefully and end their tragedy or comedy with a grateful bow! I have had a generous share of pleasure; I thank the world for it; I make my adieu to-night, and tranquilly go home to rest."

Spoken with an untroubled smile the words were both touching and impressive, and the friendly Coventry was obliged to clear his voice before he could answer with an assumption of cheery unbelief:

"Not yet, my dear fellow, not yet; we cannot spare you this forty years, and with such a wife what right have you to talk of ending the happy drama which all predict your life will be?" then glad to change the subject, he added: "Apropos of predictions, do take pity on my curiosity and tell me if it is true that you entertained a party with some very remarkable prophecies, or something of that sort, just before your marriage with Miss Forrest. Hay once spoke mysteriously of it, but he went to the bad so soon after that I never made him satisfy me."

"I did comply with a lady's wish, but entertainment was not the result. I told Hay, what all the world knew, the next day, that certain dishonorable transactions of his were discovered, and warrants out for his arrest, and they hurried home to find my warning true."

"Yes, no one dreamed of such an end for the gay captain. I don't ask how your discovery was made, but I do venture to inquire if Miss Heath's tragical death was foretold that night?"

"That which indirectly caused her death was made known to her that night, but for her sake you will pardon me that I keep the secret."

"A thousand pardons for asking, and yet I am tempted to put one more question. You look propitious, so pray tell me if your other predictions were fulfilled with equal success?"

"Yes; sooner or later they always are."

"Upon my life, that's very singular! Just for the amusement of the thing make one now, and let me see if your skill remains undiminished. Nothing personal, you know, but some general prediction that any one may know and verify."

Stähl paused a moment, bending his eyes on Ursula, who stood unseen by his companion, then answered slowly with a memorable tone and aspect:

"I prophesy that before the month is out the city will be startled by a murder, and the culprit will elude justice by death."

Coventry's florid countenance paled visibly, and hastily returning thanks for the undesirable favor so complacently granted, he took himself away to whisper the evil portent in the ears of all he met. As he disappeared Stähl advanced to his wife, asking with an air of soft solicitude:

"Are you weary, love? or will you dance? Your cousin is negligent to-night."

"Oh, no, I have not wished to dance. Let us go now, and Evan, come to me to-morrow evening, when you will find a few friends and much music," she answered, with an unquiet glance at her husband, a significant one at her cousin, who obeyed it by leaving them with a silent bow.

The homeward drive was as quiet as the other had been, and when they alighted Stähl followed his wife into the drawing-room; there, dropping wearily into a seat, he removed the handkerchief which had been pressed to his lips, and she saw that it was steeped in blood.

"Pardon me — it was unavoidable. Please ring for Marjory," he said, feebly.

Ursula neither spoke nor stirred, but stood regarding him with an expression which alarmed him, it was so full of a strange, stern triumph. It gave him strength to touch the bell, and when the faithful old woman who had nursed him from his babyhood came hurrying in, to say quietly:

"Take that ugly thing away, and bring my drops; also your mistress's vinaigrette, she needs it."

"Not she, the icicle," muttered Marjory, who adored her master, and heartily disliked her mistress because she did not do likewise.

When the momentary faintness had cleared away Stähl's quick eye at once took in the scene before him. Marjory was carefully preparing the draught, and Ursula stood watching her with curious intentness.

"What is that?" she asked, as the old woman put down the tiny vial, containing a colorless and scentless liquid.

"Poison, madam, one drop of which will restore life, while a dozen will bring a sure and sudden death."

Ursula took up the little vial, read the label containing both the medicine and its maker's name, and laid it back again with a slight motion of head and lips, as if she gave a mute assent to some secret suggestion. Marjory's lamentations as she moved about him drew the wife's eyes to her husband, and meeting his she asked coldly:

"Can I help you?"

"Thanks, Marjory will tend me. Good-night, you'll not be troubled with me long."

"No, I shall not; I have borne enough."

She spoke low to herself, but both listeners heard her, and the old woman sternly answered:

"May the Lord forgive you for that speech, madam."

"He will, for He sees the innocent and the guilty, and He knows my sore temptation."

Then without another look or word she left them with the aspect of one walking in an evil dream.

All night Marjory hovered about her master, and early in the morning his physician came. A few words assured Stähl that his hour was drawing very near, and that whatever work remained to be done must be accomplished speedily. He listened calmly to the truth which he had forced from the reluctant doctor, and when he paused made no lament, but said, with more than his accustomed gentleness:

"You will oblige me by concealing this fact from my wife. It is best to let it break upon her by merciful degrees."

"I understand, sir, I will be dumb; but I must caution you not to exert or agitate yourself in the least, for any undue exertion or excitement would be fatal in your weak state."

The worthy doctor spoke earnestly, but to his infinite amazement and alarm his patient rose suddenly from the couch on which he lay half dressed, and standing erect before him, said forcibly, while his hollow cheeks burned crimson, and his commanding eye almost enforced belief in his assertion:

"You are mistaken; I am not weak, for I have done with fear as well as hope, and if I choose to barter my month of life for one hour, one moment of exertion or excitement, I have the right to do it."

He paused, took breath and added:

"My wife intended to receive her friends tonight; she must not be disappointed, therefore you will not only tell her I am in no danger, but add that an unexpected crisis in my malady has come, and that with care and a season at the South I shall yet be a hale and hearty man. Grant me this favor, I shall not forget it."

The doctor was both a poor and a timid man; his generous but eccentric patient was a fortune to him; the falsehood seemed a kind one; the hint of a rich remembrance was irresistible, and bowing his acquiescence, he departed to obey directions to the letter.

All that day Ursula sat in her room writing steadily, and all that

day her husband watched and waited for her coming, but sent no
invitation and received no message. At dusk she went out alone.
Her departure was unheard and unseen by any but the invalid,
whose every sense was alert; his quick ear caught the soft rustle of
her dress as she passed his door, and dragging himself to the window he saw her glide away, wrapped in a shrouding cloak. At that
sight Stähl's hand was lifted to the bell, but he dropped it, saying
to himself:

"No, if she did not mean to return she would have taken care to
tell me she was coming back; women always betray themselves by
too much art. I have it! she has been writing, Marjory says; the
letter is to Evan; she fears he may not come to-night, and trusts no
one but herself to post it. I must assure myself of this."

Nerved with new strength, he went down into the dainty room
so happily prepared and dedicated to Ursula's sole use. It was
empty, but the charm of her presence lingered there, and every
graceful object spoke of her. Lights burned upon the writing-table;
the ink was still wet in the pen, and scattered papers confirmed the
report of her day's employment; but no written word was visible,
no note or packet anywhere appeared. A brief survey satisfied her
husband, and assured him of the truth of his suspicion.

"Oh, for an hour of my old strength to end this entanglement
like a man, instead of being forced to wait for time and chance to
aid me like a timorous woman," he sighed, looking out into the wild
March night, tormented by an impotent desire to follow his truant
wife, yet conscious that it was impossible unless he left a greater
work undone, for hourly he felt his power decline, and one dark
purpose made him tenacious of the life fast slipping from his hold.

For many moments he stood thinking deeply, so deeply that the
approach of a light, rapid step roused him too late for escape. It
was his wife's step; why was she returning so soon? had her heart
failed her? had some unforeseen occurrence thwarted her? She had
not been absent long enough to post a letter to reach Evan's lodgings, or the house of any friend, then where had she been? An
uncontrollable impulse caused Stähl to step noiselessly into the
shadow of a curtained recess as these thoughts flashed through his
mind, and hardly had he done so when Ursula hurried in wet,

wild-eyed and breathless, but wearing a look of pale determination which gave place to an expression of keen anxiety as she glanced about the room as if in search of something. Presently she murmured half aloud, "He shall never say again that I do not trust his honor. Lie there in safety till I need you, little friend," and lifting the cover of a carved ivory casket that ornamented the low chimneypiece, she gave some treasure to its keeping, saying, as she turned away with an air of feverish excitement, "Now for Evan and — my liberty!"

Nothing stirred in the room but the flicker of the fire and the softly moving pendulum of the clock that pointed to the hour of seven, till the door of Ursula's distant dressing-room closed behind her and a bell had summoned her maid. Then, from the recess, Stähl went straight to the ivory ornament and laid his hand upon its lid, yet paused long before he lifted it. The simple fact of her entire trust in him at any other time would have been the earnest safeguard of her secret; even now it restrained him by appealing to that inconsistent code of honor which governs many a man who would shoot his dearest friend for a hot word, and yet shrink with punctilious pride from breaking the seal of any letter that did not bear his name. Stähl hesitated till her last words stung his memory, making his own perfidy seem slight compared to hers. "I have a right to know," he said, "for when she forgets her honor I must preserve mine at any cost." A rapid gesture uncovered the casket, and showed him nothing but a small, sealed bottle, lying alone upon the velvet lining. A harmless little thing it looked, yet Stähl's face whitened terribly, and he staggered to a seat, as if the glance he gave had shown him his own death-warrant. He believed it had, for in size, shape, label and colorless contents the little vial was the counterpart of another last seen in Ursula's hand, one difference only in the two — that had been nearly empty, this was full to the lip.

In an instant her look, tone, gesture of the preceding night returned to him, and with the vivid recollection came the firm conviction that Ursula had yielded to a black temptation, and in her husband's name had purchased her husband's death. Till now no feeling but the intensest love had filled his heart towards her; Evan

Discovery of the Poison

he had learned to hate, himself to despise, but of his wife he had made an idol and worshipped her with a blind passion that would not see defects, own disloyalty or suspect deceit.

From any other human being the treachery would not have been so base, but from her it was doubly bitter, for she knew and owned her knowledge of his exceeding love. "Am I not dying fast enough for her impatience? Could she not wait a little, and let me go happy in my ignorance?" he cried within himself, forgetting in the anguish of that moment the falsehood told her at his bidding, for the furtherance of another purpose as sinful but less secret than her own. How time passed he no longer knew nor cared, as leaning his head upon his hands, he took counsel with his own unquiet heart, for all the evil passions, the savage impulses of his nature were aroused, and raged rebelliously in utter defiance of the feeble prison that confined them. Like all strong yet selfish souls, the wrongs he had committed looked to him very light compared with this, and seeing only his own devotion, faith and patience, no vengeance seemed too heavy for a crime that would defraud him of his poor remnant of unhappy life. Suddenly he lifted up his head, and on his face was stamped a ruthless, reckless purpose, which no earthly power could change or stay. An awesome smile touched his white lips, and the ominous fierceness glittered in his eye — for he was listening to a devil that sat whispering in his heart.

"I shall have my hour of excitement sooner than I thought," he said low to himself, as he left the room, carrying the vial with him. "My last prediction will be verified, although the victim and the culprit are one, and Evan shall live to wish that Ursula had died before me."

An hour later Ursula came to him as he sat gloomily before his chamber fire, while Marjory stood tempting him to taste the cordial she had brought. As if some impassable and unseen abyss already yawned between them, she gave him neither wifely caress nor evening greeting, but pausing opposite, said, with an inclination of her handsome head, which would have seemed a haughty courtesy but for the gentle coldness of her tone:

"I have obeyed the request you sent me, and made ready to receive the friends whose coming would else have been delayed. Is it your pleasure that I excuse you to them, or will you join us as you have often done when other invalids would fear to leave their beds?"

Her husband looked at her as she spoke, wondering what woman's whim had led her to assume a dress rich in itself, but lustreless and sombre as a mourning garb; its silken darkness relieved only by the gleam of fair arms through folds of costly lace, and a knot of roses, scarcely whiter than the bosom they adorned.

"Thanks for your compliance, Ursula. I will come down later in the evening for a moment to receive congratulations on the restoration promised me. Shall I receive yours then?"

"No, now, for now I can wish you a long and happy life, can rejoice that time is given you to learn a truer faith, and ask you to forgive me if in thought, or word, or deed I have wronged or wounded you."

Strangely sweet and solemn was her voice, and for the first time in many months her old smile shed its serenest sunshine on her face, touching it with a meeker beauty than that which it had lost. Her husband shot one glance at her as the last words left her lips, then veiled the eyes that blazed with sudden scorn and detestation. His voice was always under his control, and tranquilly it answered her, while his heart cried out within him:

"I forgive as I would be forgiven, and trust that the coming years will be to you all that I desire to have them. Go to your pleasures, Ursula, and let me hear you singing, whether I am there or here."

"Can I do nothing else for you, Felix, before I go?" she asked, pausing, as she turned away, as if some involuntary impulse ruled her.

Stähl smiled a strange smile as he said, pointing to the goblet and the minute bottle Marjory had just placed on the table at his side:

"You shall sweeten a bitter draught for me by mixing it, and I will drink to you when I take it by-and-by."

His eye was on her now, keen, cold and steadfast, as she drew near to serve him. He saw the troubled look she fixed upon the cup, he saw her hand tremble as she poured the one safe drop, and heard a double meaning in her words:

"This is the first, I hope it may be the last time that I shall need to pour this dangerous draught for you."

She laid down the nearly emptied vial, replaced the cup and turned to go. But, as if bent on trying her to the utmost, though each test tortured him, Stähl arrested her by saying, with an unwonted tremor in his voice, a rebellious tenderness in his eyes:

"Stay, Ursula, I may fall asleep and so not see you until — morning. Bid me good-night, my wife."

She went to him, as if drawn against her will, and for a moment they stood face to face, looking their last on one another in this life. Then Stähl snatched her to him with an embrace almost savage in its passionate fervor, and Ursula kissed him once with the cold lips, that said, without a smile, "Good-night, my husband, sleep in peace!"

"Judas!" he muttered, as she vanished, leaving him spent with the controlled emotions of that brief interview. Old Marjory heard the word, and from that involuntary betrayal seemed to gather courage for a secret which had burned upon her tongue for two mortal hours. As Stähl sunk again into his cushioned seat, and seemed about to relapse into his moody reverie, she leaned towards him, saying in a whisper:

"May I tell you something, sir?"

"Concerning what or whom, my old gossip?" he answered, listlessly, yet with even more than usual kindliness, for now this humble, faithful creature seemed his only friend.

"My mistress, sir," she said, nodding significantly.

His face woke then, he sat erect, and with an eager gesture bade her speak.

"I've long mistrusted her; for ever since her cousin came she has not been the woman or the wife she was at first. It's not for me to meddle, but it's clear to see that if you were gone there'd be a wedding soon."

Stähl frowned, eyed her keenly, seemed to catch some helpful hint from her indignant countenance, and answered, with a pensive smile:

"I know it, I forgive it; and am sure that, for my sake, you will

"Good-night, my husband, sleep in peace!"

be less frank to others.·Is this what you wished to tell me, Marjory?"

"Bless your unsuspecting heart, I wish it was, sir. I heard her
words last night, I watched her all to-day, and when she went out
at dusk I followed her, and saw her buy it."

Stähl started, as if about to give vent to some sudden passion,
but repressed it, and with a look of well-feigned wonder, asked:

"Buy what?"

Marjory pointed silently to the table, upon which lay three ob-
jects, the cup, the little vial and a rose that had fallen from Ursula's
bosom as she bent to render her husband the small service he had
asked of her. There was no time to feign horror, grief or doubt, for
a paroxysm of real pain seized him in its gripe, and served him
better than any counterfeit of mental suffering could have done.
He conquered it by the power of an inflexible spirit that would not
yield yet, and laying his thin hand on Marjory's arm, he whispered,
hastily:

"Hush! Never hint that again, I charge you. I bade her get it,
my store was nearly gone, and I feared I should need it in the
night."

The old woman read his answer as he meant she should, and laid
her withered cheek down on his hand, saying, with the tearless
grief of age:

"Always so loving, generous and faithful! You may forgive her,
but I never can."

Neither spoke for several minutes, then Stähl said:

"I will lie down and try to rest a little before I go — "

The sentence remained unfinished, as, with a weary yet wistful
air, he glanced about the shadowy room, asking, dumbly, "Where?"
Then he shook off the sudden influence of some deeper sentiment
than fear that for an instant thrilled and startled him.

"Leave me, Marjory, set the door ajar, and let me be alone until
I ring."

She went, and for an hour he lay listening to the steps of gathering guests, the sound of music, the soft murmur of conversation,
and the pleasant stir of life that filled the house with its social
charm, making his solitude doubly deep, his mood doubly bitter.

Once Ursula stole in, and finding him apparently asleep, paused for a moment studying the wan face, with its stirless lids, its damp forehead and its pale lips, scarcely parted by the fitful breath, then, like a sombre shadow, flitted from the room again, unconscious that the closed eyes flashed wide to watch her go.

Presently there came a sudden hush, and borne on the wings of an entrancing air Ursula's voice came floating up to him, like the sweet, soft whisper of some better angel, imploring him to make a sad life noble by one just and generous action at its close. No look, no tone, no deed of patience, tenderness or self-sacrifice of hers but rose before him now, and pleaded for her with the magic of that unconscious lay. No ardent hope, no fair ambition, no high purpose of his youth, but came again to show the utter failure of his manhood, and in the hour darkened by a last temptation his benighted soul groped blindly for a firmer faith than that which superstition had defrauded of its virtue. Like many another man, for one short hour Felix Stähl wavered between good and evil, and like so many a man in whom passion outweighs principle, evil won. As the magical music ceased, a man's voice took up the strain, a voice mellow, strong and clear, singing as if the exultant song were but the outpouring of a hopeful, happy heart. Like some wild creature wounded suddenly, Stähl leaped from his couch and stood listening with an aspect which would have appalled the fair musician and struck the singer dumb.

"She might have spared me that!" he panted, as through the heavy beating of his heart he heard the voice he hated lending music to the song he loved, a song of lovers parting in the summer night, whose dawn would break upon their wedding-day. Whatever hope of merciful relenting might have been kindled by one redeeming power was for ever quenched by that ill-timed air, for with a gesture of defiant daring, Stähl drew the full vial from his breast, dashed its contents into the cup, and drained it to the dregs.

A long shudder crept over him as he set it down, then a pale peace dawned upon his face, as, laying his weary head upon the pillow it would never find sleepless any more, he pressed the rose against his lips, saying, with a bitter smile that never left his face again:

"I won my rose, and her thorns have pierced me to the heart; but my blight is on her, and no other man will wear her in his bosom when I am gone."

PART III

"STAY, EVAN, when the others go; I have much to say to you, and a packet of valuable papers to entrust to you. Do not forget."

"You regard me with a strange look, Ursula, you speak in a strange tone. What has happened?"

"They tell me that Felix will live, with care and a journey to the South."

"I catch your meaning now. You will go with him."

"No, my journey will be made alone."

She looked beyond him as she spoke, with a rapt yet tranquil glance, and such a sudden brightness shone upon her face that her cousin watched her half bewildered for a moment; then caught at a hope that filled him with a troubled joy, and whispered with beating heart and lowered voice:

"Shall I not follow you, Ursula?"

Her eye came back to him, clear and calm, yet very tender in its wistfulness, and though her words sounded propitious his hope died suddenly.

"I think you will follow soon, and I shall wait for you in the safe refuge I am seeking."

They stood silent for many minutes, thinking thoughts for which they had no words, then as a pause fell after music, Ursula said:

"Now I must sing again. Give me a draught of water, my throat is parched."

Her cousin served her, but before the water touched her lips the glass fell shattered at her feet, for a wild, shrill cry rang through the house silencing the gay sounds below, and rudely breaking the long hush that had reigned above. For one breathless instant all stood like living images of wonder, fear and fright, all waited for what should follow that dread cry. An agitated servant appeared upon the threshold seeking his mistress. She saw him, yet stood as if incapable of motion, as he made his way to her through a crowd of pale, expectant faces.

"What is it?" she asked, with lips that could hardly syllable the words.

"My master, madam — dead in his bed — old Marjory has just found him. I've sent for Doctor Keen," began the man, but Ursula only seemed to hear and understand one word:

"Dead!" she echoed — "so suddenly, so soon — it cannot be true. Evan, take me to him."

She stretched out her hands as if she had gone blind, and led by her cousin, left the room, followed by several guests, in whom curiosity or sympathy was stronger than etiquette or fear. Up they went, a strange procession, and entering the dusky room, lighted only by a single shaded lamp, found Marjory lamenting over her dead master in a paroxysm of the wildest grief. Evan passed in before his cousin, bent hastily and listened at the breathless lips, touched the chill forehead, and bared the wrist to feel if any flutter lingered in the pulse. But as he pushed back the loose sleeve of the wrapper, upon the wasted arm appeared a strange device. Two slender serpents twined together like the ring, and in the circle several Hindoo characters traced in the same deep red lines. At that sight the arm dropped from his hold, and he fell back daunted by a nameless fear which he could neither master nor divine.

As Ursula appeared the old woman's grief changed to an almost fierce excitement, for rising she pointed from the dead husband to the living wife, crying shrilly:

"Come; come and see your work, fair-faced devil that you are! Here he lies, safe in the deadly sleep you gave him. Look at him and deny it if you dare!"

Ursula did look, and through the horror that blanched her face many eyes saw the shadow of remorse, the semblance of guilt. Stähl lay as she left him, his head pillowed on his arm with the easy grace habitual to him, but the pallor of that sleeping face was now changed to the awful grayness that living countenances never wear. A bitter smile still lingered on the white lips, and those mysterious eyes were wide open, full of a gloomy intelligence that appalled the beholder with the scornful triumph which still lurked there unconquered even by death. These defiant eyes appeared fixed on Ursula alone; she could not look away, nor break the spell that held her own, and through the hurried scene that followed she seemed to address her dead husband, not her living accuser.

"My work? the sleep I gave? what dare I not deny?" she said, below her breath, like one bewildered.

"See her feign innocence with guilt stamped on her face!" cried Marjory, in a passion of indignant sorrow. "You killed him, that is your work. You drugged that cup with the poison I saw you buy to-day — that is the sleep you gave him — and you dare not deny that you hated him, wished him dead, and said last night you'd not be troubled long, for you had borne enough."

"I did not kill him! You saw me prepare his evening draught, and what proof have you that he did not pass away in sleep?" demanded Ursula, more firmly, yet with an awestruck gaze still fixed upon her husband's face.

"This is my proof!" and Marjory held up the empty counterpart of the little vial that lay on the table.

"That here! I left it in my — "

A hand at Ursula's lips cut short the perilous admission, as Evan whispered:

"Hush! for God's sake, own nothing yet."

"Too late for that," screamed Marjory, more and more excited by each word. "I found it in the ashes where she flung it in her haste, believing it was destroyed. I saw it glitter when I went to mend the fire before I woke my master. I knew it by the freshness of the label, and in a moment felt that my poor master was past all waking of mine, and found it so. I saw her buy it, I told him of it, but he loved her still and tried to deceive me with the kind lie that he bade her do it. I showed him that I knew the truth, and he only said, 'I know it, I forgive her, keep the secret for my sake,' and trusting her to the last, paid for his blind faith with his life."

"No, no, I never murdered him! I found him sleeping like a child an hour ago, and in that sleep he died," said Ursula, wringing her hands like one well nigh distraught.

"An hour ago! hear that and mark it all of you," cried Marjory.

"Two hours ago she bade him good night before me, and he called her 'Judas,' as she kissed him and went. Now she owns that she returned and found him safely sleeping — God forgive me that I ever left him! for then she must have remixed the draught in which he drank his death. Oh, madam! could you have no pity, could you not remember how he loved you? see your rose fast shut in his poor dead hand — could you not leave him the one little month of life he had to live before you were set free?"

"One month!" said Ursula, with a startled look. "They told me he would live to be a hale, old man. Why was I so deceived?"

"Because he would not mar your pleasure even for a single night. He meant to tell you the sad truth gently, for he thought you had a woman's heart, and would mourn him a little though you could not love."

Paler Ursula could not become, but as mesh after mesh of the net in which she had unconsciously helped to snare herself appeared, her husband's purpose flashed upon her, yet seemed too horrible for belief, till the discovery of that last deceit was made; then like one crushed by an overwhelming blow, she covered up her face and sunk down at Evan's feet. He did not raise her up, and though a gust of eager, agitated voices went whispering through the room, no one spoke to her, no one offered comfort to the widow, counsel to the woman, pity to the culprit. They listened only to old Marjory, who poured forth her story with such genuine grief, such perfect sincerity, that all felt its pathos and few doubted its entire truth. Evan alone believed in Ursula's denial, even while to himself he owned that she had borne enough to make any means of liberation tempting. He saw more clearly than the rest how every act, look and word of hers condemned her; and felt with a bitter pang that such an accusation, even if proved false, must cast a shadow on her name and darken all her life.

Suddenly, when the stir was at its height, Ursula rose, calm, cold and steady; yet few who saw her then ever forgot the desolate despair which made that beautiful face a far more piteous sight than the dead one. Turning with all her wonted dignity, she confronted the excited group, and without a tear in her eye, a falter in her voice, a trace of shame, guilt or fear in mien or manner, she said clearly, solemnly,

"I am guilty of murder in my heart, for I did wish that man dead; but I did not kill him. The words I spoke that night were the expression of a resolve made in a moment of despair, a resolve to end my own life, when I could bear no more. To-day I was told that he would live; then my time seemed come, and believing this to be my last night on earth, I bade my husband farewell as we parted, and in a few hours hoped to lay down the burden he had made heavier than I could bear. That poison was purchased for myself, not him; he discovered it, believed I meant his death, and with a black art, which none can fathom but myself, so distorted my acts and words, before a witness, that the deed committed by himself should doom me to ignominy and avenge his wrong. I have no hope that any one will credit so wild a tale, and therein his safety lies; but God knows I speak the truth, and He will judge between us at a more righteous bar than any I can stand at here. Now do with me as you will, I am done."

Through all the bitter scenes of public accusation, trial and condemnation Ursula preserved the same mournful composure, as if having relinquished both hope and fear, no emotion remained to disturb the spirit of entire self-abnegation which had taken possession of her. All her cousin's entreaties, commands and prayers failed to draw from her the key to the mystery of her strange marriage; even when, after many merciful delays, sentence was at length pronounced upon her, and captivity for life was known to be her doom, she still refused to confess, saying:

"This fate is worse than death; but till I lie on my deathbed I will prove faithful to the promise made that man, traitorous as he was to me. I have done with the world, so leave me to such peace as I can know, and go your way, dear Evan, to forget that such a mournful creature lives."

But when all others fell away, when so-called friends proved timid, when enemies grew insolent and the whole world seemed to cast her off, one man was true to her, one man still loved, believed and honored her, still labored to save her when all others gave her up as lost, still stood between her and the curious, sharp-tongued, heavy-handed world, earning a great compassion for himself, and, in time, a juster, gentler sentiment in favor of the woman whose sin and shame he had so nobly helped to bear.

Weeks and months went heavily by, the city wearied itself with excited conjectures, conflicting rumors, varying opinions, and slowly came to look with more lenient eyes upon the beautiful culprit, whose tragic fate, with its unexplained mystery, began to plead for her more eloquently than the most gifted advocate. Few doubted her guilt, and, as she feared, few believed the accusations she brought against her dead husband; but the plea of temporary insanity had been made by her counsel, and though she strenuously denied its truth, there were daily growing hopes of pardon for an offense which, thanks to Evan's tireless appeals, now wore a far less heinous aspect than at first.

All the long summer days Ursula sat alone in her guarded room, tranquilly enjoying the sunshine that flickered through the leaves with which Evan had tried to mask the bars that shut out liberty but not heaven's light. All the balmy summer nights she lay on her narrow bed, haunted by dreams that made sleep a penance and not a pleasure, or watched, with wakeful eyes, the black shadow of a cross the moon cast upon her breast as it peered through the barred window like a ghostly face. To no one did she reveal the thoughts that burdened her, whitening her hair, furrowing her face and leaving on her forehead the impress of a great grief which no human joy could ever efface.

One autumn day Evan came hastening in full of a glad excitement, which for the moment seemed to give him back the cheery youthfulness he was fast losing. He found his cousin lying on the couch he had provided for her, for even the prison officers respected that faithful love, and granted every favor in their power. She, too, seemed to be blessed with a happy mood, for the gloom had left her eyes, a peaceful smile sat on her lips, and when she spoke her voice was musical, with an undertone of deep emotion.

"Bless your tranquil face, Ursula! One would think you guessed my tidings without telling. Yes, it is almost certain that the pardon will be granted, in answer to my prayers. One more touch will win

Ursula in Prison

the men who hold your fate in their hands, and that touch you can give by clearing up the mystery of Stähl's strange power over you. For your own sake and for mine do not deny me now."

"I will not."

The joy, surprise and satisfaction of the moment caused Evan to forget the sad condition upon which this confidence could be accorded. He thought only of all they had suffered, all they might yet enjoy if the pardon could be gained, and holding that thin hand fast in both his own, he listened, with absorbing interest, to the beloved voice that unfolded to him the romance within a romance, which had made a tragedy of three lives.

"I must take you far back into the past, Evan, for my secret is but the sequel of one begun long before our birth. Our grandfather, as you know, was made governor of an Indian province while still a young and comely man. One of the native princes, though a conquered subject, remained his friend, and the sole daughter of this prince loved the handsome Englishman with the despotic fervor of her race. The prince offered the hand of the fair Naya to his friend, but being already betrothed to an English girl, he courteously declined the alliance. That insult, as she thought it, never was forgiven or forgotten by the haughty princess; but, with the subtle craft of her half-savage nature, she devised a vengeance which should not only fall upon the offender, but pursue his descendants to the very last. No apparent breach was made in the friendship of the prince and governor, even when the latter brought his young wife to the residence. But from that hour Naya's curse was on his house, unsuspected and unsleeping, and as years went by the Fate of the Forrests became a tragical story throughout British India, for the brothers, nephews and sons of Roger Forrest all died violent or sudden deaths, and the old man himself was found murdered in the jungle when at the height of fame and favor.

"Two twin lads alone remained of all who had borne the name, and for a time the fatal doom seemed averted, as they grew to manhood, married and seemed born to know all the blessings which virtue and valor could deserve. But though the princess and her father were dead, the curse was still relentlessly executed by some of her kindred, for in the year of your birth your father vanished suddenly, utterly, in broad day, yet left no trace behind, and from that hour to this no clue to the lost man was ever found beyond a strong suspicion, which was never confirmed. In that same year a horrible discovery was made, which shocked and dismayed all Christian India, and was found hard of belief across the sea. Among the tribes that infested certain provinces, intent on mischief and difficult to subdue, was one class of assassins unknown even to the native governments of the country, and entirely unsuspected by the English. This society was as widely spread and carefully organized as it was secret, powerful and fanatical. Its members worshipped a gloomy divinity called Bohwanie, who, according to their heathen belief, was best propitiated by human sacrifices. The name of these devotees was Phansegars, or Brothers of the Good Work; and he who offered up the greatest number of victims was most favored by the goddess, and received a high place in the Hindoo heaven. All India was filled with amazement and affright at this discovery, and mysteries, till then deemed unfathomable, became as clear as day. Among others the Fate of the Forrests was revealed; for by the confession of the one traitor who betrayed the society, it appeared that the old prince and his sons had been members of the brotherhood, which had its higher and its lower grades, and when the young governor drew down upon himself the wrath of Naya, her kindred avenged her by propitiating Bohwanie with victim after victim from our fated family, always working so secretly that no trace of their art remained but the seal of death.

"This terrible discovery so dismayed my father that, taking you, an orphan then, and my mother, he fled to England, hoping to banish the dreadful past from his mind. But he never could, and it preyed upon him night and day. No male Forrest had escaped the doom since the curse was spoken, and an unconquerable foreboding haunted him that sooner or later he too should be sacrificed, though continents and oceans lay between him and the avengers. The fact that the black brotherhood was discovered and destroyed weighed little with him, for still a fear pursued him that Naya's kindred would hand down the curse from generation to generation, and execute with that tenacity of purpose which in that climate of the passions makes the humblest foe worthy of fear. He doubted all men, confided his secret to none, not even to his wife, and led a wandering life with us until my mother died. You remember, Evan, that the same malady that destroyed her fell likewise upon you, and that my father was forced to leave us in Paris, that he might comply with my mother's last desire and lay her in English ground. Before he went he took me apart and told me the dark history of our unfortunate family, that I might be duly impressed with the necessity of guarding you with a sleepless vigilance; for even then he could not free himself from that ominous foreboding, soon, alas! to be confirmed. It was a strange confidence to place in a girl of seventeen, but he had no friend at hand, and knowing how wholly I loved you, how safe I was from the Fate of the Forrests, he gave you to my charge and left us for a week. You know he never came again, but found his ghostly fear a sad reality in England, and on the day that was to give my mother's body to the earth he was discovered dead in his bed, with the marks of fingers at his throat, yet no other trace of his murderer ever appeared, and another dark secret was buried in the grave. You remember the horror and the grief that nearly killed me when the tidings came, and how from that hour there was a little cloud between us, a cloud I could not lift because I had solemnly promised my father that I would watch over you, yet conceal the fate that menaced you, lest it should mar your peace as it had done his own. Evan, I have kept my word till the danger is for ever past."

She paused there, but for a moment her cousin could only gaze at her, bewildered by the sudden light let in by the gloomy past. Presently he said, impetuously:

"You have, my faithful Ursula, and I will prove that I am grateful by watching over you with a vigilance as sleepless and devoted as your own. But tell me, was there nowhere in the world justice, power or wit enough to stay that savage curse? Why did not my father, or yours, appeal to the laws of either country and obtain redress?"

"They did, and, like others, appealed in vain; for, till the Phansegars were discovered, they knew not whom to accuse. After that, as Naya's kindred were all gone but a few newly-converted women and harmless children, no magistrate in India would condemn the innocent for the crimes of their race, and my father had no proofs to bring against them. Few in England believed the seemingly incredible story when it was related to them in the Indian reports. No, Evan, the wily princess entrusted her revenge to able hands, and well they did the work to the very last, as we have bitter cause to know. Every member of the brotherhood, and every helper of the curse, bore on his left arm the word 'Bohwanie!' in Hindoo characters. You saw the sign on that dead arm. Do you understand the secret now?"

"Great heavens, Ursula! Do you mean that Stähl, a Christian man, belonged to this heathen league? Surely you wrong him there."

"You will not think so when I have told all. It seemed as horrible, as incredible to me as now to you, when I first saw and comprehended on the night that changed both our lives. Stähl suspected, from many unconscious betrayals of mine (my dislike of India, my anxiety for you, then absent, and a hundred indications unseen by other eyes) that I knew the secret of the curse; he proved it by whispering the hated name of Bohwanie in my ear, and showing me the fatal sign — I knew it, for my father had told me that also. Need I tell you what recollections rushed upon me when I saw it, what visions of blood rose red before my panic-stricken eyes, how instantly I felt the truth of my instinctive aversion to him, despite his charms of mind and manner, and, above all, how utterly I was overpowered by a sense of your peril in the presence of your unknown enemy? A single thought, hope, purpose ruled me, to save you at any cost, and guard the secret still; for I felt that I possessed some power over that dread man, and resolved to use it to the uttermost. You left us, and then I learned at what a costly price I could purchase the life so dear to me. Stähl briefly told me that his mother and one old woman were the last of Naya's race, and when his grandfather, who belonged to the brotherhood, suffered death with them, he charged her to perpetuate the curse, as all the members of the family had pledged themselves to do. She promised, and when my father left India she followed, but could not discover his hiding-place, and with a blind faith in destiny, as native to her as her superstition, she left time to bring her victim to her. While

resting from her quest in Germany she met and married Felix
Stähl, the elder, a learned man, fond of the mysticism and wisdom
of the East, who found an irresistible charm in the dark-eyed
woman, who, for his sake, became a Christian in name, though she
still clung to her Pagan gods in secret. With such parents what
wonder that the son was the man we found him? for his father
bequeathed him his features, feeble health, rare learning and accomplishments; his mother those Indian eyes that I never can forget, his fiery yet subtle nature, the superstitious temperament and
the fatal vow.

"While the father lived she kept her secret hidden; when he died,
Felix, then a man, was told it, and having been carefully prepared
by every art, every appeal to the pride and passion of his race,
every shadow years of hatred could bring to blacken the memory
of the first Forrest and the wrong he was believed to have done
their ancestors, Felix was induced to take upon himself the fulfil-
ment of the family vow. Yet living in a Christian community, and
having been bred up by a virtuous father, it was a hard task to
assume, and only the commands of the mother whom he adored
would have won compliance. He was told that but two Forrests
now remained, one a girl who was to go scatheless, the other a boy,
who, sooner or later, was to fall by his hand, for he was now the
last male of his race as you of ours. How his mother discovered
these facts he never knew, unless from the old woman who came
to them from England to die near her kin. I suspect that she was
the cause of my poor father's death, though Stähl swore that he
never knew of it until I told him.

"After much urging, many commands, he gave the promise, asking only freedom to do the work as he would, for though the savage
spirit of his Hindoo ancestors lived again in him, the influence of
civilization made the savage modes of vengeance abhorrent to him.
His mother soon followed the good professor, then leaving our
meeting still to chance, Felix went roaming up and down the world
a solitary, studious man, for ever haunted by the sinful deed he had
promised to perform, and which grew ever more and more repug-
nant to him.

"In an evil hour we met; my name first arrested him; my beauty

The Mystery Revealed

(I may speak of it now for it is gone) attracted him; my evident aversion piqued his pride and roused his will to overcome it; and then the knowledge of my love for you fanned his smouldering passion to a blaze and confirmed his wavering purpose. You asked on that sad night if I had learned to love while you were gone? I spoke truly when I answered yes, for absence proved how dear you had become to me, and I only waited your return to gratefully accept the love with which I knew your heart was overflowing. You came, and seeing Stähl's devotion, doubted the affection I never had confessed. He saw it plainly, he divined your passion, and in an hour decided upon gratifying his own desire, keeping the promise he made his mother, yet sparing himself the crime of murder, well knowing that for you life without me would be a fate more dark than any death he could devise. I pleaded, prayed and wept, but he was inexorable. To tell you was to destroy you, for he feared nothing; to keep the secret was to forfeit your love and sacrifice myself. One hope alone remained to me, a sinful yet a pardonable one in such a strait as mine; Felix could not live long; I might support life for a time by the thought that I had saved you, by the hope that I might soon undeceive and recompense you for the loss you had sustained. Evan, it was a natural yet unrighteous act, for I did evil that good might come of it, and such deeds never prosper. Better have left you in God's hand, better even have seen you dead and at peace than have condemned you to the life you have led and still must lead for years perhaps. I was a weak, loving, terror-stricken woman, and in that dreadful hour one fear overwhelmed all other passions, principles and thoughts. I could save you, and to accomplish that I would so gladly have suffered death in any shape. Believe that, dearest Evan, and forgive me for the fate to which I have condemned the man I love, truly, tenderly even to the end."

Her voice died in a broken sob as Evan gathered her close to his sore heart, and she clung there spent and speechless, as if the pain of parting were for ever over and her refuge found at last. Evan spoke first, happily and hopefully for, the future opened clearly, and the long twilight seemed about to break into a blissful dawn.

"You shall be repaid for your exceeding love, Ursula, with a devotion such as man never gave to woman until now. There is no longer any cloud between us, nor shall there be between you and the world. Justice shall be done, and then we will leave this city of bitter memories behind us, and go away together to begin the new life that lies before us."

"We shall begin a new life, but not together, Evan," was the low answer, as she tenderly laid her pale cheek to his, as if to soften the hard truth.

"But, love, you will be free at once; there can be no doubt of the pardon now."

"Yes, I shall soon be free, but human hands will not open my prison doors, and I humbly trust that I may receive pardon, but not from human lips. Evan, I told you I would never tell my secret till I lay on my deathbed; I lie there now."

If she had stabbed him with the hand folded about his neck, the act would not have shocked and startled him like those last words. They pierced him to the heart, and as if in truth he had received a mortal wound, he could only gaze at her in dumb dismay, with eyes full of anguish, incredulity and grief.

"Let me seem cruel that I may be merciful, and end both suspense and fear by telling all at once. There is no hope for me. I have prayed to live, but it cannot be, for slowly yet surely Felix has killed me. I said I would gladly die for you, God takes me at my word, and now I am content. Let me make my sacrifice cheerfully, and let the suffering I have known be my atonement for the wrong I did myself and you."

As she spoke so tranquilly, so tenderly, a veil seemed to fall from before her cousin's eyes. He looked into the face that smiled at him, saw there the shadow which no human love can banish, read perfect peace in its pale serenity, felt that life was a poor boon to ask for her, and with a pang that rent that faithful heart of his, silently relinquished the one sustaining hope which had upheld him through that gloomy year. Calm with a grief too deep for tears, he drew the wan and wasted creature who had given herself for him closer to the shelter of his arms, and changed her last fear to loving pride by saying, with a manful courage, a meek resignation that ennobled him by its sincerity:

"Rest here in peace, my Ursula. No selfish grief shall cloud your sunset or rob you of one hour of happy love. I can bear the parting, for I shall follow soon; and thank God that after the long bewilderment of this sad world we may enjoy together the new life which has no end."

THE END

A Double Tragedy. An Actor's Story

$\longrightarrow\!\!\!\!\prec\!\!\!\!\longrightarrow$

CHAPTER I

LOTILDE WAS IN HER element that night, for it was a Spanish play, requiring force and fire in its delineation, and she threw herself into her part with an *abandon* that made her seem a beautiful embodiment of power and passion. As for me I could not play ill, for when with her my acting was not art but nature, and I *was* the lover that I seemed. Before she came I made a business, not a pleasure, of my profession, and was content to fill my place, with no higher ambition than to earn my salary with as little effort as possible, to resign myself to the distasteful labor to which my poverty condemned me. She changed all that; for she saw the talent I neglected, she understood the want of motive that made me indifferent, she pitied me for the reverse of fortune that placed me where I was; by her influence and example she roused a manlier spirit in me, kindled every spark of talent I possessed, and incited me to win a success I had not cared to labor for till then.

She was the rage that season, for she came unheralded and almost unknown. Such was the power of beauty, genius, and character, that she made her way at once into public favor, and before the season was half over had become the reigning favorite. My position in the theatre threw us much together, and I had not played the lover to this beautiful woman many weeks before I found I was one in earnest. She soon knew it, and confessed that she returned my love; but when I spoke of marriage, she answered with a look and tone that haunted me long afterward.

"Not yet, Paul; something that concerns me alone must be settled first. I cannot marry till I have received the answer for which I am waiting; have faith in me till then, and be patient for my sake."

I did have faith and patience; but while I waited I wondered much and studied her carefully. Frank, generous, and deep-hearted, she won all who approached her; but I, being nearest and dearest, learned to know her best, and soon discovered that some past loss, some present anxiety or hidden care, oppressed and haunted her. A bitter spirit at times possessed her, followed by a heavy melancholy, or an almost fierce unrest, which nothing could dispel but some stormy drama, where she could vent her pent-up gloom or desperation in words and acts which seemed to have a double significance to her. I had vainly tried to find some cause or explanation of this one blemish in the nature which, to a lover's eyes, seemed almost perfect, but never had succeeded till the night of which I write.

The play was nearly over, the interest was at its height, and Clotilde's best scene was drawing to a close. She had just indignantly refused to betray a state secret which would endanger the life of her lover; and the Duke had just wrathfully vowed to denounce her to the Inquisition if she did not yield, when I her lover, disguised as a monk, saw a strange and sudden change come over her. She should have trembled at a threat so full of terror, and have made one last appeal to the stern old man before she turned to defy and dare all things for her lover. But she seemed to have forgotten time, place, and character, for she stood gazing straight before her as if turned to stone. At first I thought it was some new presentiment of fear, for she seldom played a part twice alike, and left much to the inspiration of the moment. But an instant's scrutiny convinced me that this was not acting, for her face paled visibly, her eyes dilated as they looked beyond the Duke, her lips fell apart, and she looked like one suddenly confronted by a ghost. An inquiring glance from my companion showed me that he, too, was disturbed by her appearance, and fearing that she had over-exerted herself, I struck into the dialogue as if she had made her appeal. The sound of my voice seemed to recall her; she passed her hand across her eyes, drew a long breath, and looked about her. I thought she had recovered herself and was about to resume her part, but, to my great surprise, she only clung to me, saying in a shrill whisper, so full of despair, it chilled my blood —

"The answer, Paul, the answer: it has come!"

The words were inaudible to all but myself; but the look, the gesture were eloquent with terror, grief, and love; and taking it for a fine piece of acting, the audience applauded loud and long. The accustomed sound roused Clotilde, and during that noisy moment a hurried dialogue passed between us.

"What is it? Are you ill?" I whispered.

"He is here, Paul, alive; I saw him. Heaven help us both!"

"Who is here?"

"Hush! not now; there is no time to tell you."

"You are right; compose yourself; you must speak in a moment."

"What do I say? Help me, Paul; I have forgotten every thing but that man."

She looked as if bewildered; and I saw that some sudden shock had entirely unnerved her. But actors must have neither hearts nor nerves while on the stage. The applause was subsiding, and she must speak. Fortunately I remembered enough of her part to prompt her as she struggled through the little that remained; for, seeing her condition, Denon and I cut the scene remorselessly, and brought it to a close as soon as possible. The instant the curtain fell we were assailed with questions, but Clotilde answered none; and though hidden from her sight, still seemed to see the object that had wrought such an alarming change in her. I told them she was ill, took her to her dressing-room, and gave her into the hands of her maid, for I must appear again, and delay was impossible.

How I got through my part I cannot tell, for my thoughts were with Clotilde; but an actor learns to live a double life, so while Paul Lamar suffered torments of anxiety Don Felix fought a duel, killed his adversary, and was dragged to judgment. Involuntarily my eyes often wandered toward the spot where Clotilde's had seemed fixed. It was one of the stage-boxes, and at first I thought it empty, but presently I caught the glitter of a glass turned apparently on myself. As soon as possible I crossed the stage, and as I leaned haughtily upon my sword while the seconds adjusted the preliminaries, I searched the box with a keen glance. Nothing was visible, however, but a hand lying easily on the red cushion; a man's hand, white and shapely; on one finger shone a ring, evidently a woman's ornament, for it was a slender circlet of diamonds that flashed with every gesture.

"Some fop, doubtless; a man like that could never daunt Clotilde," I thought. And eager to discover if there was not another occupant in the box, I took a step nearer, and stared boldly into the soft gloom that filled it. A low derisive laugh came from behind the curtain as the hand gathered back as if to permit me to satisfy myself. The act showed me that a single person occupied the box, but also effectually concealed that person from my sight; and as I was recalled to my duty by a warning whisper from one of my comrades, the hand appeared to wave me a mocking adieu. Baffled and angry, I devoted myself to the affairs of Don Felix, wondering the while if Clotilde would be able to reappear, how she would bear herself, if that hidden man was the cause of her terror, and why? Even when immured in a dungeon, after my arrest, I beguiled the tedium of a long soliloquy with these questions, and executed a better stage-start than any I had ever practised, when at last she came to me, bringing liberty and love as my reward.

I had left her haggard, speechless, overwhelmed with some mysterious woe, she reappeared beautiful and brilliant, with a joy that seemed too lovely to be feigned. Never had she played so well; for some spirit, stronger than her own, seemed to possess and rule her royally. If I had ever doubted her love for me, I should have been assured of it that night, for she breathed into the fond words of her part a tenderness and grace that filled my heart to overflowing, and inspired me to play the grateful lover to the life. The last words came all too soon for me, and as she threw herself into my arms she turned her head as if to glance triumphantly at the defeated

Duke, but I saw that again she looked beyond him, and with an indescribable expression of mingled pride, contempt, and defiance. A soft sound of applause from the mysterious occupant of that box answered the look, and the white hand sent a superb bouquet flying to her feet. I was about to lift and present it to her, but she checked me and crushed it under foot with an air of the haughtiest disdain. A laugh from behind the curtain greeted this demonstration, but it was scarcely observed by others; for that first bouquet seemed a signal for a rain of flowers, and these latter offerings she permitted me to gather up, receiving them with her most gracious smiles, her most graceful obeisances, as if to mark, for one observer at least, the difference of her regard for the givers. As I laid the last floral tribute in her arms I took a parting glance at the box, hoping to catch a glimpse of the unknown face. The curtains were thrown back and the door stood open, admitting a strong light from the vestibule, but the box was empty.

Then the green curtain fell, and Clotilde whispered, as she glanced from her full hands to the rejected bouquet —

"Bring that to my room; I must have it."

I obeyed, eager to be enlightened; but when we were alone she flung down her fragrant burden, snatched the stranger's gift, tore it apart, drew out a slip of paper, read it, dropped it, and walked to and fro, wringing her hands, like one in a paroxysm of despair. I seized the note and looked at it, but found no key to her distress in the enigmatical words —

"I shall be there. Come and bring your lover with you, else — "

There it abruptly ended; but the unfinished threat seemed the more menacing for its obscurity, and I indignantly demanded,

"Clotilde, who dares address you so? Where will this man be? You surely will not obey such a command? Tell me; I have a right to know."

"I cannot tell you, now; I dare not refuse him; he will be at Keen's; we *must* go. How will it end! How will it end!"

I remembered then that we were all to sup *en costume*, with a brother actor, who did not play that night. I was about to speak yet more urgently, when the entrance of her maid checked me. Clotilde composed herself by a strong effort —

"Go and prepare," she whispered; "have faith in me a little longer, and soon you shall know all."

There was something almost solemn in her tone; her eye met mine, imploringly, and her lips trembled as if her heart were full. That assured me at once; and with a reassuring word I hurried away to give a few touches to my costume, which just then was fitter for a dungeon than a feast. When I rejoined her there was no trace of past emotion; a soft color bloomed upon her cheek, her eyes were tearless and brilliant, her lips were dressed in smiles. Jewels shone on her white forehead, neck, and arms, flowers glowed in her bosom; and no charm that art or skill could lend to the rich dress or its lovely wearer, had been forgotten.

"What an actress!" I involuntarily exclaimed, as she came to meet me, looking almost as beautiful and gay as ever.

"It is well that I am one, else I should yield to my hard fate without a struggle. Paul, hitherto I have played for money, now I play for love; help me by being a calm spectator to-night, and whatever happens promise me that there shall be no violence."

I promised, for I was wax in her hands; and, more bewildered than ever, followed to the carriage, where a companion was impatiently awaiting us.

CHAPTER II

WE WERE LATE; and on arriving found all the other guests assembled. Three strangers appeared; and my attention was instantly fixed upon them, for the mysterious "he" was to be there. All three seemed gay, gallant, handsome men; all three turned admiring eyes upon Clotilde, all three were gloved. Therefore, as I had seen no face, my one clue, the ring, was lost. From Clotilde's face and manner I could learn nothing, for a smile seemed carved upon her lips, her drooping lashes half concealed her eyes, and her voice was too well trained to betray her by a traitorous tone. She received the greetings, compliments, and admiration of all alike, and I vainly looked and listened till supper was announced.

As I took my place beside her, I saw her shrink and shiver slightly, as if a chilly wind had blown over her, but before I could ask if she were cold a bland voice said,

"Will Mademoiselle Varian permit me to drink her health?"

It was one of the strangers; mechanically I offered her glass; but the next instant my hold tightened till the slender stem snapped, and the rosy bowl fell broken to the table, for on the handsome hand extended to fill it shone the ring.

"A bad omen, Mr. Lamar. I hope my attempt will succeed better," said St. John, as he filled another glass and handed it to Clotilde, who merely lifted it to her lips, and turned to enter into an animated conversation with the gentleman who sat on the other side. Some one addressed St. John, and I was glad of it; for now all my interest and attention was centered in him. Keenly, but covertly, I examined him, and soon felt that in spite of that foppish ornament he *was* a man to daunt a woman like Clotilde. Pride and passion, courage and indomitable will met and mingled in his face, though the obedient features wore whatever expression he imposed upon them. He was the handsomest, most elegant, but least attractive of the three, yet it was hard to say why. The others gave themselves freely to the enjoyment of a scene which evidently possessed the charm of novelty to them; but St. John unconsciously wore the half sad, half weary look that comes to those who have led lives of pleasure and found their emptiness. Although the wittiest, and most brilliant talker at the table, his gaiety seemed fitful, his manner absent at times. More than once I saw him knit his black brows as he met my eye, and more than once I caught a long look fixed on Clotilde, — a look full of the lordly admiration and pride which a master bestows upon a handsome slave. It made my blood boil, but I controlled myself, and was apparently absorbed in Miss Damareau, my neighbor.

We seemed as gay and care-free a company as ever made midnight merry; songs were sung, stories told, theatrical phrases added sparkle to the conversation, and the varied costumes gave an air of romance to the revel. The Grand Inquisitor still in his ghostly garb, and the stern old Duke were now the jolliest of the group; the page flirted violently with the princess; the rivals of the play were

bosom-friends again, and the fair Donna Olivia had apparently forgotten her knightly lover, to listen to a modern gentleman.

Clotilde sat leaning back in a deep chair, eating nothing, but using her fan with the indescribable grace of a Spanish woman. She
was very lovely, for the dress became her, and the black lace mantilla falling from her head to her shoulders, heightened her charms
by half concealing them; and nothing could have been more genial
and gracious than the air with which she listened and replied to the
compliments of the youngest stranger, who sat beside her and was
all devotion.

I forgot myself in observing her till something said by our opposite neighbors arrested both of us. Some one seemed to have been
joking St. John about his ring, which was too brilliant an ornament
to pass unobserved.

"Bad taste, I grant you," he said, laughing, "but it is a *gage
d'amour*, and I wear it for a purpose."

"I fancied it was the latest Paris fashion," returned Keen. "And
apropos to Paris, what is the latest gossip from the gay city?"

A slow smile rose to St. John's lips as he answered, after a moment's thought and a quick glance across the room.

"A little romance; shall I tell it to you? It is a love story, ladies,
and not long."

A unanimous assent was given; and he began with a curious glitter in his eyes, a stealthy smile coming and going on his face as the
words dropped slowly from his lips.

"It begins in the old way. A foolish young man fell in love with
a Spanish girl much his inferior in rank, but beautiful enough to
excuse his folly, for he married her. Then came a few months of
bliss; but Madame grew jealous. Monsieur wearied of domestic
tempests, and, after vain efforts to appease his fiery angel, he proposed a separation. Madame was obdurate, Monsieur rebelled; and
in order to try the soothing effects of absence upon both, after set-
tling her in a charming chateau, he slipped away, leaving no trace
by which his route might be discovered."

"Well, how did the experiment succeed?" asked Keen. St. John
shrugged his shoulders, emptied his glass, and answered tranquilly.

"Like most experiments that have women for their subjects, for the amiable creatures always devise some way of turning the tables, and defeating the best laid plans. Madame waited for her truant spouse till rumors of his death reached Paris, for he had met with mishaps, and sickness detained him long in an obscure place, so the rumors seemed confirmed by his silence, and Madame believed him dead. But instead of dutifully mourning him, this inexplicable woman shook the dust of the chateau off her feet and disappeared, leaving everything, even to her wedding ring, behind her."

"Bless me, how odd! what became of her?" exclaimed Miss Damareau, forgetting the dignity of the Princess in the curiosity of the woman.

"The very question her repentant husband asked when, returning from his long holiday, he found her gone. He searched the continent for her, but in vain; and for two years she left him to suffer the torments of suspense."

"As he had left her to suffer them while he went pleasuring. It was a light punishment for his offence."

Clotilde spoke; and the sarcastic tone for all its softness, made St. John wince, though no eye but mine observed the faint flush of shame or anger that passed across his face.

"Mademoiselle espouses the lady's cause, of course, and as a gallant man I should do likewise, but unfortunately my sympathies are strongly enlisted on the other side."

"Then you know the parties?" I said, impulsively, for my inward excitement was increasing rapidly, and I began to feel rather than to see the end of this mystery.

"I have seen them, and cannot blame the man for claiming his beautiful wife, when he found her," he answered, briefly.

"Then he did find her at last? Pray tell us how and when," cried Miss Damareau.

"She betrayed herself. It seems that Madame had returned to her old profession, and fallen in love with an actor; but being as virtuous as she was fair, she would not marry till she was assured beyond a doubt of her husband's death. Her engagements would not allow her to enquire in person, so she sent letters to various places asking for proofs of his demise; and as ill, or good fortune would have it, one of these letters fell into Monsieur's hands, giving

him an excellent clue to her whereabouts, which he followed indefatigably till he found her."

"Poor little woman, I pity her! How did she receive Monsieur
De Trop?" asked Keen.

"You shall know in good time. He found her in London playing
at one of the great theatres, for she had talent, and had become a
star. He saw her act for a night or two, made secret inquiries concerning her, and fell more in love with her than ever. Having tried
almost every novelty under the sun he had a fancy to attempt something of the dramatic sort, so presented himself to Madame at a
party."

"Heavens! what a scene there must have been," ejaculated Miss
Damareau.

"On the contrary, there was no scene at all, for the man was not
a Frenchman, and Madame was a fine actress. Much as he had
admired her on the stage he was doubly charmed with her performance in private, for it was superb. They were among strangers,
and she received him like one, playing her part with the utmost
grace and self-control, for with a woman's quickness of perception,
she divined his purpose, and knowing that her fate was in his
hands, endeavored to propitiate him by complying with his caprice.
Mademoiselle, allow me to send you some of these grapes, they are
delicious."

As he leaned forward to present them he shot a glance at her that
caused me to start up with a violence that nearly betrayed me. Fortunately the room was close, and saying something about the heat,
I threw open a window, and let in a balmy gust of spring air that
refreshed us all.

"How did they settle it, by duels and despair, or by repentance
and reconciliation all round, in the regular French fashion?"

"I regret that I'm unable to tell you, for I left before the affair
was arranged. I only know that Monsieur was more captivated than
before, and quite ready to forgive and forget, and I suspect that
Madame, seeing the folly of resistance, will submit with a good
grace, and leave the stage to play 'The Honey Moon' for a second
time in private with a husband who adores her. What is the Mademoiselle's opinion?"

She had listened, without either question or comment, her fan at rest, her hands motionless, her eyes downcast; so still it seemed as if she had hushed the breath upon her lips, so pale despite her rouge, that I wondered no one observed it, so intent and resolute that every feature seemed under control, — every look and gesture guarded. When St. John addressed her, she looked up with a smile as bland as his own, but fixed her eyes on him with an expression of undismayed defiance and supreme contempt that caused him to bite his lips with ill-concealed annoyance.

"My opinion?" she said, in her clear, cold voice, "I think that Madame, being a woman of spirit, would *not* endeavor to propitiate that man in any way except for her lover's sake, and having been once deserted would not subject herself to a second indignity of that sort while there was a law to protect her."

"Unfortunately there is no law for her, having once refused a separation. Even if there were, Monsieur is rich and powerful, she is poor and friendless; he loves her, and is a man who never permits himself to be thwarted by any obstacle; therefore, I am convinced it would be best for this adorable woman to submit without defiance or delay — and I do think she will," he added, significantly.

"They seem to forget the poor lover; what is to become of him?" asked Keen.

"*I* do not forget him;" and the hand that wore the ring closed with an ominous gesture, which I well understood. "Monsieur merely claims his own, and the other, being a man of sense and honor, will doubtless withdraw at once; and though 'desolated,' as the French say, will soon console himself with a new *inamorata*. If he is so unwise as to oppose Monsieur, who by the by is a dead shot, there is but one way in which both can receive satisfaction."

A significant emphasis on the last word pointed his meaning, and the smile that accompanied it almost goaded me to draw the sword I wore, and offer him that satisfaction on the spot. I felt the color rise to my forehead, and dared not look up, but leaning on the back of Clotilde's chair, I bent as if to speak to her.

"Bear it a little longer for my sake, Paul," she murmured, with a look of love and despair, that wrung my heart. Here some one spoke of a long rehearsal in the morning, and the lateness of the hour.

"A farewell toast before we part," said Keen. "Come, Lamar, give us a sentiment, after that whisper you ought to be inspired."

"I am. Let me give you — The love of liberty and the liberty of love."

"Good! That would suit the hero and heroine of St. John's story, for Monsieur wished much for his liberty, and, no doubt, Madame will for her love," said Denon, while the glasses were filled.

Then the toast was drunk with much merriment and the party broke up. While detained by one of the strangers, I saw St. John approach Clotilde, who stood alone by the window, and speak rapidly for several minutes. She listened with half-averted head, answered briefly, and wrapping the mantilla closely about her, swept away from him with her haughtiest mien. He watched for a moment, then followed, and before I could reach her, offered his arm to lead her to the carriage. She seemed about to refuse it, but something in the expression of his face restrained her; and accepting it, they went down together. The hall and little ante-room were dimly lighted, but as I slowly followed, I saw her snatch her hand away, when she thought they were alone; saw him draw her to him with an embrace as fond as it was irresistible; and turning her indignant face to his, kiss it ardently, as he said in a tone, both tender and imperious —

"Good night, my darling. I give you one more day, and then I claim you."

"Never!" she answered, almost fiercely, as he released her. And wishing me pleasant dreams, as he passed, went out into the night, gaily humming the burden of a song Clotilde had often sung to me.

The moment we were in the carriage all her self-control deserted her, and a tempest of despairing grief came over her. For a time, both words and caresses were unavailing, and I let her weep herself calm before I asked the hard question —

"Is all this true, Clotilde?"

"Yes, Paul, all true, except that he said nothing of the neglect, the cruelty, the insult that I bore before he left me. I was so young, so lonely, I was glad to be loved and cared for, and I believed that he would never change. I cannot tell you all I suffered, but I rejoiced when I thought death had freed me; I would keep nothing that reminded me of the bitter past, and went away to begin again, as if it had never been."

"Why delay telling me this? Why let me learn it in such a strange and sudden way?"

"Ah, forgive me! I am so proud I could not bear to tell you that any man had wearied of me and deserted me. I meant to tell you before our marriage, but the fear that St. John was alive haunted me, and till it was set at rest I would not speak. To-night there was no time, and I was forced to leave all to chance. He found pleasure in tormenting me through you, but would not speak out, because he is as proud as I, and does not wish to hear our story bandied from tongue to tongue."

"What did he say to you, Clotilde?"

"He begged me to submit and return to him, in spite of all that has passed; he warned me that if we attempted to escape it would be at the peril of your life, for he would most assuredly follow and find us, to whatever corner of the earth we might fly; and he will, for he is as relentless as death."

"What did he mean by giving you one day more?" I asked, grinding my teeth with impatient rage as I listened.

"He gave me one day to recover from my surprise, to prepare for my departure with him, and to bid you farewell."

"And will you, Clotilde?"

"No!" she replied, clenching her hands with a gesture of dogged resolution, while her eyes glittered in the darkness. "I never will submit; there must be some way of escape; I shall find it, and if I do not — I can die."

"Not yet, dearest; we will appeal to the law first; I have a friend whom I will consult to-morrow, and he may help us."

"I have no faith in law," she said, despairingly, "money and influence so often outweigh justice and mercy. I have no witnesses, no friends, no wealth to help me; he has all, and we shall only be defeated. I must devise some surer way. Let me think a little; a woman's wit is quick when her heart prompts it."

I let the poor soul flatter herself with vague hopes; but I saw no help for us except in flight, and that she would not consent to, lest it should endanger me. More than once I said savagely within my-self, "I will kill him," and then shuddered at the counsels of the devil, so suddenly roused in my own breast. As if she divined my thought by instinct, Clotilde broke the heavy silence that followed her last words, by clinging to me with the imploring cry,

"Oh, Paul, shun him, else your fiery spirit will destroy you. He promised me he would not harm you unless we drove him to it. Be careful, for my sake, and if any one must suffer let it be miserable me."

I soothed her as I best could, and when our long, sad drive ended, bade her rest while I worked, for she would need all her strength on the morrow. Then I left her, to haunt the street all night long, guarding her door, and while I paced to and fro without, I watched her shadow come and go before the lighted window as she paced within, each racking our brains for some means of help till day broke.

CHAPTER III

EARLY ON THE FOLLOWING morning I consulted my friend, but when I laid the case before him he gave me little hope of a happy issue should the attempt be made. A divorce was hardly possible, when an unscrupulous man like St. John was bent on opposing it; and though no decision could force her to remain with him, we should not be safe from his vengeance, even if we chose to dare everything and fly together. Long and earnestly we talked, but to little purpose, and I went to rehearsal with a heavy heart.

Clotilde was to have a benefit that night, and what a happy day I had fancied this would be; how carefully I had prepared for it; what delight I had anticipated in playing Romeo to her Juliet; and how eagerly I had longed for the time which now seemed to ap-proach with such terrible rapidity, for each hour brought our part-ing nearer! On the stage I found Keen and his new friend amusing themselves with fencing, while waiting the arrival of some of the company. I was too miserable to be dangerous just then, and when St. John bowed to me with his most courteous air, I returned the greeting, though I could not speak to him. I think he saw my suffering, and enjoyed it with the satisfaction of a cruel nature, but he treated me with the courtesy of an equal, which new demonstration surprised me, till, through Denon, I discovered that having inquired much about me he had learned that I was a gentleman by birth and education, which fact accounted for the change in his demeanor. I roamed restlessly about the gloomy green room and stage, till Keen, dropping his foil, confessed himself outfenced and called to me.

"Come here, Lamar, and try a bout with St. John. You are the best fencer among us, so, for the honor of the company, come and do your best instead of playing Romeo before the time."

A sudden impulse prompted me to comply, and a few passes proved that I was the better swordsman of the two. This annoyed St. John, and though he complimented me with the rest, he would not own himself outdone, and we kept it up till both grew warm and excited. In the midst of an animated match between us, I observed that the button was off his foil, and a glance at his face assured me that he was aware of it, and almost at the instant he made a skilful thrust, and the point pierced my flesh. As I caught the foil from his hand and drew it out with an exclamation of pain, I saw a gleam of exultation pass across his face, and knew that his promise to Clotilde was but idle breath. My comrades surrounded me with anxious inquiries, and no one was more surprised and solicitous than St. John. The wound was trifling, for a picture of Clotilde had turned the thrust aside, else the force with which it was given might have rendered it fatal. I made light of it, but hated him with a redoubled hatred for the cold-blooded treachery that would have given to revenge the screen of accident.

The appearance of the ladies caused us to immediately ignore the mishap, and address ourselves to business. Clotilde came last, looking so pale it was not necessary for her to plead illness; but she went through her part with her usual fidelity, while her husband watched her with the masterful expression that nearly drove me wild. He haunted her like a shadow, and she listened to him with

"My comrades surrounded me with anxious inquiries."

the desperate look of a hunted creature driven to bay. He might have softened her just resentment by a touch of generosity or compassion, and won a little gratitude, even though love was impossible; but he was blind, relentless, and goaded her beyond endurance, rousing in her fiery Spanish heart a dangerous spirit he could not control. The rehearsal was over at last, and I approached Clotilde with a look that mutely asked if I should leave her. St. John said something in a low voice, but she answered sternly, as she took my arm with a decided gesture.

"This day is mine; I will not be defrauded of an hour," and we went away together for our accustomed stroll in the sunny park.

A sad and memorable walk was that, for neither had any hope with which to cheer the other, and Clotilde grew gloomier as we talked. I told her of my fruitless consultation, also of the fencing match; at that her face darkened, and she said, below her breath, "I shall remember that."

We walked long together, and I proposed plan after plan, all either unsafe or impracticable. She seemed to listen, but when I paused she answered with averted eyes —

"Leave it to me; I have a project; let me perfect it before I tell you. Now I must go and rest, for I have had no sleep, and I shall need all my strength for the tragedy to-night."

All that afternoon I roamed about the city, too restless for anything but constant motion, and evening found me ill prepared for my now doubly arduous duties. It was late when I reached the theatre, and I dressed hastily. My costume was new for the occasion, and not till it was on did I remember that I had neglected to try it since the finishing touches were given. A stitch or two would remedy the defects, and, hurrying up to the wardrobe room, a skilful pair of hands soon set me right. As I came down the winding-stairs that led from the lofty chamber to a dimly-lighted gallery below, St. John's voice arrested me, and pausing I saw that Keen was doing the honors of the theatre in defiance of all rules. Just as they reached the stair-foot some one called to them, and throwing open a narrow door, he said to his companion —

"From here you get a fine view of the stage; steady yourself by the rope and look down. I'll be with you in a moment."

He ran into the dressing-room from whence the voice proceeded, and St. John stepped out upon a little platform, hastily built for the launching of an aeriel-car in some grand spectacle. Glad to escape meeting him, I was about to go on, when, from an obscure corner, a dark figure glided noiselessly to the door and leaned in. I caught a momentary glimpse of a white extended arm and the glitter of steel, then came a cry of mortal fear, a heavy fall; and flying swiftly down the gallery the figure disappeared. With one leap I reached the door, and looked in; the raft hung broken, the platform was empty. At that instant Keen rushed out, demanding what had happened, and scarcely knowing what I said, I answered hurriedly,

"The rope broke and he fell."

Keen gave me a strange look, and dashed down stairs. I followed, to find myself in a horror-stricken crowd, gathered about the piteous object which a moment ago had been a living man. There was no need to call a surgeon, for that headlong fall had dashed out life in the drawing of a breath, and nothing remained to do but to take the poor body tenderly away to such friends as the newly-arrived stranger possessed. The contrast between the gay crowd rustling before the curtain and the dreadful scene transpiring behind it, was terrible; but the house was filling fast; there was no time for the indulgence of pity or curiosity, and soon no trace of the accident remained but the broken rope above, and an ominous damp spot on the newly-washed boards below. At a word of command from our energetic manager, actors and actresses were sent away to re-touch their pale faces with carmine, to restoring their startled nerves with any stimulant at hand, and to forget, if possible, the awesome sight just witnessed.

I returned to my dressing-room hoping Clotilde had heard nothing of this sad, and yet for us most fortunate accident, though all the while a vague dread haunted me, and I feared to see her. Mechanically completing my costume, I looked about me for the dagger with which poor Juliet was to stab herself, and found that it was gone. Trying to recollect where I put it, I remembered having it in my hand just before I went up to have my sword-belt altered; and fancying that I must have inadvertently taken it with me, I reluctantly retraced my steps. At the top of the stairs leading to that upper gallery a little white object caught my eye, and, taking it up, I found it to be a flower. If it had been a burning coal I should not have dropped it more hastily than I did when I recognized it was one of a cluster I had left in Clotilde's room because she loved them. They were a rare and delicate kind, no one but herself was likely to possess them in that place, nor was she likely to have given one away, for my gifts were kept with jealous care; yet how came it there? And as I asked myself the question, like an answer returned the remembrance of her face when she said, "I shall remember this." The darkly-shrouded form was a female figure, the white arm a woman's, and horrible as was the act, who but that sorely-tried and tempted creature would have committed it. For a moment my heart stood still, then I indignantly rejected the black thought, and thrusting the flower into my breast went on my way, trying to convince myself that the foreboding fear which oppressed me was caused by the agitating events of the last half hour. My weapon was not in the wardrobe-room; and as I returned, wondering what I had done with it, I saw Keen standing in the little doorway with a candle in his hand. He turned and asked what I was looking for. I told him, and explained why I was searching for it there.

"Here it is; I found it at the foot of these stairs. It is too sharp for a stage-dagger, and will do mischief unless you dull it," he said, adding, as he pointed to the broken rope, "Lamar, that was cut; I have examined it."

The light shone full in my face, and I knew that it changed, as did my voice, for I thought of Clotilde, and till that fear was at rest resolved to be dumb concerning what I had seen, but I could not repress a shudder as I said, hastily,

"Don't suspect me of any deviltry, for heaven's sake. I've got to go on in fifteen minutes, and how can I play unless you let me forget this horrible business."

"Forget it then, if you can; I'll remind you of it to-morrow." And, with a significant nod, he walked away, leaving behind him a new trial to distract me. I ran to Clotilde's room, bent on relieving myself, if possible, of the suspicion that would return with redoubled pertinacity since the discovery of the dagger, which I was sure I had not dropped where it was found. When I tapped at her door, her voice, clear and sweet as ever, answered "Come!" and entering, I found her ready, but alone. Before I could open my lips she put up her hand as if to arrest the utterance of some dreadful intelligence.

"Don't speak of it; I have heard, and cannot bear a repetition of the horror. I must forget it till to-morrow, then — ." There she stopped abruptly, for I produced the flower, asking as naturally as I could —

"Did you give this to any one?"

"No; why ask me that?" and she shrunk a little, as I bent to count the blossoms in the cluster on her breast. I gave her seven; now there were but six, and I fixed on her a look that betrayed my fear, and mutely demanded its confirmation or denial. Other eyes she might have evaded or defied, not mine; the traitorous blood dyed her face, then fading, left it colorless; her eyes wandered and fell, she clasped her hands imploringly, and threw herself at my feet, crying in a stifled voice,

"Paul, be merciful; that was our only hope, and the guilt is mine alone!"

But I started from her, exclaiming with mingled incredulity and horror —

"Was this the tragedy you meant? What devil devised and helped you execute a crime like this?"

"Hear me! I did not plan it, yet I longed to kill him, and all day the thought would haunt me. I have borne so much, I could bear no more, and he drove me to it. To-night the thought still clung to me, till I was half mad. I went to find you, hoping to escape it; you were gone, but on your table lay the dagger. As I took it in my hand I heard his voice, and forgot every thing except my wrongs and the great happiness one blow could bring us. I followed then, meaning to stab him in the dark; but when I saw him leaning where a safer stroke would destroy him, I gave it, and we are safe."

"Safe!" I echoed. "Do you know you left my dagger behind you? Keen found it; he suspects me, for I was near; and St. John has told him something of the cause I have to wish you free."

She sprung up, and seemed about to rush away to proclaim her guilt, but I restrained her desperate purpose, saying sternly —

"Control yourself and be cautious. I may be mistaken; but if either must suffer, let it be me. I can bear it best, even if it comes to the worst, for my life is worthless now."

"And I have made it so? Oh, Paul, can you never forgive me and forget my sin?"

"Never, Clotilde; it is too horrible."

I broke from her trembling hold, and covered up my face, for suddenly the woman whom I once loved had grown abhorrent to me. For many minutes neither spoke or stirred; my heart seemed dead within me, and what went on in that stormy soul I shall never know. Suddenly I was called, and as I turned to leave her, she seized both my hands in a despairing grasp, covered them with tender kisses, wet them with repentant tears, and clung to them in a paroxysm of love, remorse, and grief, till I was forced to go, leaving her alone with the memory of her sin.

That night I was like one in a terrible dream; every thing looked unreal, and like an automaton I played my part, for always before me I seemed to see that shattered body and to hear again that beloved voice confessing a black crime. Rumors of the accident had crept out, and damped the spirits of the audience, yet it was as well, perhaps, for it made them lenient to the short-comings of the actors, and lent another shadow to the mimic tragedy that slowly darkened to its close. Clotilde's unnatural composure would have been a marvel to me had I not been past surprise at any demonstration on her part. A wide gulf now lay between us, and it seemed impossible for me to cross it. The generous, tender woman whom I first loved, was still as beautiful and dear to me as ever, but as much lost as if death had parted us. The desperate, despairing creature I had learned to know within an hour, seemed like an embodiment of the murderous spirit which had haunted me that day, and though by heaven's mercy it had not conquered me, yet I now hated it with remorseful intensity. So strangely were the two images blended in my troubled mind that I could not separate them, and they exerted a mysterious influence over me. When with Clotilde she seemed all she had ever been, and I enacted the lover with a power I had never known before, feeling the while that it might be for the last time. When away from her the darker impression returned, and the wildest of the poet's words were not too strong to embody my own sorrow and despair. They told me long afterwards that never had the tragedy been better played, and I could believe it, for the hapless Italian lovers never found better representatives than in us that night.

Worn out with suffering and excitement, I longed for solitude and silence with a desperate longing, and when Romeo murmured, "With a kiss I die," I fell beside the bier, wishing that I too was done with life. Lying there, I watched Clotilde, through the little that remained, and so truly, tenderly, did she render the pathetic scene that my heart softened; all the early love returned strong, and warm as ever, and I felt that I *could* forgive. As she knelt to draw my dagger, I whispered, warningly,

"Be careful, dear, it is very sharp."

"I know it," she answered with a shudder, then cried aloud,

"Oh happy dagger! this is thy sheath; there rust, and let me die."

Again I saw the white arm raised, the flash of steel as Juliet struck the blow that was to free her, and sinking down beside her lover, seemed to breathe her life away.

"I thank God it's over," I ejaculated, a few minutes later, as the curtain slowly fell. Clotilde did not answer, and feeling how cold the cheek that touched my own had grown, I thought she had given way at last.

"She has fainted; lift her, Denon, and let me rise," I cried, as Count Paris sprang up with a joke.

"Good God, she has hurt herself with that cursed dagger!" he exclaimed, as raising her he saw a red stain on the white draperies she wore.

I staggered to my feet, and laid her on the bier she had just left, but no mortal skill could heal that hurt, and Juliet's grave-clothes were her own. Deaf to the enthusiastic clamor that demanded our re-appearance, blind to the confusion and dismay about me, I leaned over her passionately, conjuring her to give me one word of pardon and farewell. As if my voice had power to detain her, even when death called, the dark eyes, full of remorseful love, met mine again, and feebly drawing from her breast a paper, she motioned

Keen to take it, murmuring in a tone that changed from solemn affirmation to the tenderest penitence,

"Lamar is innocent — I did it. This will prove it. Paul, I have tried to atone — oh, forgive me, and remember me for my love's sake."

I did forgive her; and she died, smiling on my breast. I did remember her through a long, lonely life, and never played again since the night of that DOUBLE TRAGEDY.

Ariel. A Legend of the Lighthouse

———✧———

PART I

GOOD MORNING, Mr. Southesk. Aren't you for the sea, to-day?"

"Good morning, Miss Lawrence. I am only waiting for my boat to be off."

As he answered her blithe greeting, the young man looked up from the rock where he was lounging, and a most charming object rewarded him for the exertion of lifting his dreamy eyes. Some women have the skill to make even a bathing costume graceful and picturesque; and Miss Lawrence knew that she looked well in her blue suit, with loosened hair blowing about her handsome face, glimpses of white ankles through the net-work of her bathing-sandals, and a general breeziness of aspect that became her better than the most elaborate toilet she could make. A shade of disappointment was visible on receiving the answer to her question, and her voice was slightly imperious, for all its sweetness, as she said, pausing beside the indolent figure that lay basking in the sunshine.

"I meant bathing, not boating, when I spoke of the sea. Will you not join our party and give us another exhibition of your skill in aquatic gymnastics?"

"No, thank you; the beach is too tame for me; I prefer deep water, heavy surf and a spice of danger, to give zest to my pastime."

The languid voice was curiously at variance with the words; and Miss Lawrence almost involuntarily exclaimed —

"You are the strangest mixture of indolence and energy I ever knew! To see you now, one would find it difficult to believe the stories told of your feats by land and sea; yet I know that you deserve your soubriquet of 'Bayard,' as well as the other they give you of *'Dolce far niente.'* You are as changeable as the ocean which you love so well; but we never see the moon that rules your ebb and flow."

Ignoring the first part of her speech, Southesk replied to the last sentence with sudden animation.

"I *am* fond of the sea, and well I may be, for I was born on it, both my parents lie buried in it, and out of it my fate is yet to come."

"Your fate?" echoed Miss Lawrence, full of the keenest interest, for he seldom spoke of himself, and seemed anxious to forget the past in the successful present, and the promising future. Some passing mood made him unusually frank, for he answered, as his fine eyes roved far across the glittering expanse before them —

"Yes, I once had my fortune told by a famous wizard, and it has haunted me ever since. I am not superstitious, but I cannot help attaching some importance to her prediction:

'Watch by the sea-shore early and late,
For out of its depths will rise your fate,
Both love and life will be darkly crossed,
And a single hour see all won or lost.'

"That was the prophecy; and though I have little faith in it, yet I am irresistibly drawn towards the sea, and continually find myself watching and waiting for the fate it is to bring me."

"May it be a happy one."

All the imperiousness was gone from the woman's voice, and her eyes turned as wistfully as her companion's, to the mysterious ocean which had already brought *her* fate. Neither spoke for a moment. Southesk, busied with some fancy of his own, continued to scan the blue waves that rolled to meet the horizon, and Helen scanned his face with an expression which many men would have given much to have awakened, for the world said that Miss Lawrence was as proud and cold as she was beautiful. Love and longing met and mingled in the glance she fixed on that unconscious countenance; and once, with an involuntary impulse, her small hand was raised to smooth away the wind-tossed hair that streaked his forehead, as he sat with uncovered head, smiling to himself — forgetful of her presence. She caught back her hand in time and turned away to hide the sudden color that dyed her cheeks at the momentary impulse which would have betrayed her to a less absorbed companion. Before she could break the silence, there came a call from a group gathered on the smoother beach beyond, and, glad of another chance to gain her wish, she said, in a tone that would have won compliance from any man except Southesk:

"They are waiting for us; can I not tempt you to join the mermaids yonder, and let the boat wait till it's cooler?"

But he shook his head with a wilful little gesture, and looked about him for his hat, as if eager to escape, yet answered smiling —

"I've a prior engagement with the mermaid of the island, and, as a gallant man, must keep it, or expect shipwreck on my next voyage. Are you ready, Jack?" he added, as Miss Lawrence moved away, and he strolled towards an old boatman, busy with his wherry.

"In a jiffy, sir. So you've seen her, have you?" said the man, pausing in his work.

"Seen whom?"

"The mermaid at the island."

"No; I only fabricated that excuse to rid myself of the amiable young ladies who bore me to death. You look as if you had a yarn to spin; so spin away while you work, for I want to be off."

"Well, sir, I jest thought you'd like to know that there *is* a mermaid down there, as you're fond of odd and pretty things. No one has seen her but me, or I should a heard of it, and I've told no one but my wife, being afraid of Rough Ralph, as we call the lighthouse-keeper. He don't like folks comin' round his place; and if I said a word about the marmaid, every one would go swarmin' to the island to hunt up the pretty creeter, and drive Ralph into a rage."

"Never mind Ralph; tell me how and where you saw the mermaid; asleep in your boat, I fancy."

"No, sir; wide awake and sober. I had a notion one day to row round the island, and take a look at the chasm, as they call a great split in the rock that stands up most as high as the lighthouse. It goes from top to bottom of the Gull's Perch, and the sea flows through it, foamin' and ragin' like mad, when the tide rises. The waves have worn holes in the rocks on both sides of the chasm, and in one of these basins I see the marmaid, as plain as I see you."

"What was she doing, Jack?"

"Singin' and combin' her hair; so I knew she was gennywine."

"Her hair was green or blue, of course," said Southesk, with such visible incredulity that old Jack was nettled and answered gruffly.

"It was darker and curlier than the lady's that's jest gone; so was her face handsomer, her voice sweeter, and her arms whiter; believe it or not as you please."

"How about the fins and scales, Jack?"

"Not a sign of 'em, sir. She was half in the water, and had on some sort of white gown, so I couldn't see whether there were feet or a tail. But I'll swear I saw her; and I've got her comb to prove it."

"Her comb! let me see it, and I shall find it easier to believe the story," said the young man, with a lazy sort of curiosity.

Old Jack produced a dainty little comb, apparently made of a pearly shell, cut and carved with much skill, and bearing two letters on its back.

"Faith! it *is* a pretty thing, and none but a mermaid could have owned it. How did you get it?" asked Southesk, carefully examining the delicate lines and letters, and wishing that the tale could be true, for the vision of the fair-faced mermaiden pleased his romantic fancy.

"It was this way, sir," replied Jack. "I was so took aback that I sung out before I'd had a good look at her. She see me, give a little screech, and dived out of sight. I waited to see her come up, but she didn't; so I rowed as nigh as I dared, and got the comb she'd dropped; then I went home and told my wife. She advised me to hold my tongue and not go agin, as I wanted to; so I give it up; but I'm dreadful eager to have another look at the little thing, and I guess you'd find it worth while to try for a sight of her."

"I can see women bathing without that long row, and don't believe Ralph's daughter would care to be disturbed again."

"He ain't got any, sir — neither wife nor child; and no one on the island but him and his mate — a gruff chap that never comes ashore, and don't care for nothin' but keepin' the lantern tidy."

Southesk stood a moment measuring the distance between the main land and the island, with his eye, for Jack's last speech gave an air of mystery to what before had seemed a very simple matter.

"You say Ralph is not fond of having visitors, and rarely leaves the lighthouse; what else do you know about him?" he asked.

"Nothing, sir, only he's a sober, brave, faithful man that does his duty well, and seems to like that bleak, lonesome lighthouse more than most folks would. He's seen better days, I guess, for there's something of the gentleman about him in spite of his rough ways. Now she's ready, sir, and you're just in time to find the little mermaid doin' up her hair."

"I want to visit the light-house, and am fond of adventures, so I think I'll follow your advice. What will you take for this comb, Jack?" asked Southesk, as the old man left his work, and the wherry danced invitingly upon the water.

"Nothing from you, sir; you're welcome to it, for my wife's fretted ever since I had it, and I'm glad to be rid of it. It ain't every one I give it to, or tell about what I saw; but you've done me more'n one good turn, and I'm eager to give you a bit of pleasure to pay for 'em. On the further side of the island you'll find the chasm. It's a dangerous place, but you're a reg'lar fish; so I'll risk you. Good luck, and let me know how you get on."

"What do you suppose the letters stand for?" asked Southesk, as he put the comb in his pocket, and trimmed his boat.

"Why, A. M. stands for a Mermaid; don't it?" answered Jack, soberly.

"I'll find another meaning for them before I come back. Keep your secret, and I'll do the same, for I want the mermaid all to myself."

With a laugh the young man skimmed away, deaf to the voices of the fashionable syrens, who vainly endeavored to detain him, and blind to the wistful glances following the energetic figure that bent to the oars with a strength and skill which soon left the beach and its gay groups far behind.

The light-house was built on the tallest cliff of the island, and the only safe landing place appeared to be at the foot of the rock, whence a precipitous path and an iron ladder led to the main entrance of the tower. Barren and forbidding it looked, even in the glow of the summer sun, and remembering Ralph's dislike of visitors, Southesk resolved to explore the chasm alone, and ask leave of no one. Rowing along the craggy shore he came to the enormous rift that cleft the rocks from top to bottom. Bold and skillful as he was he dared not venture very near, for the tide was coming in, and each advancing billow threatened to sweep the boat into the chasm, where angry waves chafed and foamed, filling the dark hollow with a cloud of spray and reverberating echoes that made a mellow din.

Intent on watching the splendid spectacle he forgot to look for the mermaid, till something white flashed by, and turning with a start he saw a human face rise from the sea, followed by a pair of white arms, that beckoned as the lips smiled and the bright eyes watched him while he sat motionless, till, with a sound of musical laughter, the phantom vanished.

Uttering an exclamation, he was about to follow, when a violent shock made him reel in his seat, and a glance showed him the peril he was in, for the boat had drifted between two rocks; the next wave would shatter it.

The instinct of self-preservation being stronger than curiosity, he pulled for his life and escaped just in time.

Steering into calmer water he took an observation, and decided to land if possible, and search the chasm where the watery sprite or bathing-girl had seemed to take refuge. It was some time, how-

ever, before he found any safe harbor, and with much difficulty he
at last gained the shore, breathless, wet and weary.

Guided by the noise of the waves he came at length to the brink
of the precipice and looked down. There were ledges and crannies
enough to afford foothold for a fearless climber, and full of the plea-
surable excitement of danger and adventures, Southesk swung himself down with a steady head, strong hand and agile foot. Not many
steps were taken when he paused suddenly, for the sound of a voice
arrested him. Fitfully it rose and fell through the dash of advancing
and retreating billows, but he heard it distinctly, and with redoubled eagerness looked and listened.

Half-way down the chasm lay a mass of rock, firmly wedged
between the two sides by some convulsion of nature which had
hurled it there. Years had evidently passed since it fell, for a tree
had taken root and shot up, fed by a little patch of earth, and shel-
tered from wind and storm in that secluded spot. Wild vines, led
by their instinct for the light, climbed along either wall and draped
the cliff with green. Some careful hand had been at work, however,
for a few hardy plants blossomed in the almost sunless nook; every
niche held a delicate fern, every tiny basin was full of some rare
old weed, and here and there a suspended shell contained a tuft of
greenish moss, or a bird's eggs, or some curious treasure gathered
from the deep. The sombre verdure of the little pine concealed a
part of this airy nest, but from the hidden nook the sweet voice rose
singing a song well suited to the scene —

"Oh, come unto the yellow sands."

Feeling as if he had stepped into a fairy tale, the young man
paused with suspended breath till the last soft note and its softer
echo had died away, then he noiselessly crept on. Soon his quick
eye discovered a rope ladder, half hidden by the vines and evidently
used as a path to the marine bower below. Availing himself of it he
descended a few steps, but not far, for a strong gust blew up the
rift, and swaying aside the leafy screen disclosed the object of his
search. No mermaid but a young girl, sitting and singing like a bird
in her green nest.

[*155*]

As the pine waved to and fro, Southesk saw that the unknown sat in a thoughtful attitude, looking out through the wide rift into the sunny blue beyond. He saw, too, that a pair of small, bare feet shone white against the dark bottom of a rocky basin, full of newly fallen rain; that a plain grey gown defined the lithe outlines of a girlish figure, and that the damp dark rings of hair were fastened back with a pretty band of shells.

So intent on looking was he that he leaned nearer and nearer, till a sudden gesture caused the comb to slip from his pocket and fall into the basin with a splash that roused the girl from her reverie. She started, seized it eagerly, and looking upward exclaimed with a joyful accent,

"Why, Stern, where did you find my comb?"

There was no answer to her question, and the smile died on her lips, for instead of Stern's rough, brown countenance she saw, framed in green leaves, a young and comely face.

Blonde and blue-eyed, flushed and eager, the pleasant apparition smiled down upon her with an aspect which brought no fear, but woke wonder and won confidence by the magic of a look. Only a moment did she see it; then the pine boughs came between them. The girl sprang up, and Southesk, forgetting safety in curiosity, leaped down.

He had not measured the distance; his foot slipped and he fell, striking his head with a force that stunned him for a moment. The cool drip of water on his forehead roused him, and he soon collected himself, although somewhat shaken by his fall. Half-opening his eyes he looked into a dark yet brilliant face, of such peculiar beauty that it struck and charmed him at a single glance. Pity, anxiety and alarm were visible in it, and glad of a pretext for prolonging the episode, he resolved to feign the suffering he did not feel. With a sigh he closed his eyes again, and for a moment lay enjoying the soft touch of hands about his head, the sound of a quickly-beating heart near him, and the pleasant consciousness that he was an object of interest to this sweet-voiced unknown. Too generous to keep her long in suspense, he soon raised his head and looked about him, asking faintly,

"Where am I?"

"In the chasm, but quite safe with me," replied a fresh young voice.

"Who is this gentle 'me' whom I mistook for a mermaid, and whose pardon I ask for this rude intrusion?"

"I'm Ariel, and I forgive you willingly."

"Pretty name — is it really yours?" asked Southesk, feeling that his simplest manner was the surest to win her confidence, for the girl spoke with the innocent freedom of a child.

"I have no other, except March, and that is not pretty."

"Then, 'A. M.' on the comb does not mean 'A mermaid,' as old Jack thought when he gave it to me?"

A silvery laugh followed his involuntary smile, as, still kneeling by him, Ariel regarded him with much interest, and a very frank expression of admiration in her beautiful eyes.

"Did you come to bring it back to me?" she asked, turning the recovered treasure in her hand.

"Yes; Jack told me about the pretty water-sprite he saw, so I came to find her, and am not yet sure that you're not a Lorelei, for you nearly wrecked me, and vanished in a most unearthly manner."

"Ah!" she said, with the blithe laugh again, "I lead the life of a mermaid though I'm not one, and when I'm disturbed I play pranks, for I know every cranny of the rocks, and learned swimming and diving from the gulls."

"Flying also, I should think, by the speed with which you reached this nook, for I made all haste, and nearly killed myself, as you see."

As he spoke, Southesk tried to rise, but a sharp twinge in his arm made him pause, with an exclamation of pain.

"Are you much hurt? Can I do anything more for you?" and the voice was womanly pitiful, as the girl watched him.

"I've cut my arm, I think, and lamed my foot; but a little rest will set them right. May I wait here a few minutes, and enjoy your lovely nest; though it's no place for a clumsy mortal like me?"

"Oh, yes; stay as long as you please, and let me bind up your wound. See how it bleeds."

"You are not afraid of me then?"

"No; why should I be?" and the dark eyes looked fearlessly into his as Ariel bent to examine the cut. It was a deep one, and he fancied she would cry out or turn pale; but she did neither, and having skilfully bound a wet handkerchief about it, she glanced from the strong arm and shapely hand to their owner's face, and said, naively,

"What a pity there will be a scar."

Southesk laughed outright, in spite of the smart, and, leaning on the uninjured arm, prepared to enjoy himself, for the lame foot was a fiction.

"Never mind the scar. Men consider them no blemish, and I shall be prouder of this than half a dozen others I have, because by means of it I get a glimpse into fairy land. Do you live here on foam and sunshine, Ariel?"

"No; the lighthouse is my home now."

There was evident reluctance in her manner. She seemed to weigh her words, yet longed to speak out, and it was plain to see that the newcomer was very welcome to her solitude. With all his boldness, Southesk unconsciously tempered his manner with respect, and neither by look nor tone caused any touch of fear to disturb the innocent creature whose retreat he had discovered.

"Then you are Ralph's daughter, as I fancied?" he went on, putting his questions with an engaging air that was hard to resist.

"Yes."

Again she hesitated, and again seemed eager to confide even in a stranger, but controlled the impulse, and gave brief replies to all home questions.

"No one knows you are here, and you seem to lead a hidden life like some enchanted princess. It only needs a Miranda to make a modern version of the Tempest." He spoke half aloud, as if to himself, but the girl answered readily —

"Perhaps I am to lead you to her as the real Ariel led Ferdinand to Miranda, if you've not already found her."

"Why, what do you know of Shakespeare? and how came you by your pretty name?" asked Southesk, wondering at the look and tone which suddenly gave the girl's face an expression of elfish intelligence.

"I know and love Shakespeare better than any of my other books, and can sing every song he wrote. How beautiful they are! See, I have worn out my dear book with much reading."

As she spoke, from a dry nook in the rock she drew a dilapidated volume, and turned its pages with a loving hand, while all the innocent sweetness returned to her young face, lending it new beauty.

"What a charming little sprite it is," thought Southesk, adding aloud, with an irresistible curiosity that banished politeness,

"And the name, how came that?"

"Father gave it to me." There she paused, adding hastily, "He loves Shakespeare as well as I do, and taught me to understand him."

"Here's a romantic pair, and a mystery of some sort, which I'll amuse myself by unraveling, if possible," he thought, and put another question — "Have you been here long?"

"No; I only spend the hot hours here."

"Another evasion. I shall certainly be driven into asking her, point blank, who and what she is," said Southesk to himself, and, to avoid temptation, returned to the comb which Ariel still held.

"Who carved that so daintily? I should like to bespeak one for myself it is so pretty."

"I carved it, and was very happy at my work. It's hard to find amusement on this barren island, so I invent all sorts of things to while away the time."

"Did you invent this hanging garden and make this wilderness blossom?" asked Southesk, trying the while to understand the lights and shadows that made her face as changeful as an April sky.

"Yes; I did it, and spend half my time here, for here I escape seeing people on the beach, and so forget them."

A little sigh followed, and her eyes turned wistfully to the dark rift, that gave her but a glimpse of the outer world.

"You can scarcely see the beach, much less the people on it, I should think," said Southesk, wondering what she meant.

"I can see well with the telescope from the tower, and often watch the people on the shore — they look so gay and pretty."

"Then, why wish to forget them?"

"Because since they came it is more lonely than before."

"Do you never visit the mainland? Have you no friends or companions to enliven your solitude?"

"No."

Something in the tone in which the monosyllable was uttered checked further inquiries, and prompted him to say smilingly:

"Now it is your turn; ask what you will."

But Ariel drew back, answering with an air of demure propriety that surprised him more than her self-possession or her rebuke.

"No, thank you, it is ill-bred to question strangers."

Southesk colored at the satirical glance she gave him, and rising, he made his most courtly bow, saying, with a pleasant mixture of candor and contrition:

"Again I beg pardon for my rudeness. Coming so suddenly upon a spirit singing to itself between sea and sky, I forgot myself, and fancied the world's ways out of place. Now I see my mistake, and though it spoils the romance, I will call you Miss March, and respectfully take my leave."

The silvery laugh broke in on the last sentence, and in her simplest manner Ariel replied:

"No, don't call me that nor go away, unless you are quite out of pain. I like your rudeness better than your politeness, for it made you seem like a pleasant boy, and now you are nothing but a fine gentleman."

Both amused and relieved by her reply, he answered, half in jest, half in earnest,

"Then, I'll be a boy again, and tell you who I am, as you are too well bred to ask, and it is but proper to introduce myself. Philip Southesk by name, gentleman by birth, poet by profession; but I don't deserve the title, though certain friendly persons do me the honor to praise a few verses I once wrote. Stay, I forgot two things that ladies usually take an interest in. Fortune ample — age four-and-twenty."

"You did not ask me either of these two questions," said Ariel, with a flicker of merriment in her eyes, as she glanced up rather shyly at the would-be boy, who now stood straight and tall before her.

"No; even in the midst of my delusion I remembered that one never ventures to put the last of those questions to a woman — the first I cared nothing about."

"I like that," said the girl in her quick way, adding frankly, "I am poor, and seventeen."

She half rose as she spoke, but hastily sat down again, recollecting her bare feet. The change of color, and an anxious look toward a pair of little shoes that lay near by, suggested to Southesk a speedy withdrawal, and, turning toward the half-hidden ladder, he said, lingering in the act of going:

"Good-by; may I come again, if I come properly, and do not stay too long? Poets are privileged persons, you know, and this is a poet's paradise."

She looked pleased, yet troubled, and answered reluctantly:

"You are very kind to say so, but I cannot ask you to come again, for father would be displeased, and it is best for me to go on as before."

"But why hide yourself here? Why not enjoy the pleasures fitting for your age, instead of watching them afar off, and vainly longing for them?" exclaimed Southesk, impetuously, for the eloquent eyes betrayed what the tongue would not confess.

"I cannot tell you."

As she spoke her head was bowed upon her hands, her abundant hair veiled her face, and as it fell the little chaplet of shells dropped at Southesk's feet.

"Forgive me; I have no right to question you, and will not disturb your solitude again, unless your father is willing. But give me some token to prove that I have really visited an enchanted island, and heard Ariel sing. I returned the comb, may I have this in exchange?"

He spoke playfully, hoping to win a smile of pardon for his last trespass. She looked up quite calm again, and freely gave him the chain of shells for which he asked. Then he sprang up the precipitous path, and went his way, but his parting glance showed him the fair face still wistfully watching him from the green gloom of Ariel's nest.

PART II

IN THE LOWER ROOM of the lighthouse sat three persons, each apparently busy with his own thoughts, yet each covertly watching the others. Ralph March, a stern, dark-browed, melancholy-looking man, leaned back in his chair, with one hand above his eyes, which were fixed on Ariel, who sat near the narrow window cut in the thick wall, often gazing out upon the sea, glowing with the gold and purple of a sunset sky, but oftener stealing a glance toward her father, as if she longed to speak yet dared not. The third occupant of the room was a rough, sturdy-looking man, whose age it was hard to discover, for an unsightly hump disfigured his broad shoulders, and a massive head was set upon a stunted body. Shaggy-haired, tawny-bearded and bronzed by wind and weather he was a striking, not a pitiful figure, for his herculean strength was visible at a glance, and a somewhat defiant expression seemed to repel compassion and command respect. Sitting in the doorway, he appeared to be intent on mending a torn net, but his keen eye went stealthily from father to daughter, as if trying to read their faces. The long silence that had filled the room was broken by March's deep voice, saying suddenly, as he dropped his hand and turned to Ariel:

"Are you sick or sad, child, that you sigh so heavily?"

"I'm lonely, father."

Something in the plaintive tone and drooping figure touched March's heart, and, drawing the girl to his knee, he looked into her face with a tender anxiety that softened and beautified his own.

"What can I do for you, dear? Where shall I take you to make you forget your loneliness? — or whom shall I bring here to enliven you?"

Her eyes woke and her lips parted eagerly, as if a wish was ready, but some fear restrained its utterance, and, half averting her face, she answered meekly:

"I ought to be contented with you, and I try to be, but sometimes I long to do as others do, and enjoy my youth while it lasts. If you liked to mingle with people I should love to try it; as you do not, I'll endeavor to be happy where I am."

"Poor child, it is but natural, and I am selfish to make a recluse of you, because I hate the world. Shall we leave the island and begin our wandering life again?"

"Oh, no; I like the island now, and could be quite contented if I had a young companion. I never have had, and did not know how pleasant it was until two days ago."

Her eyes turned toward the open door, through which the Gull's Perch was visible, with the chasm yawning near it, and again she sighed. March saw where she looked; a frown began to gather, but some gentler emotion checked his anger, and with a sudden smile he said, stroking her smooth cheek:

"Now I know the wish you would not tell, the cause of your daily watch from the tower, and the secret of these frequent sighs. Silly child, you want young Southesk to return, yet dare not ask me to permit it."

Ariel turned her face freely to his, and leaning confidingly upon his shoulder, answered with the frankness he had taught her.

"I do wish he'd come again, and I think I deserve some reward for telling you all that happened, for bidding him go away, and for being so careful what I said."

"Hard tasks, I know, especially the last, for such an open creature is my girl. Well, you shall be rewarded, and if he come again you may see him, and so will I."

"Oh, thank you, father, that is so kind. But you look as if you thought he would not come."

"I am afraid he has already forgotten all about the lonely island and the little bare-footed maiden he saw on it. Young men's memories are treacherous things, and curiosity once gratified, soon dies."

But Ariel shook her head, as if refusing to accept the ungracious thought, and surprised her father by the knowledge of human nature which she seemed to have learned by instinct, for she answered gravely, yet hopefully:

"I think he *will* come, simply because I forbade it. He is a poet, and cares for things that have no charm for other men. He liked my nest, he liked to hear me sing, and his curiosity was not gratified, because I only told enough to make him eager for more. I have a feeling that he will come again, to find that the island is not always lonely, nor the girl always barefooted."

Her old blithe laugh broke out again as she glanced from the little mirror that reflected the glossy waves of her hair, bound with a band of rosy coral, to the well-shod feet that peeped from below the white hem of her gown. Her father watched her fondly, as she swept him a stately curtsey, looking so gay and lovely that he could not but smile and hope her wish might be granted.

"Little vanity," he said, "who taught you to make yourself so bonny, and where did you learn these airs and graces? Not from Stern or me, I fancy."

"Ah, I have not looked through the telescope and watched the fine ladies in vain, it seems, since you observe the change. I study fashion and manners at a disadvantage, but I am an apt scholar, I find. Now I'm going up to watch and wait for my reward."

As she ran up the winding-stairs that led to the great lantern, and the circular balcony that hung outside, Stern said, with the freedom of one privileged to speak his mind:

"The girl is right; the boy will come again, and mischief will grow out of it."

"What mischief?" demanded March.

"Do you suppose he can see her often and not love her?" returned Stern, almost angrily.

"Let him love her."

"Do you mean it? After hiding her so carefully, will you let her be won by this romantic boy, if his fancy last? You are making a false step, and you'll repent of it."

"I have already made a false step, and I do repent of it; but it's not this one. I have tried to keep Ariel a child, and she was happy until she became a woman. Now the old simple life is not enough for her, and her heart craves its right. I live only for her, and if her happiness demands the sacrifice of the seclusion I love, I shall make it — shall welcome anyone who can give her pleasure, and promote any scheme that spares her from the melancholy that curses me."

"Then you are resolved to let this young man come if he choose, and allow her to love him, as she most assuredly will?"

"Yes, chance brought him here at first, and if inclination brings him again let it be so. I have made inquiries concerning him, and am satisfied. He is Ariel's equal in birth, is fitted to make her happy, and has already wakened an unusual interest in her mind. Sooner or later I must leave her; she is alone in the world, and to whom can I confide her so safely as to a husband."

A dark flush had passed over Stern's face as he listened, and more than once impetuous words seemed to have risen to his lips, to be restrained by set teeth and an emotion of despair.

March saw this, and it seemed to confirm his purpose, though he made no comment on it, and abruptly closed the conversation; for, as Stern began —

"I warn you, sir — " he interrupted him, saying with decision:

"No more of this; I have had other warnings than yours, and must listen to them, for the time is not far distant when I must leave the child alone, unless I give her a guardian soon. Wild as my plan may seem, it is far safer than to take her into the world, for here I can observe this young man, and shape her future as I will. You mean kindly, Stern, but you cannot judge for me nor understand my girl as I do. Now, leave me, I must go and rest."

Stern's black eyes glowed with an ireful spark, and he clenched his strong hands as if to force himself to silence, as he went without a word, while March passed into an inner room, with the melancholy expression deeper than ever on his face.

For a few moments the deserted room was silent and solitary, but presently a long shadow fell athwart the sunny floor, and Southesk stood in the open doorway, with a portfolio and a carefully folded parcel underneath his arm. Pausing to look about him for someone to address, the sound of Ariel's voice reached his ear, and, as if no other welcome were needed, he followed it as eagerly as before. Stealing up the steep stairs, he came into the many-windowed tower, and on the balcony saw Ariel straining her eyes through a telescope, which was pointed toward the beach he had left an hour ago. As he lingered, uncertain how to accost her, she dropped the glass, exclaiming with a sigh of weariness and disappointment:

"No, he is not there!" In the act she turned, saw him, and uttered a little cry of delight, while her face brightened beautifully as she sprang forward, offering her hand with a gesture as graceful as impulsive, saying joyfully —

"I knew you would come again!"

Well pleased at such a cordial welcome, he took the hand, and still holding it, asked in that persuasive voice of his —

"For whom were you looking, Ariel?"

She colored, and turned her traitorous eyes away, yet answered with an expression of merry mischief that was very charming —

"I looked for Ferdinand!"

"And here he is," replied Southesk, laughing at her girlish evasion. "Though you forbade my return, I was obliged to break my promise, because I unconsciously incurred a debt which I wish to discharge. When I asked you for those pretty shells I did not observe that they were strung on a little gold chain, and afterward it troubled me to think I had taken a gift of value. Much as I want to keep it, I shall not like to do so unless you will let me make some return for that, and for the hospitality you showed me. May I offer you this, with many thanks?"

While speaking rapidly, he had undone the parcel, and put into her hands a beautiful volume of Shakespeare, daintily bound, richly illustrated, and bearing on the fly-leaf a graceful little poem to herself. So touched and delighted was she that she stood silent, reading the musical lines, glancing at the pictured pages, and trying to summon words expressive enough to convey her thanks. None came that suited her, but her eyes filled, and she exclaimed with a grateful warmth that well repaid the giver.

"It is too beautiful for me, and you are too kind! How did you know I wanted a new book, and would have chosen one like this?"

"I am glad I guessed so well, and now consider the mermaid's rosary my own. But tell me, did you ask if I might come again, or did you leave it to me?"

"I tell my father everything, and when I spoke of you again to-day, much to my surprise, he said you might come if you chose. But he added that you'd probably forgotten all about the island by this time."

"And you knew I had not — thank you for that. No; so far from forgetting, I've dreamed about it ever since, and should have returned before had not my arm been too lame for rowing, and I would not bring any intruder but myself. I want to sketch your nest, for some day it will get into verse, and I wish to keep it fresh before me. May I?"

"I shall be very proud to see it drawn, and to read the poem if it is as sweet as this. I think I like your songs better than Shakespeare's."

"What a compliment! It is I who am proud now. How beautiful it is up here; one feels like a bird on this airy perch. Tell me what those places are that look so like celestial cities in this magical light?"

Willingly she obeyed, and standing at her side he listened, feeling the old enchantment creep over him as he watched the girl, who seemed to glow and brighten like a flower at the coming of the sun. Nor did the charm lie in her beauty alone; language, mien, and manner betrayed the native refinement which comes from birth and breeding, and, despite her simple dress, her frank ways, and the mystery that surrounded her, Southesk felt that this lighthouse-keeper's daughter was a gentlewoman, and every moment grew more interested in her.

Presently he professed a desire to sketch a picturesque promontory not far distant; and, seated on the step of the narrow door, he drew industriously, glancing up now and then at Ariel, who leaned on the balustrade turning the pages of her book with her loveliest expression, as she read a line here and there, sung snatches of the airs she loved so well, and paused to talk, for her companion wasted little time in silence. Place, hour, and society suited him to a charm, and he luxuriated in the romance and the freedom, both being much enhanced by the strong contrast between this hour and those he had been spending among the frivolous crowds at the great hotel. He took no thought for the future but heartily enjoyed the present, and was in his gayest, most engaging mood as he feasted his eyes on the beauty all about him while endeavoring to copy the graceful figure and spirited face before him.

Quite unconscious of his purpose she pored over the book, and presently exclaimed, as she opened on a fine illustration of the Tempest —

"Here we all are! Prospero is not unlike my father, but Ferdinand is much plainer than you. Here's Ariel swinging in a vine, as I've often done, and Caliban watching her as Stern watches me. He is horrible here, however, and my Caliban has a fine face, if one can get a sight of it when he is in good humor."

"You mean the deformed man who glowered at me as I landed? I want much to know who he is, but I dare not ask, lest I get another lesson in good manners," said Southesk, with an air of timidity belied by his bold, bright eyes.

"I'll tell you without asking. He is the lighthouse-keeper, for my father only helps him a little, because he likes the wild life. People call him the master, as he goes to the mainland for all we need instead of Stern, who hates to be seen, poor soul."

"Thank you," returned Southesk, longing to ask more questions, and on the alert for any hint that might enlighten him regarding this peculiar pair.

Ariel went back to her book, smiling to herself, as she said, after a long look at one figure in the pictured group —

"This Miranda is very charming, but not so queenly as yours."

"Mine!" ejaculated Southesk, with as much amusement as surprise. "How do you know I have one?"

"She came here to look for you," stealing a glance at him from under her long lashes.

"The deuce, she did! When — how? Tell me about it, for, upon my honor, I don't know who you mean," and Southesk put down his pencil to listen.

"Yesterday a boatman rowed a lady down here, and though the steep path and the ladder rather daunted her at first, she climbed up, and asked to see the lighthouse. Stern showed it, but she was not soon satisfied, and peered about as if bent on searching every corner. She asked many questions, and examined the book for visitors' names, which hangs below. Yours was not there, but she seemed to suspect that you had been here, and Stern told her that it was so. It was not like him, but he was unusually gracious, though he said nothing about father and myself, and when she had roamed up and down for a long time, the lady went away."

"Was she tall and dark, with fine eyes and a proud air?" asked Southesk, with a frown.

"Yes; but I thought she could be very sweet and gentle when she chose, she changed so as she spoke of you."

"Did she see you, Ariel?"

"No; I ran away and hid, as I always do when strangers come; but I saw her, and longed to know her name, for she would not give it, so I called her your Miranda."

"Not she! Her name is Helen Lawrence, and I wish she was — " He checked himself, looking much annoyed, yet ashamed of his petulant tone, and added, with a somewhat disdainful smile — "less inquisitive. She must have come while I was in the city searching for your book, but she never breathed a word of it to me. I shall feel like a fly in a cobweb if she keeps such close watch over me."

"Why did she think you had been here? Did you tell her?" asked Ariel, looking as if she quite understood Miss Lawrence's motive in coming, and rather enjoyed her disappointment.

"That puppy, Dr. Haye, who dressed my arm, and found your handkerchief on it, made a story out of nothing, and set the gossips chattering. The women over yonder have nothing else to do, so a fine romance was built up, founded on the wounded arm, the little handkerchief, and the pretty chain, of which Haye caught a glimpse. Miss Lawrence must have bribed old Jack to tell her where I'd been, for I told no one, and stole off to-day so carefully that I defy them to track me here."

"Thank you for remembering that we did not wish to be disturbed; but I am sorry that you have been annoyed, and hope this handsome Helen will not come again. You think her handsome, don't you?" asked the girl, in the demure tone that she sometimes used with much effect.

"Yes; but she is not to my taste. I like spirit, character, and variety of expression in a face more than mere beauty of coloring or outline. One doesn't see faces like hers in one's dreams, or imagine it at one's fireside; it is a fine picture — not the image of the woman one would live and die for."

A soft color had risen to Ariel's cheek as she listened, wondering why those few words sounded so sweet to her. Southesk caught the fleeting emotion, and made the likeness perfect with a happy stroke or two. Pausing to survey his work with pleasure, he said low to himself —

"What more does it need?"

"Nothing — it is excellent."

The paper fluttered from his hand as a man's voice answered, and turning quickly, he saw March standing behind him. He knew who it was at once, for several times he had passed on the beach this roughly-dressed, stern-faced man, who came and went as if blind to the gaiety all about him. Now, the change in him would have greatly surprised his guest had not his interviews with Ariel prepared him for the discovery, and when March greeted him with the air and manner of a gentleman, he betrayed no astonishment, but, giving his name, repeated his desire to sketch the beauties of the island, and asked permission to do so. A satirical smile passed over March's grave face, as he glanced from the paper he had picked up to the bare cliffs below, but his tone was very courteous as he replied —

"I have no right to forbid any one to visit the island, though its solitude was the attraction that brought me here. But poets and painters are privileged; so come freely, and if your pen and pencil make it too famous for us we can emigrate to a more secluded spot, for we are only birds of passage."

"There shall be no need of that, I assure you, sir. Its solitude is as attractive to me as to yourself, and no word or act of mine shall destroy the charm." Southesk spoke eagerly, adding, with a longing glance at the paper which March still held: "I ventured to begin with the island's mistress, and, with your permission, I will finish it as you pronounce it good."

"It is excellent, and I shall be glad to bespeak a copy, for I've often tried to sketch my will-o'-the-wisp, but never succeeded. What magic did you use to keep her still so long?"

"This, father," and Ariel showed her gift, as she came to look over his shoulder, and smile and blush to see herself so carefully portrayed.

Southesk explained, and the conversation turning upon poetry, glided smoothly on till the deepening twilight warned the guest to go, and more than ever charmed and interested, he floated home-ward to find Miss Lawrence waiting for him on the beach, and to pass her with his coolest salutation.

From that day he led a double life — one gay and frivolous for all the world to see, the other sweet and secret as a lover's first romance. Hiring a room at a fisherman's cottage that stood in a lonely nook, and giving out that he was seized with a fit of inspi-ration, he secluded himself whenever he chose, without exciting comment or curiosity. Having purchased the old couple's silence regarding his movements, he came and went with perfect freedom, and passers-by surveyed with respectful interest the drawn curtains behind which the young poet was believed to be intent on songs and sonnets, while, in reality, he was living a sweeter poem than any he could write far away on the lighthouse tower, or hidden in the shadowy depths of Ariel's nest. Even Helen was deceived, for, knowing that hers were the keenest eyes upon him, he effectually blinded them for the time by slowly changing his former indiffer-ence to the gallant devotion which may mean much or little, yet which is always flattering to a woman, and doubly so to one who loves and waits for a return. Her society was more agreeable to him than that of the giddy girls and *blasé* men about him, and believing that the belle of several seasons could easily guard the heart that many had besieged, he freely enjoyed the intercourse which their summer sojourn facilitated, all unconscious of the hopes and fears that made those days the most eventful of her life.

Stern was right; the young man could not see Ariel without lov-ing her. For years, he had roamed about the world, heart-free; but his time came at last, and he surrendered without a struggle. For a few weeks he lived in an enchanted world, too happy to weigh consequences or dread disappointment. There was no cause for doubt or fear — no need to plead for love — because the artless girl gave him her heart as freely as a little child, and reading the language of his eyes, answered eloquently with her own. It was a poet's wooing; summer, romance, beauty, innocence and youth — all lent their charms, and nothing marred its delight. March watched and waited hopefully, well pleased at the success of his desire; and seeing in the young man the future guardian of his child, soon learned to love him for his own sake as well as hers. Stern was the only cloud in all this sunshine; he preserved a grim silence, and seemed to take no heed of what went on about him; but, could the cliffs have spoken, they might have told pathetic secrets of the lonely man who haunted them by night, like a despairing ghost; and the sea might have betrayed how many tears, bitter as its own billows, had been wrung from a strong heart that loved, yet knew that the passion never could be returned.

The mystery that seemed at first to surround them no longer troubled him, for a few words from March satisfied him that sorrow and misfortune made them seek solitude, and shun the scenes where they had suffered most. A prudent man would have asked more, but Southesk cared nothing for wealth or rank, and with the delicacy of a generous nature, feared to wound by questioning too closely. Ariel loved him; he had enough for all, and the present was too blissful to permit any doubt of the past — any fears for the future.

So the summer days rolled on, sunny and serene, as if tempests were unknown, and brought, at last, the hour when Southesk longed to claim Ariel for his own, and show the world the treasure he had found.

Full of this purpose, he went to his tryst one golden August afternoon, intent on seeing March first, that he might go to Ariel armed with her father's consent. But March was out upon the sea, where he often floated aimlessly for hours, and Southesk found no one but Stern, busily burnishing the great reflectors until they shone again.

"Where is Ariel?" was the young man's second question, though usually it was the first.

"Why ask me, when you know better than I where to find her," Stern answered harshly, as he frowned over the bright mirror that reflected both his own and the happy lover's face; and too light-hearted to resent a rude speech, Southesk went smiling away to find the girl, waiting for him in the chasm.

"What pretty piece of work is in hand, to-day, busy creature?" he said, as he threw himself down beside her with an air of supreme content.

"I'm stringing these for you, because you carry the others so constantly they will soon be worn out," she answered, busying herself with a redoubled assiduity, for something in his manner made her heart beat fast and her color vary. He saw it, and fearing to agitate her by abruptly uttering the ardent words that trembled on his lips, he said nothing for a moment, but leaning on his arm, looked at her with lover's eyes, till Ariel, finding silence more dangerous than speech, said hastily, as she glanced at a ring on the hand that was idly playing with the many-colored shells that strewed her lap:

"This is a curious old jewel; are those your initials on it?"

"No, my father's;" and he held it up for her to see.

"R. M., where is the S. for Southesk?" she asked, examining it with girlish curiosity.

"I shall have to tell you a little story all about myself in order to explain that. Do you care to hear it?"

"Yes, your stories are always pleasant; tell it, please."

"Then, you must know that I was born on the long voyage to India, and nearly died immediately after. The ship was wrecked, and my father and mother were lost; but, by some miracle, my faithful nurse and I were saved. Having no near relatives in the world, an old friend of my father's adopted me, reared me tenderly, and dying, left me his name and fortune."

"Philip Southesk is not your true name, then?"

"No; I took it at my good old friend's desire. But you shall choose which name you will bear, when you let me put a more precious ring than this on the dear little hand I came to ask you for. Will you marry Philip Southesk or Richard Marston, my Ariel?"

If she had leaped down into the chasm the act would not have amazed him more than the demonstration which followed these playful, yet tender words. A stifled exclamation broke from her, all the color died out of her face, in her eyes grief deepened to despair, and when he approached her she shrunk from him with a gesture of repulsion that cut him to the heart.

"What is it? Are you ill? How have I offended you? Tell me, my darling, and let me make my peace at any cost," he cried, bewildered by the sudden and entire change that had passed over her.

"No, no; it is impossible. You must not call me that. I must not listen to you. Go — go at once, and never come again. Oh, why did I not know this sooner?" and, covering up her face, she burst into a passion of tears.

"How could you help knowing that I loved you when I showed it so plainly — it seemed hardly necessary to put it into words. Why do you shrink from me with such abhorrence? Explain this strange change, Ariel. I have a right to ask it," he demanded distressfully.

"I can explain nothing till I have seen my father. Forgive me. This is harder for me to hear than it ever can be for you," she answered through her grief, and in her voice there was the tenderest regret, as well as the firmest resolution.

"You do not need your father to help you. Answer whether you love me, and that is all I ask. Speak, I conjure you." He took her hands and made her look at him. There was no room for doubt; one look assured him, for her heart spoke in her eyes before she answered, fervently as a woman, simply as a child:

"I love you more than I can ever tell."

"Then, why this grief and terror? What have I said to trouble you? Tell me that, also, and I am content."

He had drawn her toward him as the sweet confession left her lips, and was already smiling with the happiness it gave him; but Ariel banished both smile and joy by breaking from his hold, pale and steady as if tears had calmed and strengthened her, saying, in a tone that made his heart sink with an ominous foreboding of some unknown ill:

"I must not answer you without my father's permission. I have made a bitter mistake in loving you, and I must amend it if I can. Go now, and come again to-morrow; then I can speak and make all clear to you. No, do not tempt me with caresses; do not break my heart with reproaches, but obey me, and whatever comes between us, oh, remember that I shall love you while I live."

Vain were all his prayers and pleadings, questions and commands: some power more potent than love kept her firm through the suffering and sorrow of that hour. At last he yielded to her demand, and winning from her a promise to set his heart at rest early on the morrow, he tore himself away, distracted by a thousand vague doubts and dreads.

PART III

A SLEEPLESS NIGHT, an hour or two of restless pacing to and fro upon the beach, then the impatient lover was away upon his fateful errand, careless of observation now, and rowing as he had never rowed before. The rosy flush of early day shone over the island, making the grim rocks beautiful, and Southesk saw in it a propitious omen; but when he reached the lighthouse a sudden fear dashed his sanguine hopes, for it was empty. The door stood open — no fire burned upon the hearth, no step sounded on the stairs, no voice answered when he called, and the dead silence daunted him.

Rapidly searching every chamber, shouting each name, and imploring a reply, he hurried up and down like one distraught, till but a single hope remained to comfort him. Ariel might be waiting at the chasm, though she had bid him see her father first. Bounding over the cliffs, he reached the dearest spot the earth held for him, and looking down saw only desolation. The ladder was gone, the vines torn from the walls, the little tree lay prostrate; every green and lovely thing was crushed under the enormous stones that some ruthless hand had hurled upon them, and all the beauty of the rock was utterly destroyed as if a hurricane had swept over it.

"Great heavens! who has done this?"

"I did."

Stern spoke, and standing on the opposite side of the chasm, regarded Southesk with an expression of mingled exultation, hatred, and defiance, as if the emotions which had been so long restrained had found a vent at last.

"But why destroy what Ariel loved?" demanded the young man, involuntarily retreating a step from the fierce figure that confronted him.

"Because she has done with it, and no other shall enjoy what she has lost."

"Done with it," echoed Southesk, forgetting everything but the fear that oppressed him. "What do you mean? Where is she? For God's sake end this horrible suspense."

"She is gone, never to return," and as he answered Stern smiled a smile of bitter satisfaction in the blow he was dealing the man he hated.

"Where is March?"

"Gone with her."

"Where are they gone?"

"I will never tell you."

"When did they go, and why? Oh! answer me!"

"At dawn, and to shun you."

"But why let me come for weeks and then fly me as if I brought a curse with me?"

"Because you are what you are."

Questions and answers had been too rapidly exchanged to leave time for anything but intense amazement and anxiety. Stern's last words arrested Southesk's impetuous inquiries and he stood a moment trying to comprehend that enigmatical reply. Suddenly he found a clue, for in recalling his last interview with Ariel, he remembered that for the first time he had told her his father's name. The mystery was there — that intelligence, and not the avowal of his love, was the cause of her strange agitation, and some unknown act of the father's was now darkening the son's life. These thoughts flashed through his mind in the drawing of a breath, and with them came the recollection of Ariel's promise to answer him.

Lifting the head that had sunk upon his breast, as if this stroke fell heavily, he stretched his hands imploringly to Stern, exclaiming:

"Did she leave no explanation for me, no word of comfort, no farewell? Oh! be generous, and pity me; give me her message and I will go away, never to disturb you any more."

"She bade me tell you that she obeyed her father, but her heart was yours forever, and she left you this."

With a strong effort at self-control, Stern gave the message, and slowly drew from his breast a little parcel, which he flung across the chasm. It fell at Southesk's feet, and tearing it open a long, dark lock of hair coiled about his fingers with a soft caressing touch, reminding him so tenderly of his lost love, that for a moment he forgot his manhood, and covering up his face, cried in a broken voice:

"Oh! Ariel, come back to me — come back to me!"

"She will never come back to you; so cast yourself down among the ruins yonder, and lament the ending of your love dream, like a romantic boy, as you are."

The taunting speech, and the scornful laugh that followed it calmed Southesk better than the gentlest pity. Dashing away the drops he turned on Stern with a look that showed it was fortunate the chasm parted the two men, and answered in a tone of indomitable resolve:

"No, I shall not lament, but find and claim her as my own, even if I search the world till I am grey, and a thousand obstacles be between us. I leave the ruins and the tears to you, for I am rich in hope and Ariel's love."

Then they parted, Southesk full of the energy of youth, and a lover's faith in friendly fortune, sprang down the cliffs, and shot away across the glittering bay on his long search, but Stern, with despair for his sole companion, flung himself on the hard bosom of the rocks, struggling to accept the double desolation which came upon his life.

"An early row and an early ride without a moment's rest between. Why, Mr. Southesk, we shall not dare to call you *dolce far niente* any more," began Miss Lawrence, as she came rustling out upon the wide piazza, fresh from her morning toilette, to find Southesk preparing to mount his fleetest horse; but as he turned to bow silently the smile vanished from her lips, and a keen anxiety banished the gracious sweetness from her face.

"Good heavens, what has happened?" she cried, forgetting her self-betrayal in alarm at the haggard countenance she saw.

"I have lost a very precious treasure, and I am going to find it. Adieu;" and he was gone without another word.

Miss Lawrence was alone, for the gong had emptied halls and promenades of all but herself, and she had lingered to caress the handsome horse till its master came. Her eye followed the reckless rider until he vanished, and as it came back to the spot where she had caught that one glimpse of his altered face, it fell upon a little case of curiously-carved and scented Indian wood. She took it up, wondering that she had not seen it fall from his pocket as he mounted, for she knew it to be his, and opening it, found the key to his variable moods and frequent absences of late. The string of shells appeared first, and, examining it with a woman's scrutiny, she found letters carved on the inside of each. Ten rosy shells — ten delicate letters, making the name Ariel March. A folded paper came next, evidently a design for a miniature to form a locket for the pretty chain, for in the small oval, drawn with all a lover's skill, was a young girl's face, and underneath, in Southesk's hand, as if written for his eye alone, the words, "My Ariel." A long, dark lock of hair, and a little knot of dead flowers were all the case held beside.

"This is the mermaid old Jack told me of, this is the muse Southesk has been wooing, and this is the lost treasure he has gone to find."

As she spoke low to herself, Helen made a passionate gesture as if she would tear and trample on the relics of this secret love, but some hope or purpose checked her, and concealing the case, she turned to hide her trouble in solitude, thinking as she went:

"He will return for this, till then I must wait."

But Southesk did not return, for the lesser loss was forgotten in the greater, and he was wandering over land and sea, intent upon a fruitless quest. Summer passed, and Helen returned to town still hoping and waiting with a woman's patience for some tidings of the absentee.

Rumor gossiped much about the young poet — the eccentricities of genius — and prophesied an immortal work as the fruit of such varied and incessant travel.

But Helen knew the secret of his restlessness, and while she pitied his perpetual disappointment she rejoiced over it, sustaining herself with the belief that a time would come when he would weary of this vain search, and let her comfort him. It did come; for, late in the season, when winter gaieties were nearly over, Southesk returned to his old haunts, so changed that curiosity went hand in hand with sympathy.

He gave no reason for it but past illness; yet it was plain to see the malady of his mind. Listless, taciturn, and cold, with no trace of his former energy except a curiously vigilant expression of the eye and a stern folding of the lips, as if he was perpetually looking for something and perpetually meeting with disappointment. This was the change which had befallen the once gay and *debonair* Philip Southesk.

Helen Lawrence was among the first to hear of his return, and to welcome him, for, much to her surprise, he came to see her on the second day, drawn by the tender recollections of a past with which she was associated.

Full of the deepest joy at beholding him again, and the gentlest pity for his dejection, Helen had never been more charming than during that interview.

Eager to assure herself of the failure which his face betrayed, she soon inquired, with an air and accent of the friendliest interest:

"Was your search successful, Mr. Southesk? You left so suddenly, and have been so long away I hoped the treasure had been found, and that you had been busy putting that happy summer into song for us."

The color rose to Southesk's forehead, and fading left him paler than before, as he answered with a vain attempt at calmness.

"I shall never find the thing I lost, and never put that summer into song, for it was the saddest of my life;" then, as if anxious to change the direction of her thoughts, he said abruptly, "I am on another quest now, looking for a little case which I think I dropped the day I left you, but whether at the hotel or on the road I cannot tell. Did you hear anything of such a trifle being found?"

"No. Was it of much value to you?"

"Of infinite value now, for it contains the relics of a dear friend lately lost."

Helen had meant to keep what she had found, but his last words changed her purpose, for a thrill of hope shot through her heart, and, turning to a cabinet behind her, she put the case into his hand, saying in her softest tone:

"I heard nothing of it because I found it, believed it to be yours, and kept it sacred until you came to claim it, for I did not know where to find you."

Then, with a woman's tact, she left him to examine his recovered treasure, and, gliding to an inner room, she busied herself among her flowers till he rejoined her.

Sooner than she had dared to hope he came, with signs of past emotion on his face, but much of his old impetuosity of manner, as he pressed her hand, saying warmly:

"How can I thank you for this? Let me atone for my past insincerity by confessing the cause of it; you have found a part of my secret, let me add the rest. I need a confidant, will you be mine?"

"Gladly, if it will help or comfort you."

So, sitting side by side under the passion flowers, he told his story, and she listened with an interest that insensibly drew him on to further confidences than he had intended.

When he had described the parting, briefly yet very eloquently, for voice, eye, and gesture lent their magic, he added, in an altered tone, and with an expression of pathetic patience:

"There is no need to tell you how I searched for them, how often I thought myself upon their track, how often they eluded me, and how each disappointment strengthened my purpose to look till I succeeded, though I gave years to the task. A month ago I received this, and knew that my long search was ended."

He put a worn letter into her hand, and with a beating heart Helen read:

"Ariel is dead. Let her rest in peace, and do not pursue me any longer, unless you would drive me into my grave as you have driven her.

RALPH MARCH."

A little paper, more worn and stained than the other, dropped from the letter as Helen unfolded it, and seeing a woman's writing, she asked no permission, but read it eagerly, while Southesk sat with hidden face, unaware that he had given her that sacred farewell.

"Good-by, good-by," it said, in hastily-written letters, blurred by tears that had fallen long ago. "I have obeyed my father to the last, but my heart is yours for ever. Believe this, and pray, as I do, that you may meet again your Ariel."

A long silence followed, for the simple little note had touched Helen deeply, and while she could not but rejoice in the hope which this discovery gave her, she was too womanly a woman not to pity the poor child who had loved and lost the heart she coveted. As she gently laid the letter back in Southesk's hand, she asked, turning her full eyes on his,

"Are you sure that this is true?"

"I cannot doubt it, for I recognise the writing of both, and I know that neither would lend themselves to a fraud like this. No; I must accept the hard truth, and bear it as I can. My own heart confirms it, for every hope dies when I try to revive it, and the sad belief remains unshaken" was the spiritless reply.

Helen turned her face away, to hide the passionate joy that glowed in it; then, veiling her emotion with the tenderest sympathy, she gave herself up to the sweet task of comforting the bereaved lover. So well did she perform her part, so soothing did he find her friendly society, that he came often and lingered long, for with her, and her alone, he could talk of Ariel. She never checked him, but listened to the distasteful theme with unwearied patience, till, by insensible degrees and unperceived allurements, she weaned him from these mournful reminiscences, and woke a healthier interest in the present. With feminine skill she concealed her steadily-increasing love under an affectionate friendliness, which seemed a mute assurance that she cherished no hopes for herself, but knew that his heart was still Ariel's. This gave him confidence in her, while the new and gentle womanliness which now replaced her former pride, made her more attractive and more dangerous. Of course, the gossips gave them to one another, and Southesk felt aggrieved, fearing that he must relinquish the chief comfort of his solitary life. But Helen showed such supreme indifference to the clack of idle tongues, and met him with such unchanged composure, that he was reassured, and by remaining lost another point in this game of hearts.

With the summer came an unconquerable longing to revisit the island. Helen detected this wish before he uttered it, and, feeling that it would be vain to oppose it, quietly made her preparations for the sea-side, though otherwise she would have shunned it, fearing the old charm would revive and undo her work. Such visible satisfaction appeared in Southesk's face when she bade him good-by for a time, that she departed, sure that he would follow her to that summer haunt as to no other. He did follow, and resolving to have the trial over at once, during their first stroll upon the beach Helen said, in the tone of tranquil regard which she always used with him:

"I know you are longing to see your enchanted island again, yet, perhaps, dread to go alone. If it is so, let me go with you, for, much as I desire to see it, I shall never dare to trespass a second time."

Her voice trembled a little as she spoke — the first sign of emotion she had betrayed for a long time. Remembering that he had deceived her once, and recalling all he owed her since, Southesk felt that she had been very generous, very kind, and gratitude warmed his manner as he answered, turning toward the boats, which he had been eyeing wistfully:

"How well you understand me, Helen. Thank you for giving me courage to revisit the ruins of my little paradise. Come with me, for you are the only one who knows how much I have loved and lost. Shall we go now?"

"Blind and selfish, like a true man," thought Helen, with a pang, as she saw his eye kindle and the old elasticity return to his step as he went on before her. But she smiled and followed, as if glad to serve him, and a keen observer might have added, "patient and passionate, like a true woman."

Little was said between them as they made the breezy voyage. Once Southesk woke out of a long reverie, to say, pausing on his oars:

"A year to-day since I first saw Ariel."

"A year to-day since you told me that your fate was to come to you out of the sea," and Helen sighed involuntarily as she contrasted the man before her with the happy dreamer who smiled up at her that day.

"Yes, and it has come even to the hour when all was to be won or lost," he answered, little dreaming that the next hour was to verify the prophecy more perfectly than any in the past.

As they landed, he said, beseechingly:

"Wait for me at the lighthouse; I must visit the chasm alone, and I have no desire to encounter Stern, if I can help it."

"Why not?" asked Hélen, wondering at his tone.

"Because he loved her, and could not forgive me that I was more beloved than he."

"I can pity him," she said, below her breath, adding, with unusual tenderness of manner —

"Go, Philip; I know how to wait."

"And I thank you for it."

The look he gave her made her heart leap, for he had never bent such a one on her before, yet she feared that the memory of his lost love stirred and warmed him, not a dawning passion for herself, and would have wrung her hands in despair could she have known how utterly she was forgotten, as Southesk strode across the cliffs, almost as eagerly as if he knew that Ariel waited for him in her nest. It was empty; but something of its former beauty had been restored to it, for the stones were gone, green things were struggling up again, and the ladder was replaced.

"Poor Stern, he has repented of his frantic act, and tried to make the nest beautiful again as a memorial of her," thought Southesk; and descending, he threw himself down upon the newly-piled moss to dream his happy dream again, and fancy Ariel was there.

Well for him that he did not see the wrathful face that presently peered over the chasm's edge, as Stern watched him with the air of a man driven to desperation. The old hatred seemed to possess him with redoubled violence, and some new cause for detestation appeared to goad him with a hidden fear. More than once he sprang up and glanced anxiously behind him, as if he was not alone; more than once he laid his sinewy hands on a ponderous stone near by, as if tempted to hurl it down the chasm; and more than once he ground his teeth, like some savage creature who sees a stronger enemy approaching to deprive him of his prey.

The tide was coming in, the sky was over-cast, and a gale was rising; but though Southesk saw, heard and heeded nothing about him, Stern found hope in the gathering storm; for some evil spirit seemed to have been born of the tempest that raged within him, and to teach him how to make the elements his friends.

"Mr. Southesk."

Philip leaped to his feet as if a pistol had been fired at his ear, and saw Stern standing beside him with an air of sad humility, that surprised him more than the sight of his grey hair and haggard face. Pity banished resentment, and offering his hand, he said, with a generous oblivion of their parting words —

"Thank you for the change you have wrought here, and forgive me that I come back to see it once before I go away for ever. We both loved her; let us comfort one another."

A sudden color passed over Stern's swarthy face, he drew a long breath as he listened, and clenched one hand behind him as he put the other into Southesk's, answering in the same suppressed tone and with averted eyes —

"You know it, then, and try to submit as I do?"

Philip's lips were parted to reply, but no words followed, for a faint, far-off sound was heard, a woman's voice singing —

"Oh, come unto the yellow sands!"

Southesk turned pale, believing for an instant that Ariel's spirit came to welcome him; but the change in Stern's face, and the look of baffled rage and despair that played up in his eyes, betrayed him. Clutching his arm, the young man cried out, trembling with a sudden conviction —

"You have lied to me; she is not dead!"

What passed in Stern's heart during the second in which the two stood face to face, it would be impossible to tell, but with an effort that shook his strong body, he wrenched himself away and controlled his desperate desire to send his rival down the gulf. Some thought seemed to flash across him, calming the turbulence of his nature like a spell; and assuming the air of one defeated, he said slowly —

"I have lost, and I confess, I did lie to you, for March never sent the letter. I forged it, knowing that you would believe it if I added the note Ariel left for you a year ago. I could not give it to you then, but kept it with half the lock of hair. You followed them, but I followed you, and more than once thwarted you when you had nearly found them. As time passed, your persistence and her suffering began to soften March; I saw this, and tried to check you by the story of her death."

"Thank God I came, else I should never have recovered her. Give her up, Stern; she is mine, and I claim her."

Southesk turned to spring up the ladder, with no thought now but to reach Ariel; Stern arrested him, by saying with grim reluctance —

"You'll not find her, for she will not come here any more, but sit below by the basin where you saw her first. You can reach her by climbing down the steps I have made. Nay, if you doubt me, listen."

He did listen, and as the wind swept over the chasm, clearer and sweeter came the sound of that beloved voice. Southesk hesitated no longer, but swung himself recklessly downward, followed by Stern, whose black eyes glittered with a baleful light as they watched the agile figure going on before him. When they reached the basin, full to overflowing with the rising tide, they found the book her lover gave her and the little comb he knew so well, but no Ariel.

"She has gone into the cave for the weeds and shells you used to like. I'll wait for you; there is no need of me now."

Again Southesk listened; again he heard the voice, and followed it without a thought of fear; while Stern, seating himself on one of the fragments of rock cleared from the nest, leaned his head despondently upon his hand, as if his work was done.

The cave, worn by the ceaseless action of the waves at high tide, wound tortuously through the cliff to a lesser opening on the other side. Glancing rapidly into the damp nooks on either hand, Southesk hurried through this winding passage, which grew lower, narrower and darker toward the end, yet Ariel did not appear, and, standing still, he called her. Echo after echo caught up the word, and sent it whispering to and fro, but no human voice replied, though still the song came fitfully on the wind that blew coldly through the cave.

"She has ventured on to watch the waves boil in the Kelpie's Cauldron. Imprudent child, I'll punish her with a kiss," thought Southesk, smiling to himself, as he bent his tall head and groped his way toward the opening. He reached it, and looked down upon a mass of jagged rocks, over and among which the great billows dashed turbulent and dark with the approaching storm. Still no Ariel; and as he stood, more clearly than ever sounded her voice, above him now.

"She has not been here, but has climbed the Gull's Perch to watch the sky as we used to do. I have wasted all this time. Curse Stern's stupidity!"

In a fever of impatience he retraced his steps, stopping suddenly as his feet encountered a pool which had not been there when he came.

"Ah! the tide is nearer in than I thought. Thank heaven, my darling is not here!" he said, and hurried round a sharp corner, expecting to see the entrance before him. It was not there! A ponderous stone had been rolled against it, effectually closing it, and permitting only a faint ray of light to penetrate this living tomb. At first he stood panic-stricken at the horrible death that confronted him; then he thought of Stern, and in a paroxysm of wrath dashed himself against the rock, hoping to force it outward. But Stern's immense strength had served him well; and while his victim struggled vainly, wave after wave broke against the stone, wedging it more firmly still, yet leaving crevices enough for the bitter waters to flow in, bringing sure death to the doomed man, unless help came speedily from without. Not till the rapidly advancing tide drove him back did Southesk desist; then drenched, breathless and bruised he retreated to the lesser opening, with a faint hope of escape that way. Leaning over the Cauldron, he saw that the cliff sunk sheer down, and well he knew that a leap there would be fatal. As far up as he could see, the face of the cliff offered foothold for nothing but a bird. He shouted till the cave rang, but no answer came, though Ariel's song began again, for the same wind that brought her voice to him bore his away from her. There was no hope unless Stern relented, and being human, he might have, had he seen the dumb despair that seized his rival as he lay waiting for death, while far above him the woman he loved unconsciously chanted a song he had taught her, little dreaming it would be his dirge.

Left alone, Helen entered the lighthouse, and looked about her with renewed interest. The room was empty, but through a half-open door she saw a man sitting at a table covered with papers. He seemed to have been writing, but the pen had dropped from his hand, and leaning back in his deep chair he appeared to be asleep. His face was turned from her; yet when she advanced, he did not hear her, and when she spoke, he neither stirred nor answered. Something in the attitude and silence of the unknown man alarmed her; involuntarily she stepped forward and laid her hand on his. It was icy cold, and the face she saw had no life in it. Tranquil and reposeful, as if death had brought neither pain nor fear, he lay there with his dead hand on the paper, which some irresistible impulse had prompted him to write. Helen's eye fell on it, and despite the shock of this discovery, a single name made her seize the letter and devour its contents, though she trembled at the act and the solemn witness of it.

"To Philip Southesk:

"Feeling that my end is very near, and haunted by a presentiment that it will be sudden — perhaps solitary — I am prompted to write what I hope to say to you if time is given me to reach you. Thirty years ago your father was my dearest friend, but we loved the same beautiful woman and he won her, unfairly I believed and in the passionate disappointment of the moment I swore undying hatred to him and his. We parted and never met again, for the next tidings I received were of his death. I left the country and was an alien for years; thus I heard no rumor of your birth and never dreamed that you were Richard Marston's son till I learned it through Ariel. Her mother, like yours, died at her birth. I reared her with jealous care, for she was my all, and I loved her with the intensity of a lonely heart; you came; I found that you could make her happy. I knew that my life was drawing to a close; I trusted you and I gave her up. Then I learned your name, and at the cost of breaking my child's heart I kept my sinful oath. For a year you have followed me with unwearied patience; for a year Ariel's fading youth has pleaded silently, and for a year I have been struggling to harden myself against both. But love has conquered hate, and standing in the shadow of death I see the sin and folly of the past. I repent and retract my oath, I absolve Ariel from the promise I exacted, I freely give her to the man she loves, and may God deal with him as he deals with her.

RALPH MARCH, JUNE —— "

There the pen had fallen, blotting the date; but Helen saw only the last two lines and her hand closed tighter on the paper as if she felt that it would be impossible to give it up. Forgetting everything but that she held her rival's fate in her grasp, she yielded to the terrible temptation, and thrusting the paper into her bosom glided away like a guilty creature to find Southesk and prevent him from discovering that the girl lived, if it was not too late. He was nowhere to be seen, and crossing the rude bridge that spanned the chasm she ventured to call him as she passed, round the base of the tall rock named the Gull's Perch. A soft voice answered her, and turning a sharp angle she came upon a woman who sat alone looking down into the Kelpie's Cauldron that foamed far below. She had half risen with a startled look at the sound of a familiar name, and as Helen paused to recover herself, Ariel asked half imploringly, half imperiously,

"Why do you call Philip? Tell me, is he here?" But for the paper in her breast Helen would have answered no, and trusted all to chance; now, feeling sure that the girl would keep her promise more faithfully than her father had kept his oath, unless he absolved her from it, she answered:

"Yes, but I implore you to shun him. He thinks you dead; he has learned to love me, and is happy. Do not destroy my hope, and rob me of my hard-won prize, for you cannot reward him unless you break the solemn promise you have given."

Ariel covered up her face, as if confessing the hard truth, but love clamored to be heard, and, stretching her hands to Helen, she cried:

"I will not come between you; I will keep my word; but let me see him once, and I will ask no more. Where is he? I can steal a look at him unseen; then you may take him away for ever, if it must be so."

Trying to silence the upbraidings of her conscience, and thinking only of her purpose, Helen could not refuse this passionate prayer, and, pointing toward the chasm, she said anxiously:

"He went to the place you made so dear to him, but I do not see him now, nor does he answer when I call. Can he have fallen down that precipice?"

Ariel did not answer, for she was at the chasm's brink, looking into its gloom with eyes that no darkness could deceive. No one was there, and no sound answered the soft call that broke from her lips, but the dash of water far below. Glancing toward the basin, with a sudden recollection of the precious book left there, she saw, with wonder, that the stone where she had sat was gone, and that the cavern's mouth was closed. Stern's hat lay near her, and as her eye fell on it, a sudden horror shook her, for he had left her, meaning to return, yet had not come, and was nowhere to be seen.

"Have you seen Stern?" she asked, grasping Helen's arm, with a face of pale dismay.

"I saw him climbing the ladder, as if he was going to bind up his hands, which were bleeding. He looked wet and wild, and, as he did not see me, I did not speak. Why do you ask?"

"Because I fear he has shut Philip in the cave, where the rising tide will drown him. It is too horrible to believe; I must be sure."

Back she flew to the seat she had left, and flinging herself down on the edge of the sloping cliff, she called his name till she was hoarse and trembling with the effort. Once a faint noise seemed to answer, but the wind swept the sound away, and Helen vainly strained her ear to catch some syllable of the reply. Suddenly Ariel sprung up, with a cry:

"He is there! I see the flutter of his handkerchief! Help me, and we will save him."

She was gone as she spoke, and before Helen could divine her purpose or steady her own nerves, Ariel was back again, dragging the rope ladder, which she threw down, and began to tear up the plaid on which she had been sitting.

"It is too short, and even these strips will not make it long enough. What can I give to help?" cried Helen, glancing at the frail silks and muslins which composed her dress.

"You can give nothing, and there is not time to go for help. I shall lengthen it in this way."

Tying back the hair that blew about her face, and gathering the rope on her arm, Ariel slid over the edge of the cliff, and unstartled by Helen's cry of alarm, climbed with wary feet along a perilous path, where one mis-step would be her last. Half way down a ledge appeared where a tree had once grown; the pine was blasted and shattered now, but the roots held fast, and to these Ariel hung the ladder, with a stone fastened to the lower end to keep the wind from blowing it beyond the opening. Straight as a plummet it fell, and for a moment neither woman breathed; then a cry broke from both, for the ropes tightened, as if a hand tried the strength of that frail road. Another pause of terrible suspense, and out from the dark cave below came a man, who climbed swiftly upward, regardless of the gale that nearly tore the ladder from his hold, the hungry sea that wet him with its spray, the yielding roots that hardly bore his weight, or the wounded hands that marked his way with blood, for his eyes were fixed on Ariel, and on his face, white with the approach of a cruel death, shone an expression brighter than a smile, as he neared the brave girl who lent all her strength to save him, with one arm about the tree, the other clutching the ladder as if she defied all danger to herself.

Kneeling on the cliff above, Helen saw all this, and when South-esk stood upon the ledge, with Ariel gathered to the shelter of his arms, her heart turned traitor to her will, remorse made justice

"Out from the dark cave below came a man, who climbed swiftly upward."

possible, love longed to ennoble itself by sacrifice, and all that was true and tender in her nature pleaded for the rival who had earned happiness at such a cost. One sharp pang, one moment of utter despair, followed by utter self-forgetfulness, and Helen's temptation became a triumph that atoned for an hour's suffering and sin.

What went on below her she never knew, but when the lovers came to her, spent yet smiling, she gave the paper to Southesk, and laid her hand on Ariel's head with a gesture soft and solemn, as she said, wearing an expression that made her fine face strangely beautiful:

"You have won him and you deserve him; for you are nobler than I. Forgive me, Philip; and when you are happiest, remember that, though sorely tempted, I resisted, hoping to grow worthier to become your friend."

Even while she spoke he had caught the meaning of the paper, and Ariel guessed it from his face before she, too, read the words that set her free. But her tears of joy changed to tears of grief when Helen gently broke to her the sad fact of her father's death, trying to comfort her so tenderly that, by the blessed magic of sympathy, all bitterness was banished from her own sore heart. As they turned to leave that fateful cliff, Stern confronted them with an aspect that daunted even Southesk's courage. Calm with the desperate calmness of one who had staked his last throw and lost it, he eyed them steadily a moment; then with a gesture too sudden to be restrained, he snatched Ariel to him — kissed her passionately, put her from him, and springing to the edge of the cliff, turned on Southesk, saying in an accent of the intensest scorn, as he pointed downward to the whirlpool below —

"Coward! you dared not end your life when all seemed lost, but waited for a woman to save you. I will show you how a brave man dies." And as the last words left his lips he was gone.

Years have passed since then; Ariel has long been a happy wife; Philip's name has become a household word on many lips, and Helen's life has grown serenely cheerful, though still solitary. But so the legend runs: Stern yet haunts the island; for the light-house keepers tell of a wild and woeful phantom that wanders day and night among the cliffs and caverns by the sea. Sometimes they see it, in the strong glare of the lantern, leaning on the balcony, and looking out into the night, as if it watched and waited to see some ship come sailing by. Often those who visit the Kelpie's Cauldron are startled by glimpses of a dark, desperate face that seems to rise and mock them with weird scorn. But oftenest a shadowy shape is seen to flit into the chasm, wearing a look of human love and longing, as it vanishes in the soft gloom of Ariel's nest.

Taming a Tartar

CHAPTER I

DEAR MADEMOISELLE, I assure you it is an arrangement both profitable and agreeable to one, who, like you, desires change of occupation and scene, as well as support. Madame la Princesse is most affable, generous, and to those who please her, quite child-like in her affection."

"But, madame, am I fit for the place? Does it not need accomplishments and graces which I do not possess? There is a wide difference between being a teacher in a *Pensionnat pour Demoiselles* like this and the companion of a princess."

"Ah, hah, my dear, it is nothing. Let not the fear of rank disturb you; these Russians are but savages, and all their money, splendor, and the polish Paris gives them, do not suffice to change the barbarians. You are the superior in breeding as in intelligence, as you will soon discover; and for accomplishments, yours will bear the test anywhere. I grant you Russians have much talent for them, and acquire with marvelous ease, but taste they have not, nor the skill to use these weapons as we use them."

"The princess is an invalid, you say?"

"Yes; but she suffers little, is delicate and needs care, amusement, yet not excitement. You are to chat with her, to read, sing, strive to fill the place of confidante. She sees little society, and her wing of the hotel is quite removed from that of the prince, who is one of the lions just now."

"Is it of him they tell the strange tales of his princely generosity, his fearful temper, childish caprices, and splendid establishment?"

"In truth, yes; Paris is wild for him, as for some magnificent savage beast. Madame la Comtesse Millefleur declared that she never knew whether he would fall at her feet, or annihilate her, so impetuous were his moods. At one moment showing all the complaisance and elegance of a born Parisian, the next terrifying the beholders by some outburst of savage wrath, some betrayal of the Tartar blood that is in him. Ah! it is incredible how such things amaze one."

"Has the princess the same traits? If so, I fancy the situation of companion is not easy to fill."

"No, no, she is not of the same blood. She is a half-sister; her mother was a Frenchwoman; she was educated in France, and lived here till her marriage with Prince Tcherinski. She detests St. Petersburg, adores Paris, and hopes to keep her brother here till the spring, for the fearful climate of the north is death to her delicate lungs. She is a gay, simple, confiding person; a child still in many things, and since her widowhood entirely under the control of this brother, who loves her tenderly, yet is a tyrant to her as to all who approach him."

I smiled as my loquacious friend gave me these hints of my future master and mistress, but in spite of all drawbacks, I liked the prospect, and what would have deterred another, attracted me. I was alone in the world, fond of experiences and adventures, self-reliant and self-possessed; eager for change, and anxious to rub off the rust of five years' servitude in Madame Bayard's Pensionnat. This new occupation pleased me, and but for a slight fear of proving unequal to it, I should have at once accepted madame's proposition. She knew everyone, and through some friend had heard of the princess's wish to find an English lady as companion and teacher, for a whim had seized her to learn English. Madame knew

I intended to leave her, my health and spirits being worn by long and arduous duties, and she kindly interested herself to secure the place for me.

"Go then, dear mademoiselle, make a charming toilet and present yourself to the princess without delay, or you lose your opportunity. I have smoothed the way for you; your own address will do the rest, and in one sense, your fortune is made, if all goes well."

I obeyed madame, and when I was ready, took a critical survey of myself, trying to judge of the effect upon others. The long mirror showed me a slender, well-molded figure, and a pale face — not beautiful, but expressive, for the sharply cut, somewhat haughty features betrayed good blood, spirit and strength. Gray eyes, large and lustrous, under straight, dark brows; a firm mouth and chin, proud nose, wide brow, with waves of chestnut hair parted plainly back into heavy coils behind. Five years in Paris had taught me the art of dress, and a good salary permitted me to indulge my taste. Although simply made, I flattered myself that my promenade costume of silk and sable was *en règle*, as well as becoming, and with a smile at myself in the mirror I went my way, wondering if this new plan was to prove the welcome change so long desired.

As the carriage drove into the court-yard of the prince's hotel in the Champs Élysées, and a gorgeous *laquais* carried up my card, my heart beat a little faster than usual, and when I followed the servant in, I felt as if my old life ended suddenly, and one of strange interest had already begun.

The princess was not ready to receive me yet, and I was shown into a splendid *salon* to wait. My entrance was noiseless, and as I took a seat, my eyes fell on the half-drawn curtains which divided the room from another. Two persons were visible, but as neither saw me in the soft gloom of the apartment, I had an opportunity to look as long and curiously as I pleased. The whole scene was as unlike those usually found in a Parisian *salon* as can well be imagined.

Though three o'clock in the afternoon, it was evidently early morning with the gentleman stretched on the ottoman, reading a novel and smoking a Turkish chibouk — for his costume was that

of a Russian seigneur in *déshabillé*. A long Caucasian caftan of the
finest white sheepskin, a pair of loose black velvet trowsers, bound
round the waist by a rich shawl, and Kasan boots of crimson
leather, ornamented with golden embroidery on the instep, covered
a pair of feet which seemed disproportionately small compared to
the unusually tall, athletic figure of the man; so also did the head
with a red silk handkerchief bound over the thick black hair. The
costume suited the face; swarthy, black-eyed, scarlet-lipped, heavy-
browed and beardless, except a thick mustache; serfs wear beards,
but Russian nobles never. A strange face, for even in repose the
indescribable difference of race was visible; the contour of the head,
molding of the features, hue of hair and skin, even the attitude, all
betrayed a trace of the savage strength and spirit of one in whose
veins flowed the blood of men reared in tents, and born to lead
wild lives in a wild land.

This unexpected glance behind the scenes interested me much,
and I took note of everything within my ken. The book which the
slender brown hand held was evidently a French novel, but when
a lap-dog disturbed the reader, it was ordered off in Russian with
a sonorous oath, I suspect, and an impatient gesture. On a guéri-
don, or side-table, stood a velvet *porte-cigare*, a box of sweetmeats,
a bottle of Bordeaux, and a tall glass of cold tea, with a slice of
lemon floating in it. A musical instrument, something like a man-
dolin, lay near the ottoman, a piano stood open, with a sword and
helmet on it, and sitting in a corner, noiselessly making cigarettes,
was a half-grown boy, a serf I fancied, from his dress and the silent,
slavish way in which he watched his master.

The princess kept me waiting long, but I was not impatient, and
when I was summoned at last I could not resist a backward glance
at the brilliant figure I left behind me. The servant's voice had
roused him, and, rising to his elbow, he leaned forward to look,
with an expression of mingled curiosity and displeasure in the larg-
est, blackest eyes I ever met.

I found the princess, a pale, pretty little woman of not more than
twenty, buried in costly furs, though the temperature of her bou-
doir seemed tropical to me. Most gracious was my reception, and

at once all fear vanished, for she was as simple and wanting in dignity as any of my young pupils.

"Ah, Mademoiselle Varna, you come in good time to spare me from the necessity of accepting a lady whom I like not. She is excellent, but too grave; while you reassure me at once by that smile. Sit near me, and let us arrange the affair before my brother comes. You incline to give me your society, I infer from the good Bayard?"

"If Madame la Princesse accepts my services on trial for a time, I much desire to make the attempt, as my former duties have become irksome, and I have a great curiosity to see St. Petersburg."

"*Mon Dieu!* I trust it will be long before we return to that detestable climate. *Chère* mademoiselle, I entreat you to say nothing of this desire to my brother. He is mad to go back to his wolves, his ice and his barbarous delights; but I cling to Paris, for it is my life. In the spring it is inevitable, and I submit — but not now. If you come to me, I conjure you to aid me in delaying the return, and shall be forever grateful if you help to secure this reprieve for me."

So earnest and beseeching were her looks, her words, and so entirely did she seem to throw herself upon my sympathy and good-will, that I could not but be touched and won, in spite of my surprise. I assured her that I would do my best, but could not flatter myself that any advice of mine would influence the prince.

"You do not know him; but from what Bayard tells me of your skill in controlling wayward wills and hot tempers, I feel sure that you can influence Alexis. In confidence, I tell you what you will soon learn, if you remain: that though the best and tenderest of brothers, the prince is hard to manage, and one must tread cautiously in approaching him. His will is iron; and a decree once uttered is as irrevocable as the laws of the Medes and Persians. He has always claimed entire liberty for himself, entire obedience from every one about him; and my father's early death leaving him the head of our house, confirmed these tyrannical tendencies. To keep him in Paris is my earnest desire, and in order to do so I must seem indifferent, yet make his life so attractive that he will not command our departure."

"One would fancy life could not but be attractive to the prince in the gayest city of the world," I said, as the princess paused for breath.

"He cares little for the polished pleasures which delight a Parisian, and insists on bringing many of his favorite amusements with him. His caprices amuse the world, and are admired, but they annoy me much. At home he wears his Russian costume, orders the horrible dishes he loves, and makes the apartments unendurable with his samovar, chibouk and barbarous ornaments. Abroad he drives his droschky with the Ischvostchik in full St. Petersburg livery, and wears his uniform on all occasions. I say nothing, but I suffer."

It required a strong effort to repress a smile at the princess's pathetic lamentations and the martyr-like airs she assumed. She was infinitely amusing with her languid or vivacious words and attitudes; her girlish frankness and her feeble health interested me, and I resolved to stay even before she asked my decision.

I sat with her an hour, chatting of many things, and feeling more and more at ease as I read the shallow but amiable nature before me. All arrangements were made, and I was about taking my leave when the prince entered unannounced, and so quickly that I had not time to make my escape.

He had made his toilet since I saw him last, and I found it difficult to recognize the picturesque figure on the ottoman in the person who entered wearing the ordinary costume of a well-dressed gentleman. Even the face seemed changed, for a cold, haughty expression replaced the thoughtful look it had worn in repose. A smile softened it as he greeted his sister, but it vanished as he turned to me, with a slight inclination, when she whispered my name and errand, and while she explained he stood regarding me with a look that angered me. Not that it was insolent, but supremely masterful, as if those proud eyes were accustomed to command whomever they looked upon. It annoyed me, and I betrayed my annoyance by a rebellious glance, which made him lift his brows in surprise as a half smile passed over his lips. When his sister paused, he said, in the purest French, and with a slightly imperious accent:

"Mademoiselle is an Englishwoman?"

"My mother was English, my father of Russian parentage, although born in England."

I knew not by what title to address the questioner, so I simplified the matter by using none at all.

"Ah, you are half a Russian, then, and naturally desire to see your country?"

"Yes, I have long wished it," I began, but a soft cough from the princess reminded me that I must check my wish till it was safe to express it.

"We return soon, and it is well that you go willingly. Mademoiselle sets you a charming example, Nadja; I indulge the hope that you will follow it."

As he spoke the princess shot a quick glance at me, and answered, in a careless tone:

"I seldom disappoint your hopes, Alexis; but mademoiselle agrees with me that St. Petersburg at this season is unendurable."

"Has mademoiselle tried it?" was the quiet reply, as the prince fixed his keen eyes full upon me, as if suspecting a plot.

"Not yet, and I have no desire to do so — the report satisfies me," I answered, moving to go.

The prince shrugged his shoulders, touched his sister's cheek, bowed slightly, and left the room as suddenly as he had entered.

The princess chid me playfully for my *maladresse*, begged to see me on the morrow, and graciously dismissed me. As I waited in the great hall a moment for my carriage to drive round, I witnessed a little scene which made a curious impression on me. In a small ante-room, the door of which was ajar, stood the prince, drawing on his gloves, while the lad whom I had seen above was kneeling before him, fastening a pair of fur-lined overshoes. Something was amiss with one clasp, the prince seemed impatient, and after a sharp word in Russian, angrily lifted his foot with a gesture that sent the lad backward with painful violence. I involuntarily uttered an exclamation, the prince turned quickly, and our eyes met. Mine I know were full of indignation and disgust, for I resented the kick more than the poor lad, who, meekly gathering himself up, finished his task without a word, like one used to such rebukes.

The haughtiest surprise was visible in the face of the prince, but no shame; and as I moved away I heard a low laugh, as if my demonstration amused him.

"Laugh if you will, Monsieur le Prince, but remember all your servants are not serfs," I muttered, irefully, as I entered the carriage.

CHAPTER II

ALL WENT SMOOTHLY for a week or two, and I not only found my new home agreeable but altogether luxurious, for the princess had taken a fancy to me and desired to secure me by every means in her power, as she confided to Madame Bayard. I had been in a treadmill so long that any change would have been pleasant, but this life was as charming as anything but entire freedom could be. The very caprices of the princess were agreeable, for they varied what otherwise might have been somewhat monotonous, and her perfect simplicity and frankness soon did away with any shyness of mine. As madame said, rank was nothing after all, and in this case princess was but a name, for many an untitled Parisienne led a gayer and more splendid life than Nadja Tcherinski, shut up in her apartments and dependent upon those about her for happiness. Being younger than myself, and one of the clinging, confiding women who must lean on some one, I soon felt that protective fondness which one cannot help feeling for the weak, the sick, and the unhappy. We read English, embroidered, sung, talked, and drove out together, for the princess received little company and seldom joined the revels which went on in the other wing of the hotel.

The prince came daily to visit his sister, and she always exerted herself to make these brief interviews as agreeable as possible. I was pressed into the service, and sung, played, or talked as the princess signified — finding that, like most Russians of good birth, the prince was very accomplished, particularly in languages and music. But in spite of these gifts and the increasing affability of his manners toward myself, I always felt that under all the French polish was hidden the Tartar wildness, and often saw the savage in his eye while his lips were smiling blandly. I did not like him, but my vanity was gratified by the daily assurances of the princess that I possessed and exerted an unconscious influence over him. It was interesting to match him, and soon exciting to try my will against his in covert ways. I did not fear him as his sister did, because over me he had no control, and being of as proud a spirit as himself, I paid him only the respect due to his rank, not as an inferior, but an equal, for my family was good, and he lacked the real princeliness of nature which commands the reverence of the highest. I think he felt this instinctively, and it angered him; but he betrayed nothing of it in words, and was coolly courteous to the incomprehensible *dame-de-compagnie* of his sister.

My apartments were near the princess's, but I never went to her till summoned, as her hours of rising were uncertain. As I sat one day awaiting the call of Claudine, her maid came to me looking pale and terrified.

"Madame la Princesse waits, mademoiselle, and begs you will pardon this long delay."

"What agitates you?" I asked, for the girl glanced nervously over her shoulder as she spoke, and seemed eager, yet afraid to speak.

"Ah, mademoiselle, the prince has been with her, and so afflicted her, it desolates me to behold her. He is quite mad at times, I think, and terrifies us by his violence. Do not breathe to any one this that I say, and comfort madame if it is possible," and with her finger on her lips the girl hurried away.

I found the princess in tears, but the moment I appeared she dropped her handkerchief to exclaim with a gesture of despair: "We are lost! We are lost! Alexis is bent on returning to Russia and taking me to my death. *Chère* Sybil, what is to be done?"

"Refuse to go, and assert at once your freedom; it is a case which warrants such decision," was my revolutionary advice, though I well knew the princess would as soon think of firing the Tuileries as opposing her brother.

"It is impossible, I am dependent on him, he never would forgive such an act, and I should repent it to my last hour. No, my hope is in you, for you have eloquence, you see my feeble state, and you can plead for me as I cannot plead for myself."

"Dear madame, you deceive yourself. I have no eloquence, no power, and it is scarcely for me to come between you and the prince. I will do my best, but it will be in vain, I think."

"No, you do not fear him, he knows that, and it gives you power; you can talk well, can move and convince; I often see this when you read and converse with him, and I know that he would listen. Ah, for my sake make the attempt, and save me from that dreadful place!" cried the princess imploringly.

"Well, madame, tell me what passed, that I may know how to conduct the matter. Is a time for departure fixed?"

"No, thank heaven; if it were I should despair, for he would never revoke his orders. Something has annoyed him; I fancy a certain lady frowns upon him; but be that as it may, he is eager to be gone, and desired me to prepare to leave Paris. I implored, I wept, I reproached, and caressed, but nothing moved him, and he left me with the look which forebodes a storm."

"May I venture to ask why the prince does not return alone, and permit you to join him in the spring?"

"Because when my poor Feodor died he gave me into my brother's care, and Alexis swore to guard me as his life. I am so frail, so helpless, I need a faithful protector, and but for his fearful temper I should desire no better one than my brother. I owe everything to him, and would gladly obey even in this matter but for my health."

"Surely he thinks of that? He will not endanger your life for a selfish wish?"

"He thinks me fanciful, unreasonably fearful, and that I make this an excuse to have my own way. He is never ill, and knows nothing of my suffering, for I do not annoy him with complaints."

"Do you not think, madame, that if we could once convince him of the reality of the danger he would relent?"

"Perhaps; but how convince him? He will listen to no one."

"Permit me to prove that. If you will allow me to leave you for an hour I fancy I can find a way to convince and touch the prince."

The princess embraced me cordially, bade me go at once, and return soon, to satisfy her curiosity. Leaving her to rest and wonder, I went quietly away to the celebrated physician who at intervals visited the princess, and stating the case to him, begged for a written opinion which, coming from him, would, I knew, have weight with the prince. Dr. Segarde at once complied, and strongly urged the necessity of keeping the princess in Paris some months longer. Armed with this, I hastened back, hopeful and gay.

The day was fine, and wishing to keep my errand private, I had not used the carriage placed at my disposal. As I crossed one of the long corridors, on my way to the princess, I was arrested by howls of pain and the sharp crack of a whip, proceeding from an apartment near by. I paused involuntarily, longing yet fearing to enter and defend poor Mouche, for I recognized his voice. As I stood, the door swung open and the great hound sprang out, to cower behind me, with an imploring look in his almost human eyes. The prince followed, whip in hand, evidently in one of the fits of passion which terrified the household. I had seen many demonstrations of wrath, but never anything like that, for he seemed literally beside himself. Pale as death, with eyes full of savage fire, teeth set, and hair bristling like that of an enraged animal, he stood fiercely glaring at me. My heart fluttered for a moment, then was steady, and feeling no fear, I lifted my eyes to his, freely showing the pity I felt for such utter want of self-control.

It irritated him past endurance, and pointing to the dog, he said, in a sharp, low voice, with a gesture of command:

"Go on, mademoiselle, and leave Mouche to his fate."

"But what has the poor beast done to merit such brutal punishment?" I asked, coolly, remaining where I was.

"It is not for you to ask, but to obey," was the half-breathless answer, for a word of opposition increased his fury.

"Pardon; Mouche takes refuge with me; I cannot betray him to his enemy."

The words were still on my lips, when, with a step, the prince reached me, and towering above me like the incarnation of wrath, cried fiercely, as he lifted his hand menacingly:

"If you thwart me it will be at your peril!"

I saw he was on the point of losing all control of himself, and seizing the upraised arm, I looked him in the eye, saying steadily:

"Monsieur le Prince forgets that in France it is dastardly to strike a woman. Do not disgrace yourself by any Russian brutality."

The whip dropped from his hand, his arm fell, and turning suddenly, he dashed into the room behind him. I was about to make good my retreat, when a strange sound made me glance into the room. The prince had flung himself into a chair, and sat there actually choking with the violence of his passion. His face was purple, his lips pale, and his eyes fixed, as he struggled to unclasp the great sable-lined cloak he wore. As he then looked I was afraid he would have a fit, and never stopping for a second thought, I hurried to him, undid the cloak, loosened his collar, and filling a glass from the *carafe* on the sideboard, held it to his lips. He drank mechanically, sat motionless a moment, then drew a long breath, shivered as if recovering from a swoon, and glanced about him till his eye fell on me. It kindled again, and passing his hand over his forehead as if to collect himself, he said abruptly:

"Why are you here?"

"Because you needed help, and there was no one else to give it," I answered, refilling the glass, and offering it again, for his lips seemed dry.

He took it silently, and as he emptied it at a draught his eye glanced from the whip to me, and a scarlet flush rose to his forehead.

"Did I strike you?" he whispered, with a shame-stricken face.

"If you had we should not have been here."

"And why?" he asked, in quick surprise.

"I think I should have killed you, or myself, after such degradation. Unwomanly, perhaps, but I have a man's sense of honor."

It was an odd speech, but it rose to my lips, and I uttered it impulsively, for my spirit was roused by the insult. It served me better than tears or reproaches, for his eye fell after a furtive glance, in which admiration, shame and pride contended, and forcing a smile, he said, as if to hide his discomposure:

"I have insulted you; if you demand satisfaction I will give it, mademoiselle."

"I do," I said, promptly.

He looked curious, but seemed glad of anything which should divert his thoughts from himself, for with a bow and a half smile, he said quickly:

"Will mademoiselle name the reparation I shall make her? Is it to be pistols or swords?"

"It is pardon for poor Mouche.

His black brow lowered, and the thunderbolt veins on his forehead darkened again with the angry blood, not yet restored to quietude. It cost him an effort to say gravely:

"He has offended me, and cannot be pardoned yet; ask anything for yourself, mademoiselle."

I was bent on having my own way, and making him submit as a penance for his unwomanly menace. Once conquer his will, in no matter how slight a degree, and I had gained a power possessed by no other person. I liked the trial, and would not yield one jot of the advantage I had gained; so I answered, with a smile I had never worn to him before:

"Monsieur le Prince has given his word to grant me satisfaction; surely he will not break it, whatever atonement I demand! Ah, pardon Mouche, and I forget the rest."

I had fine eyes, and knew how to use them; as I spoke I fixed them on the prince with an expression half-imploring, half-commanding, and saw in his face a wish to yield, but pride would not permit it.

"Mademoiselle, I ordered the dog to follow me; he refused, and for that I would have punished him. If I relent before the chastisement is finished I lose my power over him, and the offense will be repeated. Is it not possible to satisfy you without ruining Mouche?"

"Permit one question before I reply. Did you give yourself the trouble of discovering the cause of the dog's unusual disobedience before the whip was used?"

"No; it is enough for me that the brute refused to follow. What cause could there have been for his rebelling?"

"Call him and it will appear."

The prince ordered in the dog; but in vain; Mouche crouched in the corridor with a forlorn air, and answered only by a whine. His master was about to go to him angrily, when, to prevent another scene, I called, and at once the dog came limping to my feet. Stooping, I lifted one paw, and showed the prince a deep and swollen wound, which explained the poor brute's unwillingness to follow his master on the long daily drive. I was surprised at the way in which the prince received the rebuke; I expected a laugh, a careless or a haughty speech, but like a boy he put his arm about the hound, saying almost tenderly:

"Pardon, pardon, my poor Mouche! Who has hurt thee so cruelly? Forgive the whip; thou shalt never feel it again."

Like a noble brute as he was, Mouche felt the change, understood, forgave, and returned to his allegiance at once, lifting himself to lick his master's hand and wag his tail in token of affection. It was a pretty little scene, for the prince laid his face on the smooth head of the dog, and half-whispered his regrets, exactly as a generous-hearted lad would have done to the favorite whom he had wronged in anger. I was glad to see it, childish as it was, for it satisfied me that this household tyrant had a heart, and well pleased with the ending of this stormy interview, I stole noiselessly away, carrying the broken whip with me as a trophy of my victory.

To the princess I said nothing of all this, but cheered her with the doctor's note and somewhat rash prophecies of its success. The prince seldom failed to come morning and evening to inquire for his sister, and as the time drew near for the latter visit we both grew anxious. At the desire of the princess I placed myself at the piano, hoping that "music might soothe the savage breast," and artfully prepare the way for the appeal. One of the prince's whims was to have rooms all over the hotel and one never knew in which he might be. That where I had first seen him was near the suite of the princess, and he often stepped quietly in when we least expected him. This habit annoyed his sister, but she never betrayed it, and always welcomed him, no matter how inopportune his visit might be. As I sat playing I saw the curtains that hung before the door softly drawn aside, and expected the prince to enter, but they fell again and no one appeared. I said nothing, but thundered out the Russian national airs with my utmost skill, till the soft scent of flowers and a touch on my arm made me glance down, to see Mouche holding in his mouth a magnificent bouquet, to which was attached a card bearing my name.

I was pleased, yet not quite satisfied, for in this Frenchy little performance I fancied I saw the prince's desire to spare himself any further humiliation. I did not expect it, but I did wish he had asked pardon of me as well as of the dog, and when among the flowers I found a bracelet shaped like a coiled up golden whip with a jeweled handle, I would have none of it, and giving it to Mouche, bid him take it to his master. The docile creature gravely retired, but not before I had discovered that the wounded foot was carefully bound up, that he wore a new silver collar, and had the air of a dog who had been petted to his heart's content.

The princess from her distant couch had observed but not understood the little pantomime, and begged to be enlightened. I told the story, and was amused at the impression it made upon her, for when I paused she clasped her hands, exclaiming, theatrically:

"*Mon Dieu*, that any one should dare face Alexis in one of his furies! And you had no fear? you opposed him? made him spare Mouche and ask pardon? It is incredible!"

"But I could not see the poor beast half killed, and I never dreamed of harm to myself. Of that there could be no danger, for I am a woman, and the prince a gentleman," I said, curious to know how that part of the story would affect the princess.

"Ah, my dear, those who own serfs see in childhood so much cruelty, they lose that horror of it which we feel. Alexis has seen many women beaten when a boy, and though he forbids it now, the thing does not shock him as it should. When in these mad fits he knows not what he does; he killed a man once, a servant, who angered him, struck him dead with a blow. He suffered much remorse, and for a long time was an angel; but the wild blood cannot be controlled, and he is the victim of his passion. It was like him to send the flowers, but it will mortally offend him that you refuse the bracelet. He always consoles me with some bijou after he has made me weep, and I accept it, for it relieves and calms him."

"Does he not express contrition in words?"

"Never! he is too proud for that. No one dares demand such humiliation, and since he was not taught to ask pardon when a child, one cannot expect to teach the lesson now. I fear he will not come to-night; what think you, Sybil?"

"I think he will not come, but what matter? Our plan can be executed at any time. Delay is what we wish, and this affair may cause him to forget the other."

"Ah, if it would, I should bless Mouche almost as fervently as when he saved Alexis from the wolves."

"Does the prince owe his life to the dog?"

"In truth he does, for in one of his bear hunts at home he lost his way, was beset by the ferocious beasts, and but for the gallant dog would never have been saved. He loves him tenderly, and — "

"Breaks whips over the brave creature's back," I added, rudely enough, quite forgetting etiquette in my indignation.

The princess laughed, saying, with a shrug:

"You English are such stern judges."

CHAPTER III

I WAS INTENSELY CURIOUS to see how the prince would behave when we met. Politeness is such a national trait in France, where the poorest workman lifts his cap in passing a lady, to the Emperor, who returns the salute of his shabbiest subject, that one soon learns to expect the little courtesies of daily life so scrupulously and gracefully paid by all classes, and to miss them if they are wanting. When he chose, the prince was a perfect Frenchman in this respect, but at times nothing could be more insolently haughty, or entirely oblivious of common civility. Hitherto I had had no personal experience of this, but had observed it toward others, and very unnecessarily angered myself about it. My turn came now; for when he entered his sister's apartment next day, he affected entire unconsciousness of my presence. Not a look, word, or gesture was vouchsafed me, but, half turning his back, he chatted with the princess in an unusually gay and affectionate manner.

After the first indignant impulse to leave the room had passed, I became cool enough to see and enjoy the ludicrous side of the affair. I could not help wondering if it was done for effect, but for the first time since I came I saw the prince in his uniform. I would not look openly, though I longed to do so, for covert glances, as I busied myself with my embroidery, gave me glimpses of a splendid blending of scarlet, white and gold. It would have been impossible for the prince not to have known that this brilliant costume was excessively becoming, and not to have felt a very natural desire to display his handsome figure to advantage. More than once he crossed the room to look from the window, as if impatient for the droschky, then sat himself down at the piano and played stormily for five minutes, marched back to the princess's sofa and teased Bijou the poodle, ending at length by standing erect on the rug and facing the enemy.

Finding I bore my disgrace with equanimity, he was possessed to play the master, and show his displeasure in words as well as by silence. Turning to his sister, he said, in the tone of one who does not deign to issue commands to inferiors:

"You were enjoying some book as I entered, Nadja; desire Mademoiselle Varna to continue — I go in a moment."

"*Ma chère*, oblige me by finishing the chapter," said the princess, with a significant glance, and I obeyed.

We were reading George Sand's *Consuelo*, or rather the sequel of that wonderful book, and had reached the scenes in which Frederick the Great torments the prima donna before sending her to prison, because she will not submit to his whims. I liked my task, and read with spirit, hoping the prince would enjoy the lesson as much as I did. By skillfully cutting paragraphs here and there, I managed to get in the most apposite and striking of Consuelo's brave and sensible remarks, as well as the tyrant's unjust and ungenerous commands. The prince stood with his eyes fixed upon me. I felt, rather than saw this, for I never lifted my own, but permitted a smile to appear when Frederick threatened her with his cane. The princess speedily forgot everything but the romance, and when I paused, exclaimed, with a laugh:

"Ah, you enjoy that much, Sybil, for, like Consuelo, you would have defied the Great Fritz himself."

"That I would, in spite of a dozen Spondous. Royalty and rank give no one a right to oppress others. A tyrant — even a crowned one — is the most despicable of creatures," I answered, warmly.

"But you will allow that Porporina was very cold and coy, and altogether provoking, in spite of her genius and virtue," said the princess, avoiding the word "tyrant," as the subjects of the czar have a tendency to do.

"She was right, for the humblest mortals should possess their liberty and preserve it at all costs. Golden chains are often heavier than iron ones: is it not so, Mouche?" I asked of the dog, who lay at my feet, vainly trying to rid himself of the new collar which annoyed him.

A sharp "Here, sir!" made him spring to his master, who ordered him to lie down, and put one foot on him to keep him, as he showed signs of deserting again. The prince looked ireful, his black eyes were kindling, and some imperious speech was trembling on his lips, when Claudine entered with the *mal-apropos* question.

"Does Madame la Princesse desire that I begin to make preparations for the journey?"

"Not yet. Go; I will give orders when it is time," replied the princess, giving me a glance, which said, "We must speak now."

"What journey?" demanded the prince, as Claudine vanished precipitately.

"That for which you commanded me to prepare," returned his sister, with a heavy sigh.

"That is well. You consent, then, without more useless delay?" and the prince's face cleared as he spoke.

"If you still desire it, after reading this, I shall submit, Alexis," and giving him the note, his sister waited, with nervous anxiety, for his decision.

As he read I watched him, and saw real concern, surprise, and regret in his face, but when he looked up, it was to ask:

"When did Dr. Segarde give you this, and wherefore?"

"You shall know all, my brother. Mademoiselle sees my sufferings, pities my unhappiness, and is convinced that it is no whim of mine which makes me dread this return. I implore her to say this to you, to plead for me, because, with all your love, you cannot know my state as she does. To this prayer of mine she listens, but with a modesty as great as her goodness, she fears that you may think her officious, over-bold, or blinded by regard for me. Therefore she wisely asks for Segarde's opinion, sure that it will touch and influence you. Do not destroy her good opinion, nor disappoint thy Nadja!"

The prince *was* touched, but found it hard to yield, and said, slowly, as he refolded the note, with a glance at me of annoyance not anger:

"So you plot and intrigue against me, ladies! But I have said we shall go, and I never revoke a decree."

"Go!" cried the princess, in a tone of despair.

"Yes, it is inevitable," was the answer, as the prince turned toward the fire, as if to escape importunities and reproaches.

"But when, Alexis — when? Give me still a few weeks of grace!" implored his sister, approaching him in much agitation.

"I give thee till April," replied the prince, in an altered tone.

"But that is spring, the time I pray for! Do you, then, grant my prayer?" exclaimed the princess, pausing in amazement.

"I said we must go, but not *when;* now I fix a time, and give thee yet some weeks of grace. Didst thou think I loved my own pleasure more than thy life, my sister?"

As he turned, with a smile of tender reproach, the princess uttered a cry of joy and threw herself into his arms in a paroxysm of gratitude, delight and affection. I never imagined that the prince could unbend so beautifully and entirely; but as I watched him caress and reassure the frail creature who clung to him, I was surprised to find what a hearty admiration suddenly sprung up within me for "the barbarian," as I often called him to myself. I enjoyed the pretty tableau a moment, and was quietly gliding away, lest I should be *de trop*, when the princess arrested me by exclaiming, as she leaned on her brother's arm, showing a face rosy with satisfaction:

[*213*]

"*Chère* Sybil, come and thank him for this kindness; you know how ardently I desired the boon, and you must help me to express my gratitude."

"In what language shall I thank Monsieur le Prince for prolonging his sister's life? Your tears, madame, are more eloquent than any words of mine," I replied, veiling the reproach under a tone of respectful meekness.

"She is too proud, this English Consuelo; she will not stoop to confess an obligation even to Alexis Demidoff."

He spoke in a half-playful, half-petulant tone, and hesitated over the last words, as if he would have said "a prince." The haughtiness was quite gone, and something in his expression, attitude and tone touched me. The sacrifice had cost him something, and a little commendation would not hurt him, vain and selfish though he might be. I was grateful for the poor princess's sake, and I did not hesitate to show it, saying with my most cordial smile, and doubtless some of the satisfaction I could not but feel visible in my face:

"I am not too proud to thank you sincerely for this favor to Madame la Princesse, nor to ask pardon for anything by which I may have offended you."

A gratified smile rewarded me as he said, with an air of surprise:

"And yet, mademoiselle desires much to see St. Petersburg?"

"I do, but I can wait, remembering that it is more blessed to give than to receive."

A low bow was the only reply he made, and with a silent caress to his sister he left the room.

"You have not yet seen the droschky; from the window of the ante-room the courtyard is visible; go, mademoiselle, and get a glimpse of St. Petersburg," said the princess, returning to her sofa, weary with the scene.

I went, and looking down, saw the most picturesque equipage I had ever seen. The elegant, coquettish droschky with a pair of splendid black Ukraine horses, harnessed in the Russian fashion, with a network of purple leather profusely ornamented with silver, stood before the grand entrance, and on the seat sat a handsome young man in full Ischvostchik costume. His caftan of fine cloth was slashed at the sides with embroidery; his hat had a velvet band, a silver buckle, and a bunch of rosy ribbons in it; a white-laced neck-cloth, buckskin gloves, hair and beard in perfect order; a brilliant sash and a crimson silk shirt. As I stood wondering if he was a serf, the prince appeared, wrapped in the long gray capote, lined with scarlet, which all military Russians wear, and the brilliant helmet surmounted by a flowing white plume. As he seated himself among the costly furs he glanced up at his sister's windows, where she sometimes stood to see him. His quick eye recognized me, and to my surprise he waved his hand with a gracious smile as the fiery horses whirled him away.

That smile haunted me curiously all day, and more than once I glanced into the courtyard, hoping to see the picturesque droschky again, for, though one cannot live long in Paris without seeing nearly every costume under the sun, and accustomed as I was to such sights, there was something peculiarly charming to me in the martial figure, the brilliant equipage and the wild black horses, as full of untamed grace and power as if but just brought from the steppes of Tartary.

There was a dinner party in the evening, and, anxious to gratify her brother, the princess went down. Usually I enjoyed these free hours, and was never at a loss for occupation or amusement, but on this evening I could settle to nothing till I resolved to indulge an odd whim which possessed me. Arranging palette and brushes, I was soon absorbed in reproducing on a small canvas a likeness of the droschky and its owner. Hour after hour slipped by as the little picture grew, and horses, vehicle, driver and master took shape and color under my touch. I spent much time on the principal figure, but left the face till the last. All was carefully copied from memory, the white tunic, golden cuirass, massive epaulets, and silver sash; the splendid casque with its plume, the gray cloak, and the scarlet trowsers, half-hidden by the high boots of polished leather. At the boots I paused, trying to remember something.

"Did he wear spurs?" I said, half audibly, as I leaned back to survey my work complacently.

"Decidedly yes, mademoiselle," replied a voice, and there stood the prince with a wicked smile on his lips.

I seldom lose my self-possession, and after an involuntary start, was quite myself, though much annoyed at being discovered. Instead of hiding the picture or sitting dumb with embarrassment, I held it up, saying tranquilly:

"Is it not creditable to so bad an artist? I was in doubt about the spurs, but now I can soon finish."

"The horses are wonderful, and the furs perfect. Ivan is too handsome, and this countenance may be said to lack expression."

He pointed to the blank spot where his own face should have been, and eyed me with most exasperating intelligence. But I concealed my chagrin under an innocent air, and answered simply:

"Yes; I wait to find a portrait of the czar before I finish this addition to my little gallery of kings and queens."

"The czar!" ejaculated the prince, with such an astonished expression that I could not restrain a smile, as I touched up the handsome Ivan's beard.

"I have an admiration for the droschky, and that it may be quite complete, I boldly add the czar. It always pleased me to read how freely and fearlessly he rides among his people, unattended, in the gray cloak and helmet."

The prince gave me an odd look, crossed the room, and returning, laid before me an enameled casket, on the lid of which was a portrait of a stout, light-haired, somewhat ordinary, elderly gentleman, saying in a tone which betrayed some pique and much amusement:

"Mademoiselle need not wait to finish her work: behold the czar!"

I was strongly tempted to laugh, and own the truth, but something in the prince's manner restrained me, and after gravely regarding the portrait a moment, I began to copy it. My hand was not steady nor my eye clear, but I recklessly daubed on till the prince, who had stood watching me, said suddenly in a very mild tone:

"I flatter myself that there was some mistake last evening; either Mouche failed to do his errand, or the design of the trinket displeased you. I have endeavored to suit mademoiselle's taste better, and this time I offer it myself."

A white-gloved hand holding an open jewel-case which con-

tained a glittering ring came before my eyes, and I could not retreat. Being stubborn by nature, and ruffled by what had just
passed, as well as bent on having my own way in the matter, I
instantly decided to refuse all gifts. Retreating slightly from the
offering, I pointed to the flowers on the table near me, and said,
with an air of grave decision:

"Monsieur le Prince must permit me to decline. I have already
received all that it is possible to accept."

"Nay, examine the trifle, mademoiselle, and relent. Why will
you not oblige me and be friends, like Mouche?" he said, earnestly.

That allusion to the dog nettled me, and I replied, coldly turning
from the importunate hand.

"It was not the silver collar which consoled poor Mouche for the
blows. Like him I can forgive, but I cannot so soon forget."

The dainty case closed with a sharp snap, and flinging it on to a
table as he passed, the prince left the room without a word.

I was a little frightened at what I had done for a moment, but
soon recovered my courage, resolving that since he had made it a
test which should yield, *I* would not be the one to do it, for I had
right on my side. Nor would I be appeased till he had made the
amende honorable to me as to the dog. I laughed at the foolish affair,
yet could not entirely banish a feeling of anger at the first violence
and at the lordly way in which he tried to atone for the insult.

"Let us wait and see how the sultan carries himself to-morrow,"
I said; "if he become tyrannical, I am free to go, thank heaven;
otherwise it is interesting to watch the handsome savage chafe and
fret behind the bars of civilized society."

And gathering up my work, I retired to my room to replace the
czar's face with that of the prince.

CHAPTER IV

"*CHÈRE AMIE*, you remember I told you that Alexis always gave
me some trifle after he had made me weep; behold what a charming

gift I find upon my table to-day!" cried the princess, as I joined her next morning.

She held up her slender hand, displaying the ring I had left behind me the night before. I had had but a glimpse of it, but I knew it by the peculiar arrangement of the stones. Before I could say anything the princess ran on, as pleased as a girl with her new bauble:

"I have just discovered the prettiest conceit imaginable. See, the stones spell 'Pardon;' pearl, amethyst, ruby, diamond, opal, and as there is no stone commencing with the last letter, the initial of my name is added in enamel. Is not that divine?"

I examined it, and being a woman, I regretted the loss of the jewels as well as the opportunity of ending the matter, by a kinder reply to this fanciful petition for pardon. While I hesitated to enlighten the princess, for fear of further trouble, the prince entered, and I retreated to my seat at the other end of the room.

"Dear Alexis, I have just discovered your charming souvenir; a thousand thanks," cried his sister, with effusion.

"My souvenir; of what do you speak, Nadja?" he replied, with an air of surprise as he approached.

"Ah, you affect ignorance, but I well know whose hand sends me this, though I find it lying carelessly on my table. Yes, that start is very well done, yet it does not impose upon me. I am charmed with the gift; come, and let me embrace you."

With a very ill grace the "dear Alexis" submitted to the ceremony, and received the thanks of his sister, who expatiated upon the taste and beauty of the ring till he said, impatiently:

"You are very ingenious in your discoveries; I confess I meant it for a charming woman whom I had offended; if you had not accepted it I should have flung it in the fire. Now let it pass, and bid me adieu. I go to pass a week with Bagdonoff."

The princess was, of course, desolated to lose her brother, but resigned herself to the deprivation with calmness, and received his farewell without tears. I thought he meant to ignore me entirely, but to my surprise he approached, and with an expression I had never seen before, said, in a satirical tone:

"Mademoiselle, I leave the princess to your care, with perfect faith in your fidelity. Permit me to hope that you will enjoy my absence," and with a low bow, such as I had seen him give a count- ess, he departed.

The week lengthened to three before we saw the prince, and I am forced to confess that I did *not* enjoy his absence. So monoto- nous grew my days that I joyfully welcomed a somewhat romantic little episode in which I was just then called to play a part.

One of my former pupils had a lover. Madame Bayard discovered the awful fact, sent the girl home to her parents, and sternly refused to give the young man her address. He knew me, and in his despair applied to me for help and consolation. But not daring to seek me at the prince's hotel, he sent a note, imploring me to grant him an interview in the Tuileries Garden at a certain hour. I liked Adolph, pitied my amiable ex-pupil, and believing in the sincerity of their love, was glad to aid them.

At the appointed time I met Adolph, and for an hour paced up and down the leafless avenues, listening to his hopes and fears. It was a dull April day, and dusk fell early, but we were so absorbed that neither observed the gathering twilight till an exclamation from my companion made me look up.

"That man is watching us!"

"What man?" I asked, rather startled.

"Ah, he slips away again behind the trees yonder. He has done it twice before as we approached, and when we are past he follows stealthily. Do you see him?"

I glanced into the dusky path which crossed our own, and caught a glimpse of a tall man in a cloak just vanishing.

"You mistake, he does not watch us; why should he? Your own disquiet makes you suspicious, *mon ami*," I said.

"Perhaps so; let him go. Dear mademoiselle, I ask a thousand pardons for detaining you so long. Permit me to call a carriage for you."

I preferred to walk, and refusing Adolph's entreaties to escort me, I went my way along the garden side of the Rue de Rivoli, glad to be free at last. The wind was dying away as the sun set, but as a last freak it blew my veil off and carried it several yards behind me. A gentleman caught and advanced to restore it. As he put it into my hand with a bow, I uttered an exclamation, for it was the prince. He also looked surprised, and greeted me courteously, though with a strong expression of curiosity visible in his face. A cloak hung over his arm, and as my eyes fell upon it, an odd fancy took possession of me, causing me to conceal my pleasure at seeing him, and to assume a cold demeanor, which he observed at once. Vouchsafing no explanation of my late walk, I thanked him for the little service, adjusted my veil, and walked on as if the interview was at an end.

"It is late for mademoiselle to promenade alone; as I am about to return to the hotel, she will permit me to accompany her?"

The prince spoke in his most gracious tone, and walked beside me, casting covert glances at my face as we passed, the lamps now shining all about us. I was angry, and said, with significant emphasis:

"Monsieur le Prince has already sufficiently honored me with his protection. I can dispense with it now."

"Pardon, I do not understand," he began hastily; but I added, pointing to the garment on his arm:

"Pray assume your cloak; it is colder here than in the garden of the Tuileries."

Glancing up as I spoke, I saw him flush and frown, then draw himself up as if to haughtily demand an explanation, but with a sudden impulse, pause, and ask, averting his eyes:

"Why does mademoiselle speak in that accusing tone? Are the gardens forbidden ground to me?"

"Yes; when Monsieur le Prince condescends to play the spy," I boldly replied, adding with a momentary doubt arising in my mind, "Were you not there watching me?"

To my infinite surprise he looked me full in the face, and answered briefly:

"I was."

"Adolph was right then — I also; it is well to know one's enemies," I said, as if to myself, and uttered not another word, but walked rapidly on.

Silent also the prince went beside me, till, as we were about to cross the great square, a carriage whirled round the corner, causing me to step hastily back. An old crone, with a great basket on her head, was in imminent danger of being run over, when the prince sprang forward, caught the bit and forced the spirited horses back till the old creature gathered herself up and reached the pave in safety. Then he returned to me as tranquilly as if nothing had occurred.

"Are you hurt?" I asked, forgetting my anger, as he pulled off and threw away the delicate glove, torn and soiled in the brief struggle.

"Thanks — no; but the old woman?"

"She was not injured, and went on her way, never staying to thank you."

"Why should she?" he asked, quietly.

"One likes to see gratitude. Perhaps she is used to such escapes, and so the act surprised her less than it did me."

"Ah! you wonder that I troubled myself about the poor creature, mademoiselle. I never forget that my mother was a woman, and for her sake I respect all women."

I had never heard that tone in his voice, nor seen that look in his face before, as he spoke those simple words. They touched me more than the act, but some tormenting spirit prompted me to say:

"Even when you threaten one of them with a — "

I got no further, for, with a sudden flash that daunted me, the prince cried imploringly, yet commandingly:

"No — no; do not utter the word — do not recall the shameful scene. Be generous, and forget, though you will not forgive."

"Pardon, it was unkind, I never will offend again."

An awkward pause followed, and we went on without a word, till glancing at me as we passed a brilliant lamp, the prince exclaimed:

"Mademoiselle, you are very pale — you are ill, over-wearied; let me call a carriage."

"By no means; it is nothing. In stepping back to avoid the horses, I hurt my ankle; but we are almost at the hotel, and I can reach it perfectly well."

"And you have walked all this distance without a complaint, when every step was painful? *Ma foi!* mademoiselle is brave," he said, with mingled pity, anxiety and admiration in his fine eyes.

"Women early learn to suffer in silence," I answered, rather grimly, for my foot was in agony, and I was afraid I should give out before I reached the hotel.

The prince hastened on before me, unlocked the side-door by which I usually entered, and helping me in, said earnestly:

"There are many steps to climb; let me assist you, or call some one."

"No, no, I will have no scene; many thanks; I can reach my room quite well alone. *Bon soir*, Monsieur le Prince," and turning from his offered arm, I set my teeth and walked steadily up the first seven stairs. But on reaching the little landing, pain overcame pride, and I sank into a chair with a stifled groan. I had heard the door close, and fancied the prince gone, but he was at my side in an instant.

"Mademoiselle, I shall not leave you till you are safely in your apartment. How can I best serve you?"

I pointed to the bell, saying faintly:

"I cannot walk; let Pierre carry me."

"I am stronger and more fit for such burdens. Pardon, it must be so."

And before I could utter a refusal, he folded the cloak about me, raised me gently in his arms, and went pacing quietly along the corridors, regarding me with an air of much sympathy, though in his eyes lurked a gleam of triumph, as he murmured to himself:

"She has a strong will, this brave mademoiselle of ours, but it must bend at last."

That annoyed me more than my mishap, but being helpless, I answered only with a defiant glance and an irrepressible smile at my little adventure. He looked keenly at me with an eager, yet puzzled air, and said, as he grasped me more firmly:

"Inexplicable creature! Pain can conquer her strength, but her spirit defies me still."

I hardly heard him, for as he laid me on the couch in my own little *salon*, I lost consciousness, and when I recovered myself, I was alone with my maid.

"What has happened?" I asked.

"Dear mademoiselle, I know not; the bell rings, I fly, I find you fainting, and I restore you. It is fatigue, alarm, illness, and you ring before your senses leave you," cried Jacobine, removing my cloak and furs.

A sudden pang in my foot recalled me to myself at once, and bidding the girl apply certain remedies, I was soon comfortable. Not a word was said of the prince; he had evidently vanished before the maid came. I was glad of this, for I had no desire to furnish food for gossip among the servants. Sending Jacobine with a message to the princess, I lay recalling the scene and perplexing myself over several trifles which suddenly assumed great importance in my eyes.

My bonnet and gloves were off when the girl found me. Who had removed them? My hair was damp with eau-de-cologne; who had bathed my head? My injured foot lay on a cushion; who placed it there? Did I dream that a tender voice exclaimed, "My little Sybil, my heart, speak to me"? or did the prince really utter such words?

With burning cheeks, and a half-sweet, half-bitter trouble in my heart, I thought of these things, and asked myself what all this was coming to. A woman often asks herself such questions, but seldom answers them, nor did I, preferring to let time drift me where it would.

The amiable princess came herself to inquire for me. I said nothing of her brother, as it was evident that he had said nothing even to her.

"Alexis has returned, *ma chère*; he was with me when Jacobine told me of your accident; he sends his compliments and regrets. He is in charming spirits, and looking finely."

I murmured my thanks, but felt a little guilty at my want of frankness. Why not tell her the prince met and helped me? While debating the point within myself, the princess was rejoicing that my accident would perhaps still longer delay the dreaded journey.

"Let it be a serious injury, my friend; it will permit you to enjoy life here, but not to travel; so suffer sweetly for my sake, and I will repay you with a thousand thanks," she said, pleadingly.

Laughingly I promised, and having ordered every luxury she could imagine, the princess left me with a joyful heart, while I vainly tried to forget the expression of the prince's face as he said low to himself:

"Her spirit defies me still."

CHAPTER V

FOR A WEEK I kept my room and left the princess to fabricate what tales she liked. She came to me every day reporting the preparations for departure were begun, but the day still remained unfixed, although April was half over.

"He waits for you, I am sure; he inquires for you daily, and begins to frown at the delay. To appease him, come down to-morrow, languid, lame, and in a charming dishabille. Amuse him as you used to do, and if anything is said of Russia, express your willingness to go, but deplore your inability to bear the journey now."

Very glad to recover my liberty, I obeyed the princess, and entered her room next day leaning on Jacobine, pale, languid, and in my most becoming morning toilet. The princess was reading novels on her sofa by the fire; the prince, in the brilliant costume in which I first saw him, sat in my chair, busy at my embroidery frame. The odd contrast between the man and his employment struck me so ludicrously that a half laugh escaped me. Both looked up; the prince sprang out of his chair as if about to rush forward, but checked himself, and received me with a silent nod. The princess made a great stir over me, and with some difficulty was persuaded to compose herself at last. Having answered her eager and the prince's polite inquiries, I took up my work, saying, with an irresistible smile as I examined the gentleman's progress:

"My flowers have blossomed in my absence, I see. Does M. le Prince possess all accomplishments?"

"Ah, you smile, but I assure you embroidery is one of the amusements of Russian gentlemen, and they often excel us in it. My brother scorned it till he was disabled with a wound, and when all other devices failed, this became his favorite employment."

As the princess spoke the prince stood in his usual attitude on the rug, eying me with a suspicious look, which annoyed me intensely and destroyed my interesting pallor by an uncontrollable blush. I felt terribly guilty with those piercing black eyes fixed on me, and appeared to be absorbed in a fresh bit of work. The princess chattered on till a salver full of notes and cards was brought in, when she forgot everything else in reading and answering these. The prince approached me then, and seating himself near my sofa, said, with somewhat ironical emphasis on the last two words:

"I congratulate mademoiselle on her recovery, and that her bloom is quite untouched by her *severe·sufferings*."

"The princess in her amiable sympathy doubtlessly exaggerated my pain, but I certainly *have* suffered, though my roses may belie me."

Why my eyes should fill and my lips tremble was a mystery to me, but they did, as I looked up at him with a reproachful face. I spoke the truth. I *had* suffered, not bodily but mental pain, trying to put away forever a tempting hope which suddenly came to trouble me. Astonishment and concern replaced the cold, suspicious expression of the prince's countenance, and his voice was very kind as he asked, with an evident desire to divert my thoughts from myself:

"For what luxurious being do you embroider these splendid slippers of purple and gold, mademoiselle? Or is that an indiscreet question?"

"For my friend Adolph Vernay."

"They are too large, he is but a boy," began the prince, but stopped abruptly, and bit his lip, with a quick glance at me.

Without lifting my eyes I said, coolly:

"M. le Prince appears to have observed this gentleman with much care, to discover that he has a handsome foot and a youthful face."

"Without doubt I should scrutinize any man with whom I saw mademoiselle walking alone in the twilight. As one of my household, I take the liberty of observing your conduct, and for my sister's sake ask of you to pardon this surveillance."

He spoke gravely, but looked unsatisfied, and feeling in a tormenting mood, I mystified him still more by saying, with a bow of assent:

"If M. le Prince knew all, he would see nothing strange in my promenade, nor in the earnestness of that interview. Believe me, I may seem rash, but I shall never forget what is due to the princess while I remain with her."

He pondered over my words a moment with his eyes on my face, and a frown bending his black brows. Suddenly he spoke, hastily, almost roughly:

"I comprehend what mademoiselle would convey. Monsieur Adolph is a lover, and the princess is about to lose her friend."

"Exactly. M. le Prince has guessed the mystery," and I smiled with downcast eyes.

A gilded ornament on the back of the chair against which the prince leaned snapped under his hand as it closed with a strong grip. He flung it away, and said, rapidly, with a jar in his usually musical voice:

"This gentleman will marry, it seems, and mademoiselle, with the charming freedom of an English woman, arranges the affair herself."

"Helps to arrange; Adolph has sense and courage; I leave much to him."

"And when is this interesting event to take place, if one may ask?"

"Next week, if all goes well."

"I infer the princess knows of this?"

"Oh, yes. I told her at once."

"And she consents?"

"Without doubt; what right would she have to object?"

"Ah, I forgot; in truth, none, nor any other. It is incomprehensible! She is to lose you and yet is not in despair."

"It is but for a time. I join her later if she desires it."

"Never, with that man!" and the prince rose with an impetuous gesture, which sent my silks flying.

"What man?" I asked, affecting bewilderment.

"This Adolph, whom you are about to marry."

"M. le Prince quite mistakes; I fancied he knew more of the affair. Permit me to explain."

"Quick, then; what is the mystery? who marries? who goes? who stays?"

So flushed, anxious and excited did he look, that I was satisfied with my test, and set about enlightening him with alacrity. Having told why I met the young man, I added:

"Adolph will demand the hand of Adele from her parents, but if they refuse it, as I fear they will, being prejudiced against him by Madame Bayard, he will effect his purpose in another manner. Though I do not approve of elopements in general, this is a case where it is pardonable, and I heartily wish him success."

While I spoke the prince's brow had cleared, he drew a long breath, reseated himself in the chair before me, and when I paused, said, with one of his sudden smiles and an air of much interest:

"Then you would have this lover boldly carry off his mistress in spite of all obstacles?"

"Yes. I like courage in love as in war, and respect a man who conquers all obstacles."

"Good, it is well said," and with a low laugh the prince sat regarding me in silence for a moment. Then an expression of relief stole over his face as he said, still smiling:

"And it was of this you spoke so earnestly when you fancied I watched you in the gardens?"

"Fancied! nay, M. le Prince has confessed that it was no fancy."

"How if I had not confessed?"

"I should have believed your word till you betrayed yourself, and then — "

I paused there with an uncontrollable gesture of contempt. He eyed me keenly, saying in that half-imperious, half-persuasive voice of his:

"It is well then that I obeyed my first impulse. To speak truth is one of the instincts which these polished Frenchmen have not yet conquered in the 'barbarian,' as they call me."

"I respected you for that truthful 'yes,' more than for anything you ever said or did," I cried, forgetting myself entirely.

"Then, mademoiselle has a little respect for me?"

He leaned his chin upon the arm that lay along the back of his chair, and looked at me with a sudden softening of voice, eye, and manner.

"Can M. le Prince doubt it?" I said, demurely, little guessing what was to follow.

"Does mademoiselle desire to be respected for the same virtue?" he asked.

"More than for any other."

"Then will she give me a truthful answer to the plain question I desire to ask?"

"I will;" and my heart beat rebelliously as I glanced at the handsome face so near me, and just then so dangerously gentle.

"Has not mademoiselle feigned illness for the past week?"

The question took me completely by surprise, but anxious to stand the test, I glanced at the princess, still busy at her writing-table in the distant alcove, and checking the answer which rose to my lips, I said, lowering my voice:

"On one condition will I reply."

"Name it, mademoiselle?"

"That nothing be said to Madame la Princesse of this."

"I give you my word."

"Well, then, I answer, yes;" and I fixed my eyes full on his as I spoke.

His face darkened a shade, but his manner remained unchanged.

"Thanks; now, for the reason of the ruse?"

"To delay a little the journey to Russia."

"Ha, I had not thought of that, imbecile that I am!" he exclaimed with a start.

"What other reason did M. le Prince imagine, if I may question in my turn?"

His usually proud and steady eyes wavered and fell, and he made no answer, but seemed to fall into a reverie, from which he woke presently to ask abruptly:

"What did you mean by saying you were to leave my sister for a time, and rejoin her later?"

"I must trouble you with the relation of a little affair which will probably detain me till after the departure, for but a week now remains of April."

"I listen, mademoiselle."

"Good Madame Bayard is unfortunately the victim of a cruel disease, which menaces her life unless an operation can be successfully performed. The time for this trial is at hand, and I have promised to be with her. If she lives I can safely leave her in a few days; if she dies I must remain till her son can arrive. This sad duty will keep me for a week or two, and I can rejoin madame at any point she may desire."

"But why make this promise? Madame Bayard has friends — why impose this unnecessary sacrifice of time, nerve, and sympathy upon you, mademoiselle?" And the prince knit his brows, as if ill-pleased.

"When I came to Paris long ago a poor, friendless, sorrowful girl, this good woman took me in, and for five years has been a mother to me. I am grateful, and would make any sacrifice to serve her in her hour of need."

I spoke with energy; the frown melted to the smile which always ennobled his face, as the prince replied, in a tone of forgetful acquiescence:

"You are right. I say no more. If you are detained I will leave Vacil to escort you to us. He is true as steel, and will guard you well. When must you go to the poor lady?"

"To-morrow; the princess consents to my wish, and I devote myself to my friend till she needs me no longer. May I ask when you leave Paris?" I could not resist asking.

"On the last day of the month," was the brief reply, as the prince rose, and roamed away with a thoughtful face, leaving me to ponder over many things as I wrought my golden pansies, wondering if I should ever dare to offer the purple velvet slippers to the possessor of a handsomer foot than Adolph.

On the following day I went to Madame Bayard; the operation

was performed, but failed, and the poor soul died in my arms, blessing me for my love and care. I sent tidings of the event to the princess, and received a kind reply, saying all was ready, and the day irrevocably fixed.

I passed a busy week; saw my best friend laid to her last rest; arranged such of her affairs as I could, and impatiently awaited the arrival of her son. On the second day of May he came, and I was free.

As soon as possible I hastened to the hotel, expecting to find it deserted. To my surprise, however, I saw lights in the *salon* of the princess, and heard sounds of life everywhere as I went wonderingly toward my own apartments. The windows were open, flowers filled the room with spring odors, and everything wore an air of welcome as if some one waited for me. Some one did, for on the balcony, which ran along the whole front, leaned the prince in the mild, new-fallen twilight, singing softly to himself.

"Not gone!" I exclaimed, in unfeigned surprise.

He turned, smiled, flushed, and said, as he vanished:

"I follow mademoiselle's good example in yielding my wishes to the comfort and pleasure of others."

CHAPTER VI

THE NEXT DAY WE SET OUT, but the dreaded journey proved delightful, for the weather was fine, and the prince in a charming mood. No allusion was made to the unexpected delay, except by the princess, who privately expressed her wonder at my power, and treated me with redoubled confidence and affection. We loitered by the way, and did not reach St. Petersburg till June.

I had expected changes in my life as well as change of scene, but was unprepared for the position which it soon became evident I was to assume. In Paris I had been the companion, now I was treated as a friend and equal by both the prince and princess. They entirely ignored my post, and remembering only that I was by birth a gentlewoman, by a thousand friendly acts made it impossible for me to refuse the relations which they chose to establish between us. I suspect the princess hinted to her intimates that I was a connection of her own, and my name gave color to the statement. Thus I found myself received with respect and interest by the circle in which I now moved, and truly enjoyed the free, gay life, which seemed doubly charming, after years of drudgery.

With this exception there was less alteration in my surroundings than I had imagined, for the upper classes in Russia speak nothing but French; in dress, amusements, and manners, copy French models so carefully that I should often have fancied myself in Paris, but for the glimpses of barbarism, which observing eyes cannot fail to detect, in spite of the splendor which surrounds them. The hotel of the prince was a dream of luxury; his equipages magnificent; his wealth apparently boundless; his friends among the highest in the land. He appeared to unusual advantage at home, and seemed anxious that I should observe this, exerting himself in many ways to impress me with his power, even while he was most affable and devoted.

I could no longer blind myself to the truth, and tried to meet it honestly. The prince loved me, and made no secret of his preference, though not a word had passed his lips. I had felt this since the night he carried me in his arms, but remembering the difference in rank, had taught myself to see in it only the passing caprice of a master for a servant, and as such, to regard it as an insult. Since we came to St. Petersburg the change in his manner seemed to assure me that he sought me as an equal, and desired to do me honor in the eyes of those about us. This soothed my pride and touched my heart, but, alluring as the thought was to my vanity and my ambition, I did not yield to it, feeling that I should not love, and that such an alliance was not the one for me.

Having come to this conclusion, I resolved to abide by it, and did so the more inflexibly as the temptation to falter grew stronger. My calm, cool manner perplexed and irritated the prince, who seemed to grow more passionate as test after test failed to extort any betrayal of regard from me. The princess, absorbed in her own affairs, seemed apparently blind to her brother's infatuation, till I was forced to enlighten her.

July was nearly over, when the prince announced that he was about to visit one of his estates, some versts from the city, and we were to accompany him. I had discovered that Volnoi was a solitary place, that no guests were expected, and that the prince was supreme master of everything and everybody on the estate. This did not suit me, for Madame Yermaloff, an Englishwoman, who had conceived a friendship for me, had filled my head with stories of Russian barbarity, and the entire helplessness of whomsoever dared to thwart or defy a Russian seigneur, especially when on his own domain. I laughed at her gossip, yet it influenced my decision, for of late the prince had looked ireful, and his black eyes had kept vigilant watch over me. I knew that his patience was exhausted, and feared that a stormy scene was in store for me. To avoid all further annoyance, I boldly stated the case to the princess, and decidedly refused to leave St. Petersburg.

To my surprise, she agreed with me; and I discovered, what I had before suspected, that, much as she liked me as a friend, the princess would have preferred her brother to marry one of his own rank. She delicately hinted this, yet, unwilling to give me up entirely, begged me to remain with Madame Yermaloff till she returned, when some new arrangement might be made. I consented, and feeling unequal to a scene with the prince, left his sister to inform him of my decision, and went quietly to my friend, who gladly received me. Next morning the following note from the princess somewhat reassured me:

MA CHERE SYBIL — We leave in an hour. Alexis received the news of your flight in a singular manner. I expected to see him half frantic; but no, he smiled, and said, tranquilly: "She fears and flies me; it is a sign of weakness, for which I thank her." I do not understand him; but when we are quiet at Volnoi, I hope to convince him that you are, as always, wise and prudent. Adieu! I embrace you tenderly.   N.T.

A curious sense of disappointment and uneasiness took possession of me on reading this note, and, womanlike, I began to long for that which I had denied myself. Madame Yermaloff found me a very dull companion, and began to rally me on my preoccupation. I tried to forget, but could not, and often stole out to walk past the prince's hotel, now closed and silent. A week dragged slowly by, and I had begun to think the prince had indeed forgotten me, when I was convinced that he had not in a somewhat alarming manner. Returning one evening from a lonely walk in the Place Michel, with its green English square, I observed a carriage standing near the Palace Galitzin, and listlessly wondered who was about to travel, for the coachman was in his place and a servant stood holding the door open. As I passed I glanced in, but saw nothing, for in the act sudden darkness fell upon me; a cloak was dexterously thrown over me, enveloping my head and arms, and rendering me helpless. Some one lifted me into the carriage, the door closed, and I was driven rapidly away, in spite of my stifled cries and fruitless struggles. At first I was frantic with anger and fear, and rebelled desperately against the strong hold which restrained me. Not a word was spoken, but I felt sure, after the first alarm, that the prince was near me, and this discovery, though it increased my anger, allayed my fear. Being half-suffocated, I suddenly feigned faintness, and lay motionless, as if spent. A careful hand withdrew the thick folds, and as I opened my eyes they met those of the prince fixed on me, full of mingled solicitude and triumph.

"You! Yes; I might have known no one else would dare perpetrate such an outrage!" I cried, breathlessly, and in a tone of intense scorn, though my heart leaped with joy to see him.

He laughed, while his eyes flashed, as he answered, gayly:

"Mademoiselle forgets that she once said she 'liked courage in love as in war, and respected a man who conquered all obstacles.' I remember this, and, when other means fail dare to brave even her anger to gain my object."

"What is that object?" I demanded, as my eyes fell before the ardent glance fixed on me.

"It is to see you at Volnoi, in spite of your cruel refusal."

"I will not go."

And with a sudden gesture I dashed my hand through the window and cried for help with all my strength. In an instant I was pinioned again, and my cries stifled by the cloak, as the prince said, sternly:

"If mademoiselle resists, it will be the worse for her. Submit, and no harm will befall you. Accept the society of one who adores you, and permit yourself to be conquered by one who never yields — except to you," he added, softly, as he held me closer, and put by the cloak again.

"Let me go — I will be quiet," I panted, feeling that it was indeed idle to resist now, yet resolving that he should suffer for this freak.

"You promise to submit — to smile again, and be your charming self?" he said, in the soft tone that was so hard to deny.

"I promise nothing but to be quiet. Release me instantly!" and I tried to undo the clasp of the hand that held me.

"Not till you forgive me and look kind. Nay, struggle if you will, I like it, for till now you have been the master. See, I pardon all your cruelty, and find you more lovely than ever."

As he spoke he bent and kissed me on forehead, lips and cheek with an ardor which wholly daunted me. I did pardon him, for there was real love in his face, and love robbed the act of rudeness in my eyes, for instead of any show of anger or disdain, I hid my face in my hands, weeping the first tears he had ever seen me shed. It tamed him in a moment, for as I sobbed I heard him imploring me to be calm, promising to sin no more, and assuring me that he meant only to carry me to Volnoi as its mistress, whom he loved and honored above all women. Would I forgive his wild act, and let his obedience in all things else atone for this?

I must forgive it; and if he did not mock me by idle offers of obedience, I desired him to release me entirely and leave me to compose myself, if possible.

He instantly withdrew his arm, and seated himself opposite me, looking half contrite, half exultant, as he arranged the cloak about my feet. I shrunk into the corner and dried my tears, feeling unusually weak and womanish, just when I most desired to be strong and stern. Before I could whet my tongue for some rebuke, the prince uttered an exclamation of alarm, and caught my hand. I looked, and saw that it was bleeding from a wound made by the shattered glass.

"Let it bleed," I said, trying to withdraw it. But he held it fast, binding it up with his own handkerchief in the tenderest manner, saying as he finished, with a passionate pressure:

"Give it to me, Sybil, I want it — this little hand — so resolute, yet soft. Let it be mine, and it shall never know labor or wound again. Why do you frown — what parts us?"

"This," and I pointed to the crest embroidered on the corner of the *mouchoir*.

"Is that all?" he asked, bending forward with a keen glance that seemed to read my heart.

"One other trifle," I replied sharply.

"Name it, my princess, and I will annihilate it, as all other obstacles," he said, with the lordly air that became him.

"It is impossible."

"Nothing is impossible to Alexis Demidoff."

"I do not love you."

"In truth, Sybil?" he cried incredulously.

"In truth," I answered steadily.

He eyed me an instant with a gloomy air, then drew a long breath, and set his teeth, exclaiming:

"You are mortal. I shall *make* you love me."

"How, monsieur?" I coldly asked, while my traitorous heart beat fast.

"I shall humble myself before you, shall obey your commands, shall serve you, protect you, love and honor you ardently, faithfully, while I live. Will not such devotion win you?"

"No."

It was a hard word to utter, but I spoke it, looking him full in the eye and seeing with a pang how pale he grew with real despair.

"Is it because you love already, or that you have no heart?" he said slowly.

"I love already." The words escaped me against my will, for the truth would find vent in spite of me. He took it as I meant he should, for his lips whitened, as he asked hoarsely:

"And this man whom you love, is he alive?"

"Yes."

"He knows of this happiness — he returns your love?"

"He loves me; ask no more; I am ill and weary."

A gloomy silence reigned for several minutes, for the prince seemed buried in a bitter reverie, and I was intent on watching him. An involuntary sigh broke from me as I saw the shadow deepen on the handsome face opposite, and thought that my falsehood had changed the color of a life. He looked up at the sound, saw my white, anxious face, and without a word drew from a pocket of the carriage a flask and silver cup, poured me a draught of wine, and offered it, saying gently:

"Am I cruel in my love, Sybil?"

I made no answer, but drank the wine, and asked as I returned the cup:

"Now that you know the truth, must I go to Volnoi? Be kind, and let me return to Madame Yermaloff."

His face darkened and his eyes grew fierce, as he replied, with an aspect of indomitable resolve:

"It is impossible; I have sworn to make you love me, and at Volnoi I will work the miracle. Do you think this knowledge of the truth will deter me? No; I shall teach you to forget this man, whoever he is, and make you happy in my love. You doubt this. Wait a little and see what a real passion can do."

This lover-like pertinacity was dangerous, for it flattered my woman's nature more than any submission could have done. I dared not listen to it, and preferring to see him angry rather than tender, I said provokingly:

"No man ever forced a woman to love him against her will. You will certainly fail, for no one in her senses would give her heart to *you!*"

"And why? Am I hideous?" he asked, with a haughty smile.

"Far from it."

"Am I a fool, mademoiselle?"

"Quite the reverse."

"Am I base?"

"No."

"Have I degraded my name and rank by any act?"

"Never, till to-night, I believe."

He laughed, yet looked uneasy, and demanded imperiously:

"Then, why will no woman love me?"

"Because you have the will of a tyrant, and the temper of a madman."

If I had struck him in the face it would not have startled him as my blunt words did. He flushed scarlet, drew back and regarded me with a half-bewildered air, for never had such a speech been made to him before. Seeing my success, I followed it up by saying gravely:

"The insult of to-night gives me the right to forget the respect I have hitherto paid you, and for once you shall hear the truth as plain as words can make it. Many fear you for these faults, but no one dares tell you of them, and they mar an otherwise fine nature."

I got no further, for to my surprise, the prince said suddenly, with real dignity, though his voice was less firm than before:

"One dares to tell me of them, and I thank her. Will she add to the obligation by teaching me to cure them?" Then he broke out impetuously: "Sybil, you can help me; you possess courage and power to tame my wild temper, my headstrong will. In heaven's name I ask you to do it, that I may be worthy some good woman's love."

He stretched his hands toward me with a gesture full of force and feeling, and his eloquent eyes pleaded for pity. I felt my resolution melting away, and fortified myself by a chilly speech.

"Monsieur le Prince has said that nothing is impossible to him; if he can conquer all obstacles, it were well to begin with these."

"I have begun. Since I knew you my despotic will has bent more than once to yours, and my mad temper has been curbed by the remembrance that you have seen it. Sybil, if I do conquer myself, can you, will you try to love me?"

So earnestly he looked, so humbly he spoke, it was impossible to resist the charm of this new and manlier mood. I gave him my hand, and said, with the smile that always won him:

"I will respect you sincerely, and be your friend; more I cannot promise."

He kissed my hand with a wistful glance, and sighed as he dropped it, saying in a tone of mingled hope and resignation:

"Thanks; respect and friendship from you are dearer than love and confidence from another woman. I know and deplore the faults fostered by education and indulgence, and I will conquer them. Give me time. I swear it will be done."

"I believe it, and I pray for your success."

He averted his face and sat silent for many minutes, as if struggling with some emotion which he was too proud to show. I watched him, conscious of a redoubled interest in this man, who at one moment ruled me like a despot, and at another confessed his faults like a repentant boy.

CHAPTER VII

IN RUSSIA, from the middle of May to the 1st of August, there is no night. It is daylight till eleven, then comes a soft semi-twilight till one, when the sun rises. Through this gathering twilight we drove toward Volnoi. The prince let down the windows, and the summer air blew in refreshingly; the peace of the night soothed my perturbed spirit, and the long silences were fitly broken by some tender word from my companion, who, without approaching nearer, never ceased to regard me with eyes so full of love that, for the first time in my life, I dared not meet them.

It was near midnight when the carriage stopped, and I could discover nothing but a tall white pile in a wilderness of blooming shrubs and trees. Lights shone from many windows, and as the prince led me into a brilliantly lighted *salon*, the princess came smiling to greet me, exclaiming, as she embraced me with affection:

"Welcome, my sister. You see it is in vain to oppose Alexis. We must confess this, and yield gracefully; in truth, I am glad to keep you, *chère amie*, for without you we find life very dull."

"Madame mistakes; I never yield, and am here against my will."

I withdrew myself from her as I spoke, feeling hurt that she had not warned me of her brother's design. They exchanged a few words as I sat apart, trying to look dignified, but dying with sleep. The princess soon came to me, and it was impossible to resist her caressing manner as she begged me to go and rest, leaving all disagreements till the morrow. I submitted, and, with a silent salute to the prince, followed her to an apartment next her own, where I was soon asleep, lulled by the happy thought that I was not forgotten.

The princess was with me early in the morning, and a few moments' conversation proved to me that, so far from her convincing her brother of the folly of his choice, he had entirely won her to his side, and enlisted her sympathies for himself. She pleaded his suit with sisterly skill and eloquence, but I would pledge myself to nothing, feeling a perverse desire to be hardly won, if won at all, and a feminine wish to see my haughty lover thoroughly subdued before I put my happiness into his keeping. I consented to remain for a time, and a servant was sent to Madame Yermaloff with a letter explaining my flight, and telling where to forward a portion of my wardrobe.

Professing herself satisfied for the present, and hopeful for the future, the princess left me to join her brother in the garden, where I saw them talking long and earnestly. It was pleasant to a lonely soul like myself to be so loved and cherished, and when I descended it was impossible to preserve the cold demeanor I had assumed, for all faces greeted me with smiles, all voices welcomed me, and one presence made the strange place seem like home. The prince's behavior was perfect, respectful, devoted and self-controlled; he appeared like a new being, and the whole household seemed to rejoice in the change.

Day after day glided happily away, for Volnoi was a lovely spot, and I saw nothing of the misery hidden in the hearts and homes of the hundred serfs who made the broad domain so beautiful. I seldom saw them, never spoke to them, for I knew no Russ, and in our drives the dull-looking peasantry possessed no interest for me. They never came to the house, and the prince appeared to know nothing of them beyond what his Stavosta, or steward reported. Poor Alexis! he had many hard lessons to learn that year, yet was a better man and master for them all, even the one which nearly cost him his life.

Passing through the hall one day, I came upon a group of servants lingering near the door of the apartment in which the prince gave his orders and transacted business. I observed that the French servants looked alarmed, the Russian ones fierce and threatening, and that Antoine, the valet of the prince, seemed to be eagerly dissuading several of the serfs from entering. As I appeared he exclaimed:

"Hold, he is saved! Mademoiselle will speak for him; she fears nothing, and she pities every one." Then, turning to me, he added, rapidly: "Mademoiselle will pardon us that we implore this favor of her great kindness. Ivan, through some carelessness, has permitted the favorite horse of the prince to injure himself fatally. He has gone in to confess, and we fear for his life, because Monsieur le Prince loved the fine beast well, and will be in a fury at the loss. He killed poor Androvitch for a less offense, and we tremble for Ivan. Will mademoiselle intercede for him? I fear harm to my master if Ivan suffers, for these fellows swear to avenge him."

Without a word I opened the door and entered quietly. Ivan was on his knees, evidently awaiting his doom with dogged submission. A pair of pistols lay on the table, and near it stood the prince, with the dark flush on his face, the terrible fire in his eyes which I had seen before. I saw there was no time to lose, and going to him, looked up into that wrathful countenance, whispering in a warning tone:

"Remember poor Androvitch."

It was like an electric shock; he started, shuddered, and turned pale; covered his face a moment and stood silent, while I saw drops gather on his forehead and his hand clinch itself spasmodically. Suddenly he moved, flung the pistols through the open window, and turning on Ivan, said, with a forceful gesture:

"Go. I pardon you."

The man remained motionless as if bewildered, till I touched him, bidding him thank his master and begone.

"No, it is you I thank, good angel of the house," he muttered, and lifting a fold of my dress to his lips Ivan hurried from the room.

I looked at the prince; he was gravely watching us, but a smile touched his lips as he echoed the man's last words, "'Good angel of the house'; yes, in truth you are. Ivan is right, he owes me no thanks; and yet it was the hardest thing I ever did to forgive him the loss of my noble Sophron."

"But you did forgive him, and whether he is grateful or not, the victory is yours. A few such victories and the devil is cast out for ever."

He seized my hand, exclaiming in a tone of eager delight:

"You believe this? You have faith in me, and rejoice that I conquer this cursed temper, this despotic will?"

"I do; but I still doubt the subjection of the will," I began; he interrupted me by an impetuous —

"Try it; ask anything of me and I will submit."

"Then let me return to St. Petersburg at once, and do not ask to follow."

He had not expected this, it was too much; he hesitated, demanding, anxiously:

"Do you really mean it?"

"Yes."

"You wish to leave me, to banish me now when you are all in all to me?"

"I wish to be free. You have promised to obey; yield your will to mine and let me go."

He turned and walked rapidly through the room, paused a moment at the further end, and coming back, showed me such an altered face that my conscience smote me for the cruel test. He looked at me in silence for an instant, but I showed no sign of relenting, although I saw what few had ever seen, those proud eyes wet with tears. Bending, he passionately kissed my hands, saying, in a broken voice:

"Go, Sybil. I submit."

"Adieu, my friend; I shall not forget," and without venturing another look I left him.

I had hardly reached my chamber and resolved to end the struggle for both of us, when I saw the prince gallop out of the courtyard like one trying to escape from some unfortunate remembrance or care.

"Return soon to me," I cried; "the last test is over and the victory won."

Alas, how little did I foresee what would happen before that return; how little did he dream of the dangers that encompassed him.

A tap at my door roused me as I sat in the twilight an hour later, and Claudine crept in, so pale and agitated that I started up, fearing some mishap to the princess.

"No, she is well and safe, but oh, mademoiselle, a fearful peril hangs over us all. Hush! I will tell you. I have discovered it, and we must save them."

"Save who? what peril? speak quickly."

"Mademoiselle knows that the people on the estate are poor ignorant brutes who hate the Stavosta, and have no way of reaching the prince except through him. He is a hard man; he oppresses them, taxes them heavily unknown to the prince, and they believe my master to be a tyrant. They have borne much, for when we are away the Stavosta rules here, and they suffer frightfully. I have lived long in Russia, and I hear many things whispered that do not reach the ears of my lady. These poor creatures bear long, but at last they rebel, and some fearful affair occurs, as at Bagatai, where the countess, a cruel woman, was one night seized by her serfs, who burned and tortured her to death."

"Good heavens! Claudine, what is this danger which menaces us?"

"I understand Russ, mademoiselle, have quick eyes and ears, and for some days I perceive that all is not well among the people. Ivan is changed; all look dark and threatening but old Vacil. I watch and listen, and discover that they mean to attack the house and murder the prince."

"*Mon Dieu!* but when?"

"I knew not till to-day. Ivan came to me and said, 'Mademoiselle Varna has saved my life. I am grateful. I wish to serve her. She came here against her will; she desires to go; the prince is away; I will provide a horse to-night at dusk, and she can join her friend Madame Yermaloff, who is at Baron Narod's, only a verst distant. Say this to mademoiselle, and if she agrees, drop a signal from her window. I shall see and understand.'"

"But why think that the attack is to be to-night?"

"Because Ivan was so anxious to remove you. He urged me to persuade you, for the prince is gone, and the moment is propitious. You will go, mademoiselle?"

"No; I shall not leave the princess."

"But you can save us all by going, for at the baron's you can procure help and return to defend us before these savages arrive. Ivan will believe you safe, and you can thwart their plans before the hour comes. Oh, mademoiselle, I conjure you to do this, for we are watched, and you alone will be permitted to escape."

A moment's thought convinced me that this was the only means of help in our power, and my plans were quickly laid. It was useless to wait for the prince, as his return was uncertain; it was unwise to alarm the princess, as she would betray all; the quick-witted Claudine and myself must do the work, and trust to heaven for success. I dropped a handkerchief from my window; a tall figure emerged from the shrubbery, and vanished, whispering:

"In an hour — at the chapel gate."

At the appointed time I was on the spot, and found Ivan holding the well-trained horse I often rode. It was nearly dark — for August brought night — and it was well for me, as my pale face would have betrayed me.

"Mademoiselle has not fear? If she dares not go alone I will guard her," said Ivan, as he mounted me.

"Thanks. I fear nothing. I have a pistol, and it is not far. Liberty is sweet. I will venture much for it."

"I also," muttered Ivan.

He gave me directions as to my route, and watched me ride away, little suspecting my errand.

How I rode that night! My blood tingles again as I recall the wild gallop along the lonely road, the excitement of the hour, and the resolve to save Alexis or die in the attempt. Fortunately I found a large party at the baron's, and electrified them by appearing in their midst, disheveled, breathless and eager with my tale of danger. What passed I scarcely remember, for all was confusion and alarm. I refused to remain, and soon found myself dashing homeward, followed by a gallant troop of five and twenty gentlemen. More time had been lost than I knew, and my heart sunk as a dull glare shone from the direction of Volnoi as we strained up the last hill.

Reaching the top, we saw that one wing was already on fire, and distinguished a black, heaving mass on the lawn by the flickering torchlight. With a shout of wrath the gentlemen spurred to the rescue, but I reached the chapel gate unseen, and entering, flew to find my friends. Claudine saw me and led me to the great saloon, for the lower part of the house was barricaded. Here I found the princess quite insensible, guarded by a flock of terrified French servants, and Antoine and old Vacil endeavoring to screen the prince, who, with reckless courage, exposed himself to the missiles which came crashing against the windows. A red light filled the room, and from without arose a yell from the infuriated mob more terrible than any wild beast's howl.

As I sprang in, crying, "They are here — the baron and his friends — you are safe!" all turned toward me as if every other hope was lost. A sudden lull without, broken by the clash of arms, verified my words, and with one accord we uttered a cry of gratitude. The prince flung up the window to welcome our deliverers; the red glare of the fire made him distinctly visible, and as he leaned out with a ringing shout, a hoarse voice cried menacingly:

"Remember poor Androvitch."

It was Ivan's voice, and as it echoed my words there was the sharp crack of a pistol, and the prince staggered back, exclaiming faintly:

"I forgive him; it is just."

We caught him in our arms, and as Antoine laid him down he looked at me with a world of love and gratitude in those magnificent eyes of his, whispering as the light died out of them:

"Always our good angel. Adieu, Sybil. I submit."

How the night went after that I neither knew nor cared, for my only thought was how to keep life in my lover till help could come. I learned afterward that the sight of such an unexpected force caused a panic among the serfs, who fled or surrendered at once. The fire was extinguished, the poor princess conveyed to bed, and the conquerors departed, leaving a guard behind. Among the gentlemen there fortunately chanced to be a surgeon, who extracted the ball from the prince's side.

I would yield my place to no one, though the baron implored me to spare myself the anguish of the scene. I remained steadfast, supporting the prince till all was over; then, feeling that my strength was beginning to give way, I whispered to the surgeon, that I might take a little comfort away with me:

"He will live? His wound is not fatal?"

The old man shook his head, and turned away, muttering regretfully:

"There is no hope; say farewell, and let him go in peace, my poor child."

The room grew dark before me, but I had strength to draw the white face close to my own, and whisper tenderly:

"Alexis, I love you, and you alone. I confess my cruelty; oh, pardon me, before you die!"

A look, a smile full of the intensest love and joy, shone in the eyes that silently met mine as consciousness deserted me.

One month from that night I sat in that same saloon a happy woman, for on the couch, a shadow of his former self but alive and out of danger, lay the prince, my husband. The wound was not fatal, and love had worked a marvelous cure. While life and death still fought for him, I yielded to his prayer to become his wife, that he might leave me the protection of his name, the rich gift of his rank and fortune. In my remorse I would have granted anything, and when the danger was passed rejoiced that nothing could part us again.

As I sat beside him my eyes wandered from his tranquil face to the garden where the princess sat singing among the flowers, and then passed to the distant village where the wretched serfs drudged their lives away in ignorance and misery. They were mine now, and the weight of this new possession burdened my soul.

"I cannot bear it; this must be changed."

"It shall."

Unconsciously I had spoken aloud, and the prince had answered without asking to know my thoughts.

"What shall be done, Alexis?" I said, smiling, as I caressed the thin hand that lay in mine.

"Whatever you desire. I do not wait to learn the wish, I promise it shall be granted."

"Rash as ever; have you, then, no will of your own?"

"None; you have broken it."

"Good; hear then my wish. Liberate your serfs; it afflicts me as a free-born Englishwoman to own men and women. Let them serve you if they will, but not through force or fear. Can you grant this, my prince?"

"I do; the Stavosta is already gone, and they know I pardon them. What more, Sybil?"

"Come with me to England, that I may show my countrymen the brave barbarian I have tamed."

My eyes were full of happy tears, but the old tormenting spirit prompted the speech. Alexis frowned, then laughed, and answered, with a glimmer of his former imperious pride:

"I might boast that I also had tamed a fiery spirit, but I am humble, and content myself with the knowledge that the proudest woman ever born has promised to love, honor, and — "

"*Not* obey you," I broke in with a kiss.